THE
BABY-SITTERS
CLUB®

CLAUDIA AND MEAN JANINE

DON'T MISS THE OTHER BABY-SITTERS CLUB GRAPHIC NOVELS!

KRISTY'S GREAT IDEA

THE TRUTH ABOUT STACEY

MARY ANNE SAVES THE DAY

DAWN AND THE IMPOSSIBLE THREE

ANN M. MARTIN

THE BABY-SITTERS CLUB®

CLAUDIA AND MEAN JANINE

A GRAPHIC NOVEL BY
RAINA TELGEMEIER
WITH COLOR BY BRADEN LAMB

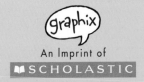

An Imprint of
■ SCHOLASTIC

Library of Congress Control Number: 2015935840

ISBN 978-0-545-88623-9 (hardcover)
ISBN 978-1-338-88826-3 (paperback)

10 9 8 7 6 5 4 3 2 1   23 24 25 26 27

Printed in China   62
This edition first printing, April 2023

Lettering by John Green
Edited by Cassandra Pelham Fulton, Sheila Keenan and David Levithan
Book design by Phil Falco
Creative Director: David Saylor

For Aunt Adele and Uncle Paul

A. M. M.

Thanks to everyone who has helped make this project a
reality! Dave Roman, Marion Vitus, John Green, Ashley Button,
Janna Morishima, David Saylor, David Levithan, Cassandra Pelham,
Ellie Berger, Sheila Keenan, Kristina Albertson, Phil Falco, Vera Brosgol,
Dr. Laurie Kane, the Green family: Bill, Martha, and MarMar,
and most especially, Ann M. Martin.

R. T.

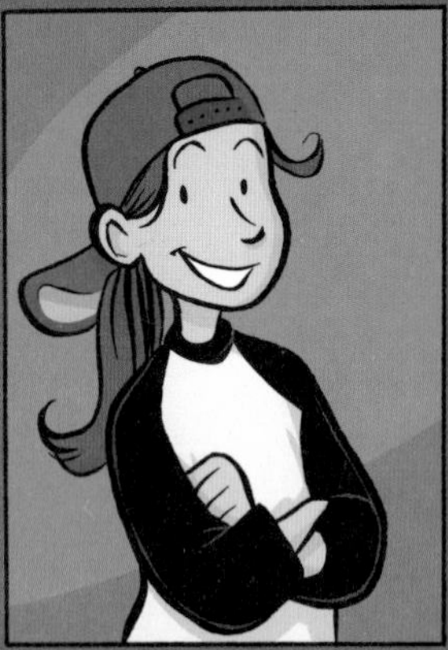

KRISTY THOMAS
PRESIDENT

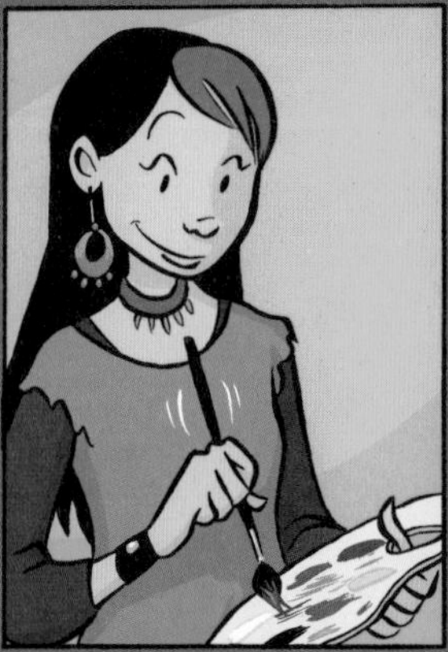

CLAUDIA KISHI
VICE PRESIDENT

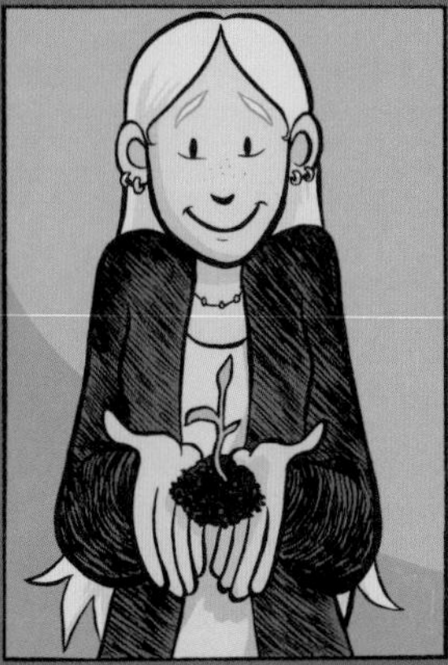

DAWN SCHAFER

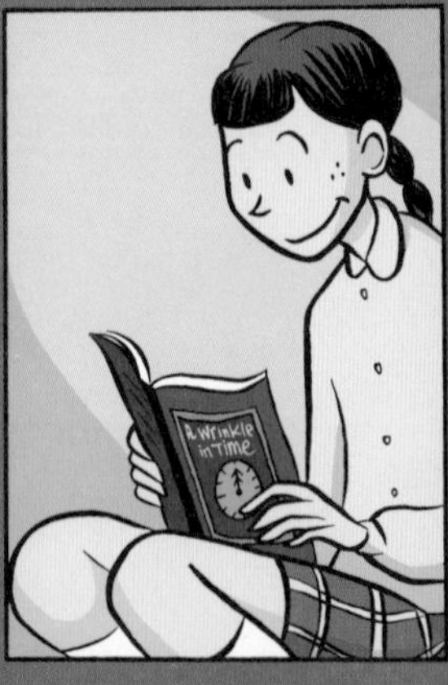
A Wrinkle in Time

MARY ANNE SPIER
SECRETARY

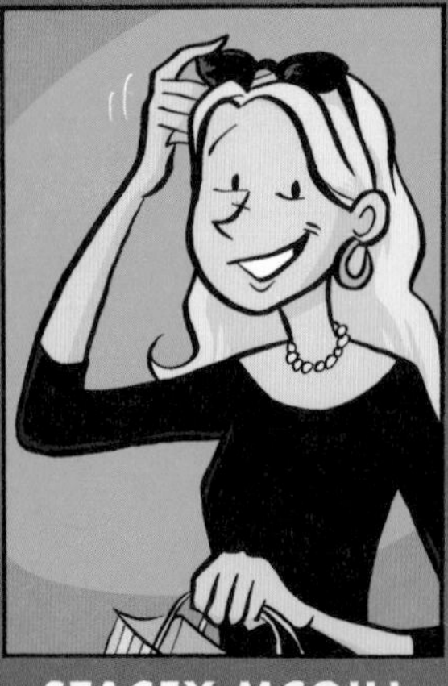

STACEY MCGILL
TREASURER

CHAPTER 1

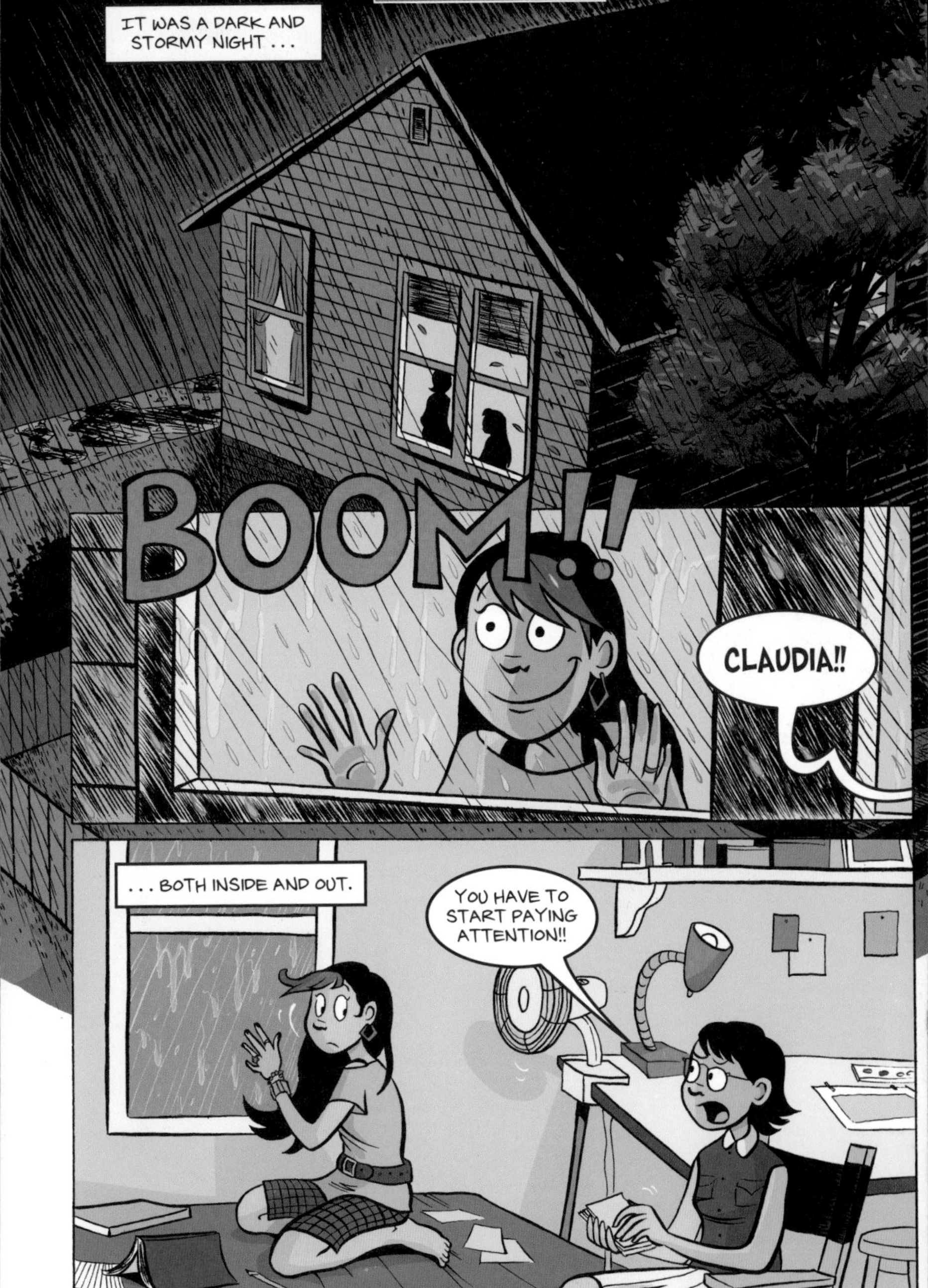
IT WAS A DARK AND STORMY NIGHT . . .
BOOM!!
CLAUDIA!!
. . . BOTH INSIDE AND OUT.
YOU HAVE TO START PAYING ATTENTION!!

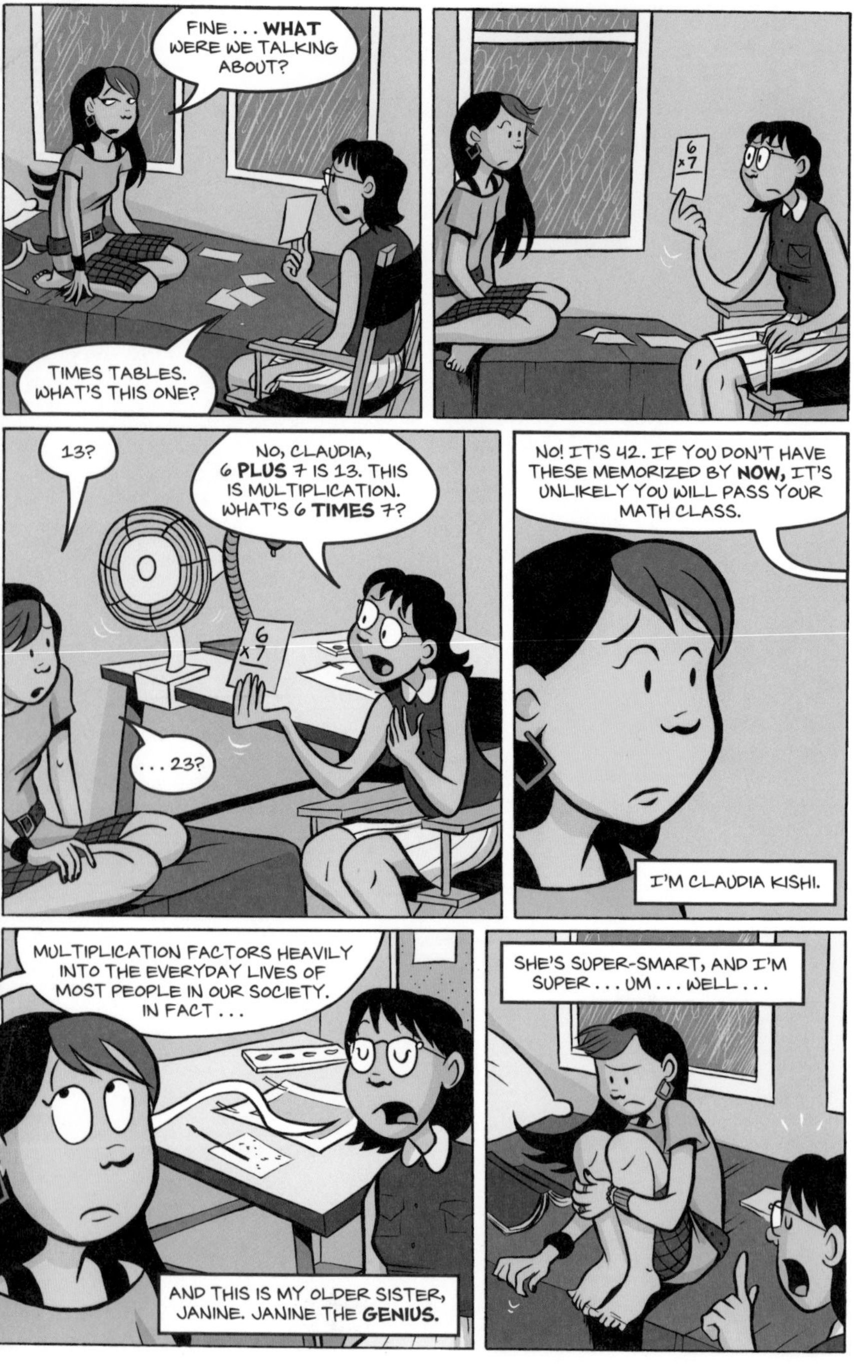
FINE . . . **WHAT** WERE WE TALKING ABOUT?
TIMES TABLES. WHAT'S THIS ONE?
6 x7
13?
NO, CLAUDIA, 6 **PLUS** 7 IS 13. THIS IS MULTIPLICATION. WHAT'S 6 **TIMES** 7?
6 x7
. . . 23?
NO! IT'S 42. IF YOU DON'T HAVE THESE MEMORIZED BY **NOW,** IT'S UNLIKELY YOU WILL PASS YOUR MATH CLASS.
I'M CLAUDIA KISHI.
MULTIPLICATION FACTORS HEAVILY INTO THE EVERYDAY LIVES OF MOST PEOPLE IN OUR SOCIETY. IN FACT . . .
AND THIS IS MY OLDER SISTER, JANINE. JANINE THE **GENIUS.**
SHE'S SUPER-SMART, AND I'M SUPER . . . UM . . . WELL . . .

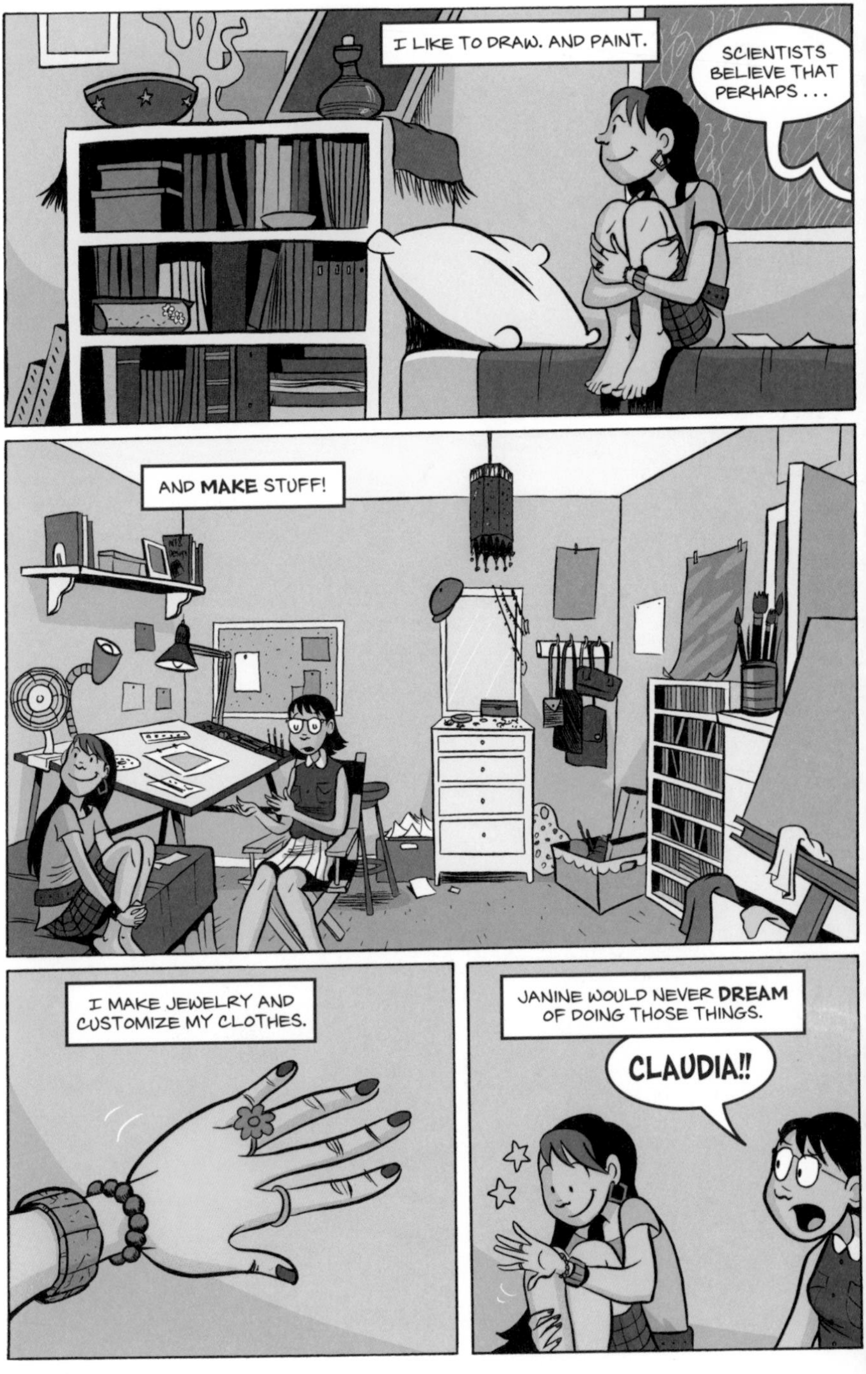
I LIKE TO DRAW. AND PAINT.
SCIENTISTS BELIEVE THAT PERHAPS . . .
AND MAKE STUFF!
I MAKE JEWELRY AND CUSTOMIZE MY CLOTHES.
JANINE WOULD NEVER DREAM OF DOING THOSE THINGS.
CLAUDIA!!

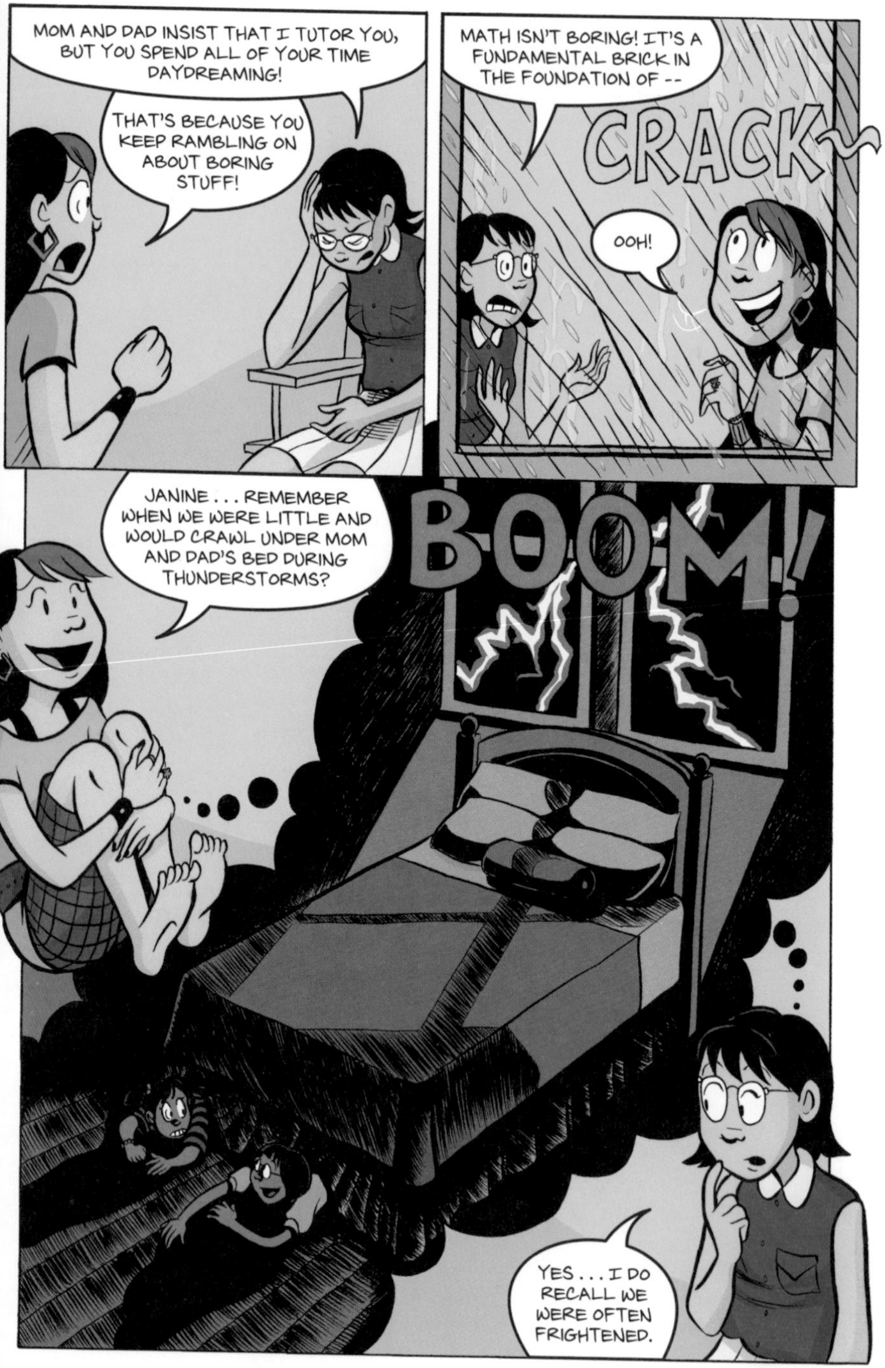
MOM AND DAD INSIST THAT I TUTOR YOU, BUT YOU SPEND ALL OF YOUR TIME DAYDREAMING!
THAT'S BECAUSE YOU KEEP RAMBLING ON ABOUT BORING STUFF!
MATH ISN'T BORING! IT'S A FUNDAMENTAL BRICK IN THE FOUNDATION OF --
CRACK
OOH!
JANINE . . . REMEMBER WHEN WE WERE LITTLE AND WOULD CRAWL UNDER MOM AND DAD'S BED DURING THUNDERSTORMS?
BOOM!
YES . . . I DO RECALL WE WERE OFTEN FRIGHTENED.

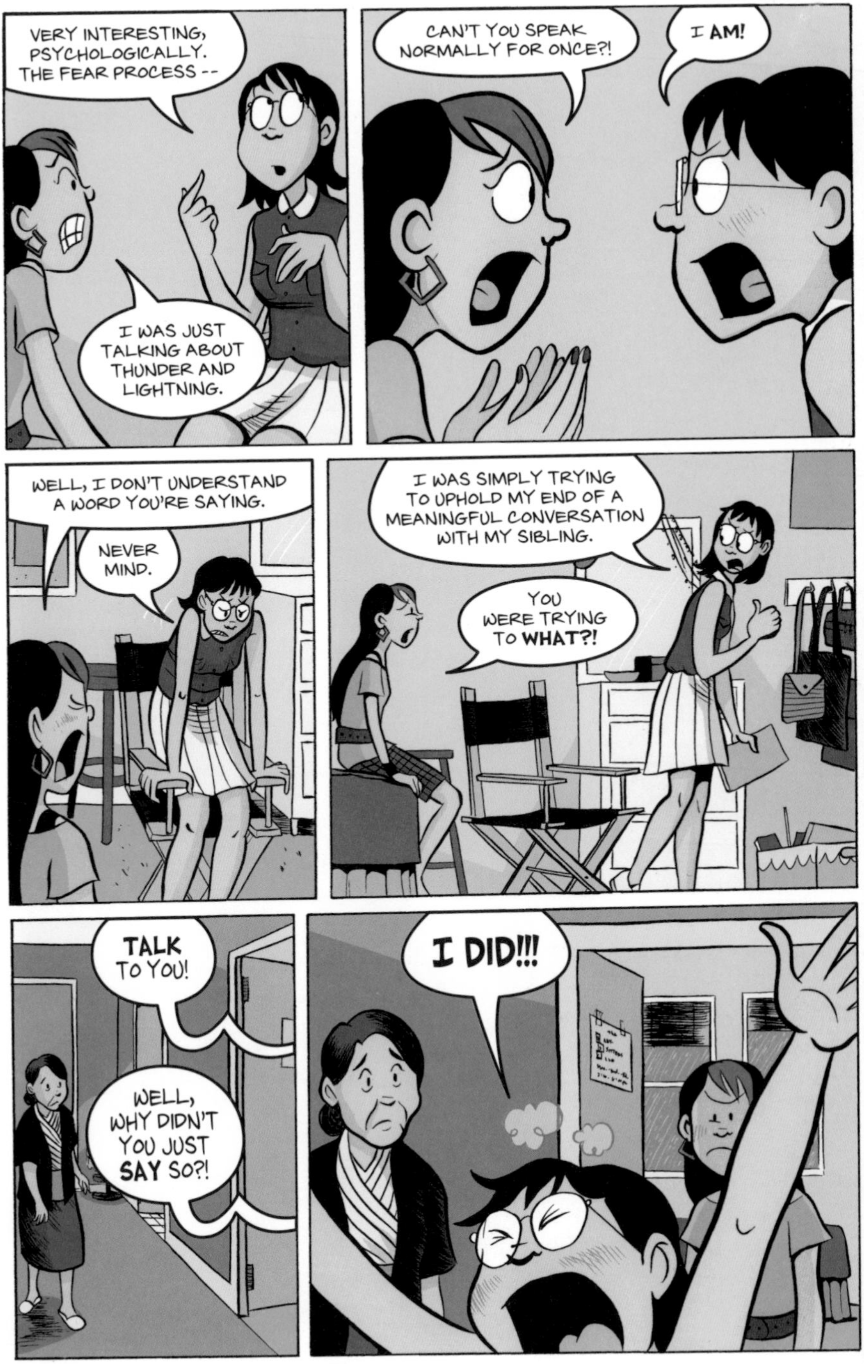
VERY INTERESTING, PSYCHOLOGICALLY. THE FEAR PROCESS --
I WAS JUST TALKING ABOUT THUNDER AND LIGHTNING.
CAN'T YOU SPEAK NORMALLY FOR ONCE?!
I AM!
WELL, I DON'T UNDERSTAND A WORD YOU'RE SAYING.
NEVER MIND.
I WAS SIMPLY TRYING TO UPHOLD MY END OF A MEANINGFUL CONVERSATION WITH MY SIBLING.
YOU WERE TRYING TO WHAT?!
TALK TO YOU!
WELL, WHY DIDN'T YOU JUST SAY SO?!
I DID!!!

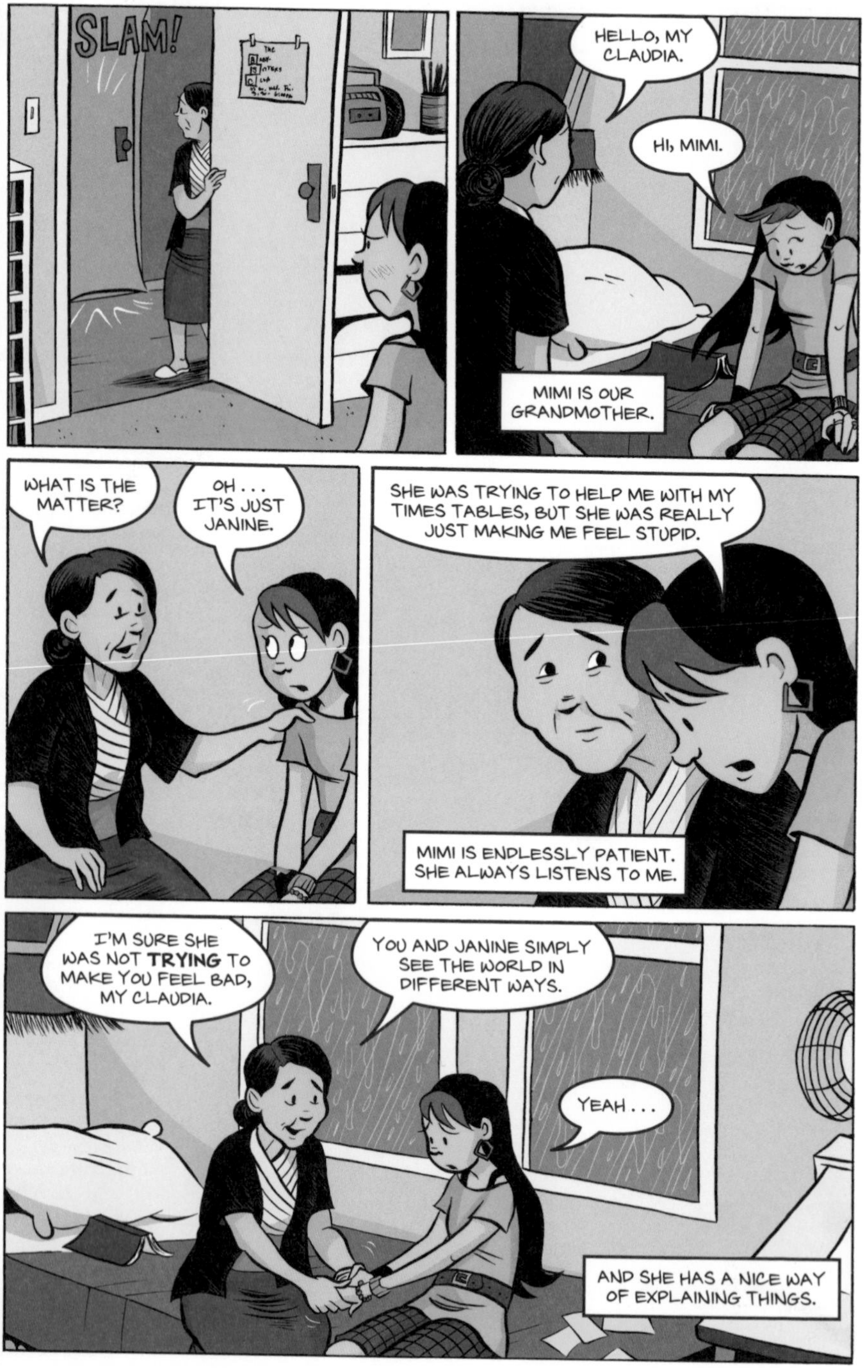
SLAM!
HELLO, MY CLAUDIA.
HI, MIMI.
MIMI IS OUR GRANDMOTHER.
WHAT IS THE MATTER?
OH . . . IT'S JUST JANINE.
SHE WAS TRYING TO HELP ME WITH MY TIMES TABLES, BUT SHE WAS REALLY JUST MAKING ME FEEL STUPID.
MIMI IS ENDLESSLY PATIENT. SHE ALWAYS LISTENS TO ME.
I'M SURE SHE WAS NOT **TRYING** TO MAKE YOU FEEL BAD, MY CLAUDIA.
YOU AND JANINE SIMPLY SEE THE WORLD IN DIFFERENT WAYS.
YEAH . . .
AND SHE HAS A NICE WAY OF EXPLAINING THINGS.

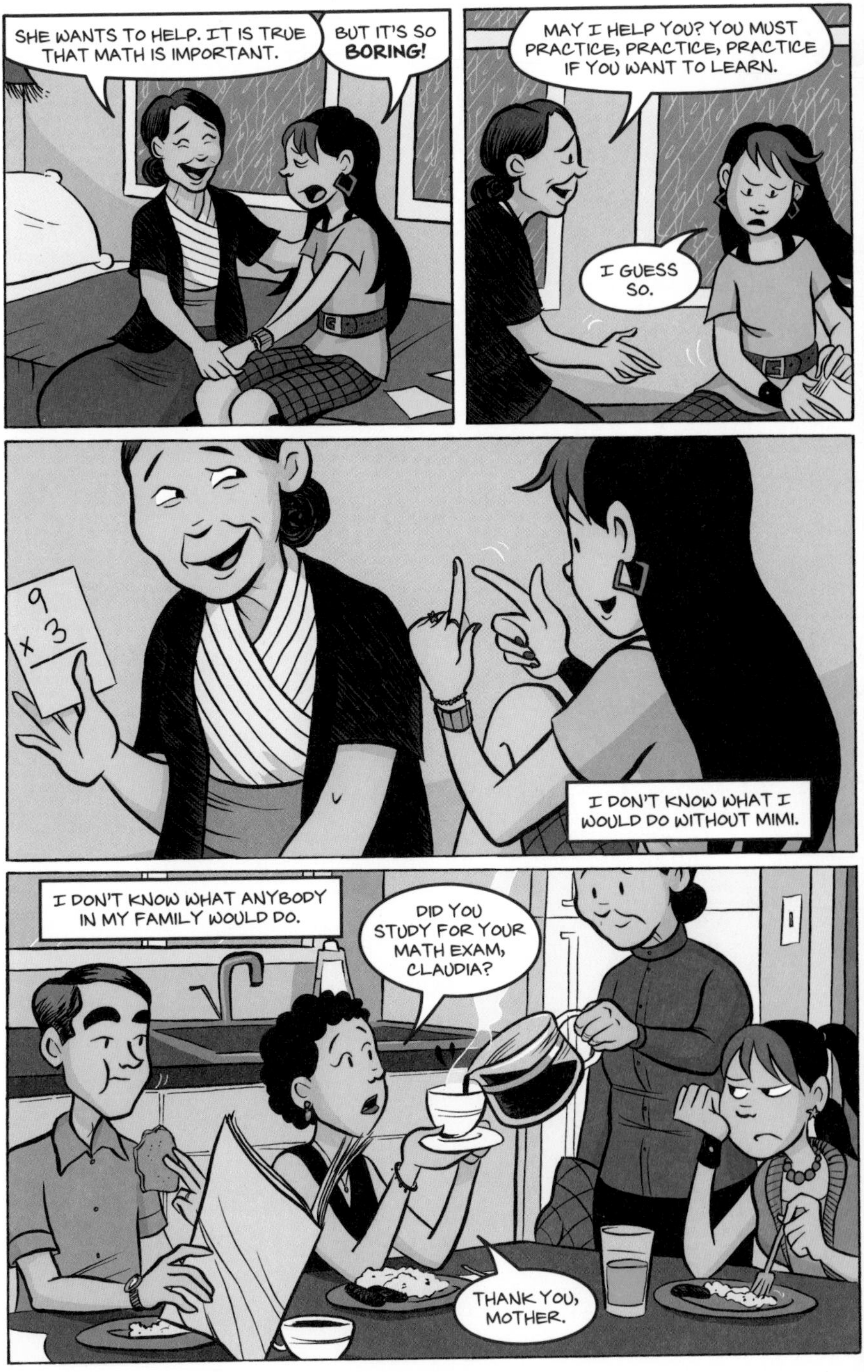
SHE WANTS TO HELP. IT IS TRUE THAT MATH IS IMPORTANT.
BUT IT'S SO **BORING!**
MAY I HELP YOU? YOU MUST PRACTICE, PRACTICE, PRACTICE IF YOU WANT TO LEARN.
I GUESS SO.
9 x 3
I DON'T KNOW WHAT I WOULD DO WITHOUT MIMI.
I DON'T KNOW WHAT ANYBODY IN MY FAMILY WOULD DO.
DID YOU STUDY FOR YOUR MATH EXAM, CLAUDIA?
THANK YOU, MOTHER.

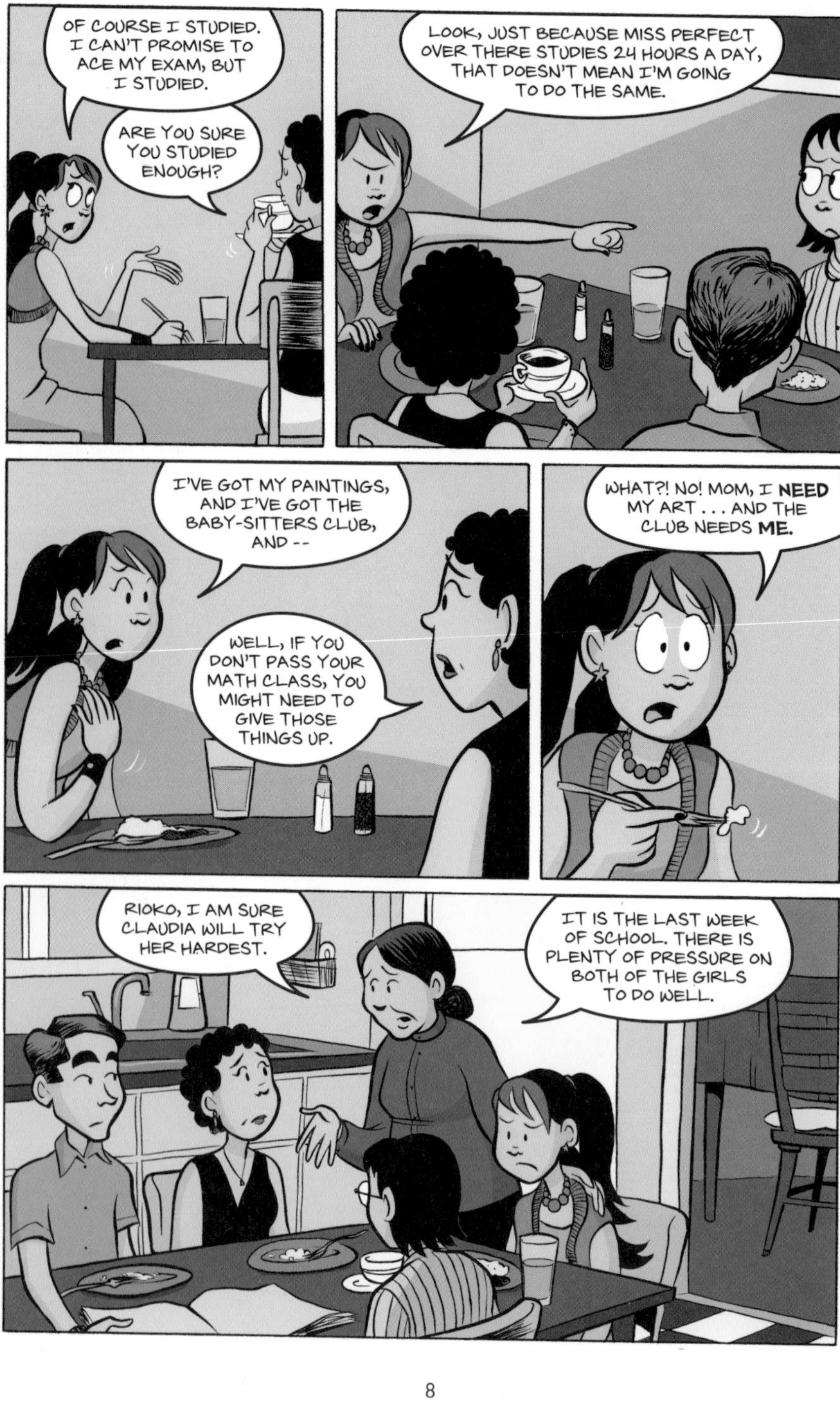
OF COURSE I STUDIED. I CAN'T PROMISE TO ACE MY EXAM, BUT I STUDIED.
ARE YOU SURE YOU STUDIED ENOUGH?
LOOK, JUST BECAUSE MISS PERFECT OVER THERE STUDIES 24 HOURS A DAY, THAT DOESN'T MEAN I'M GOING TO DO THE SAME.
I'VE GOT MY PAINTINGS, AND I'VE GOT THE BABY-SITTERS CLUB, AND --
WELL, IF YOU DON'T PASS YOUR MATH CLASS, YOU MIGHT NEED TO GIVE THOSE THINGS UP.
WHAT?! NO! MOM, I **NEED** MY ART . . . AND THE CLUB NEEDS **ME.**
RIOKO, I AM SURE CLAUDIA WILL TRY HER HARDEST.
IT IS THE LAST WEEK OF SCHOOL. THERE IS PLENTY OF PRESSURE ON BOTH OF THE GIRLS TO DO WELL.

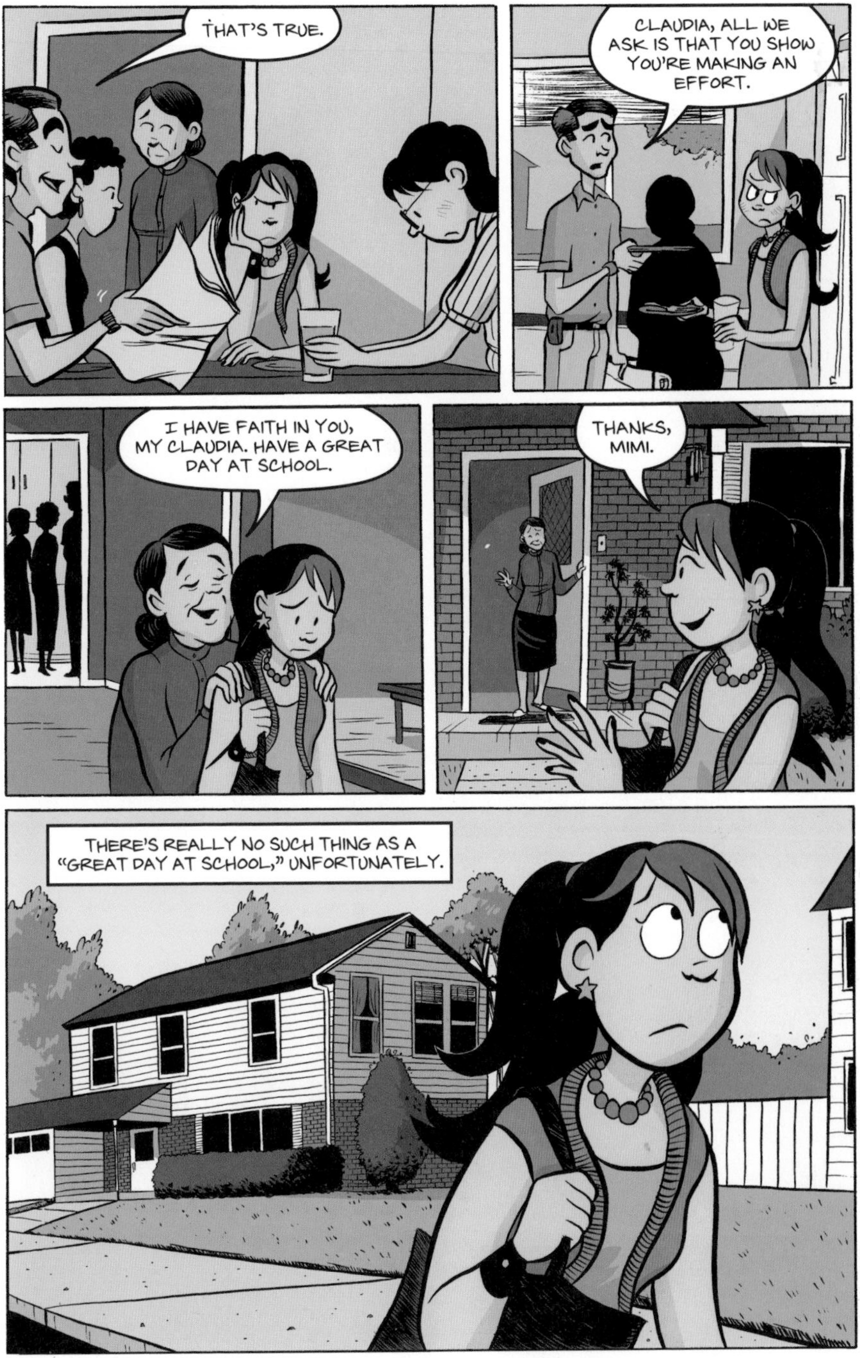
THAT'S TRUE.
CLAUDIA, ALL WE ASK IS THAT YOU SHOW YOU'RE MAKING AN EFFORT.
I HAVE FAITH IN YOU, MY CLAUDIA. HAVE A GREAT DAY AT SCHOOL.
THANKS, MIMI.
THERE'S REALLY NO SUCH THING AS A "GREAT DAY AT SCHOOL," UNFORTUNATELY.

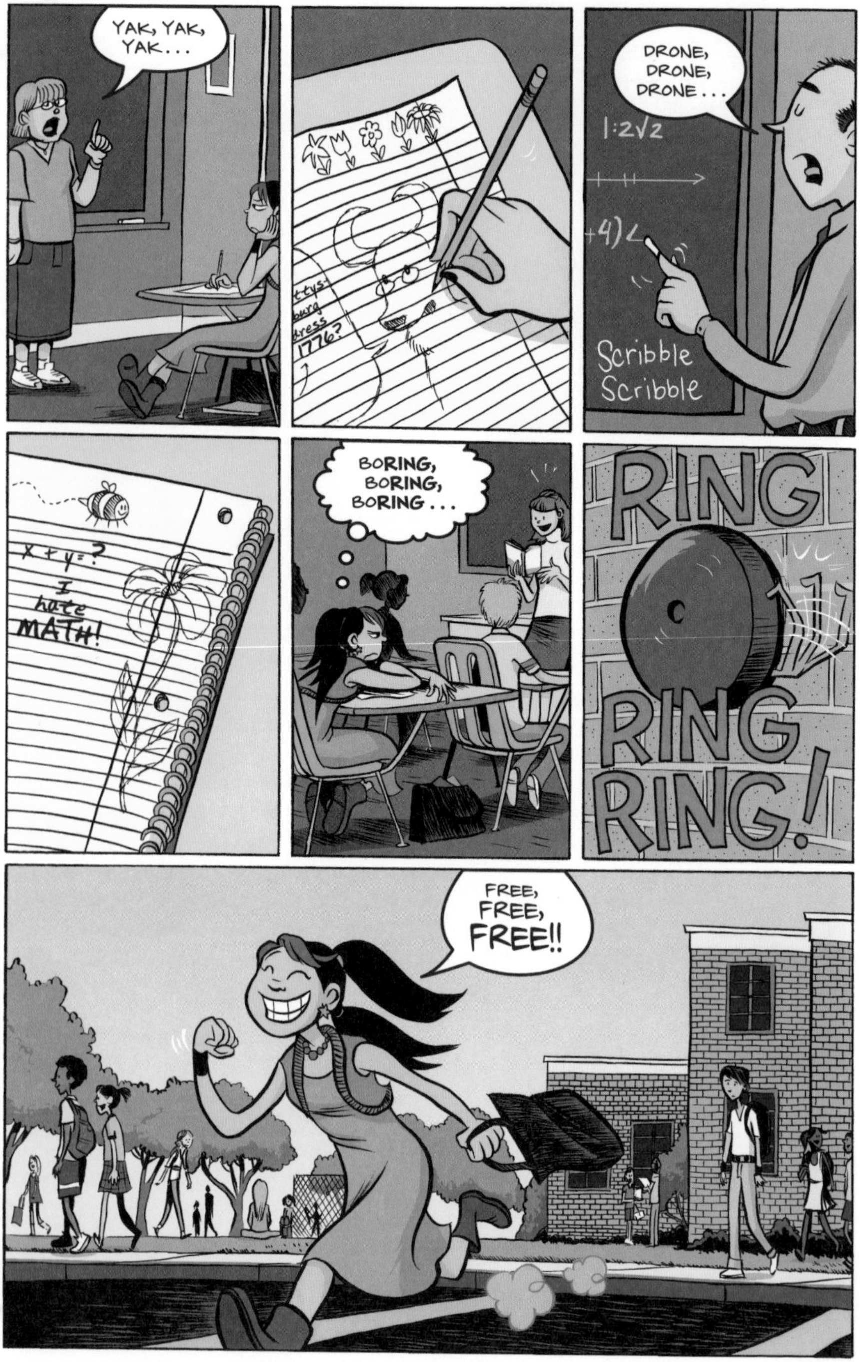
YAK, YAK, YAK...
1776?
DRONE, DRONE, DRONE...
1:2√2
Scribble Scribble
x + y = ?
I hate MATH!
BORING, BORING, BORING...
RING
RING
RING!
FREE, FREE, FREE!!

CHAPTER 2

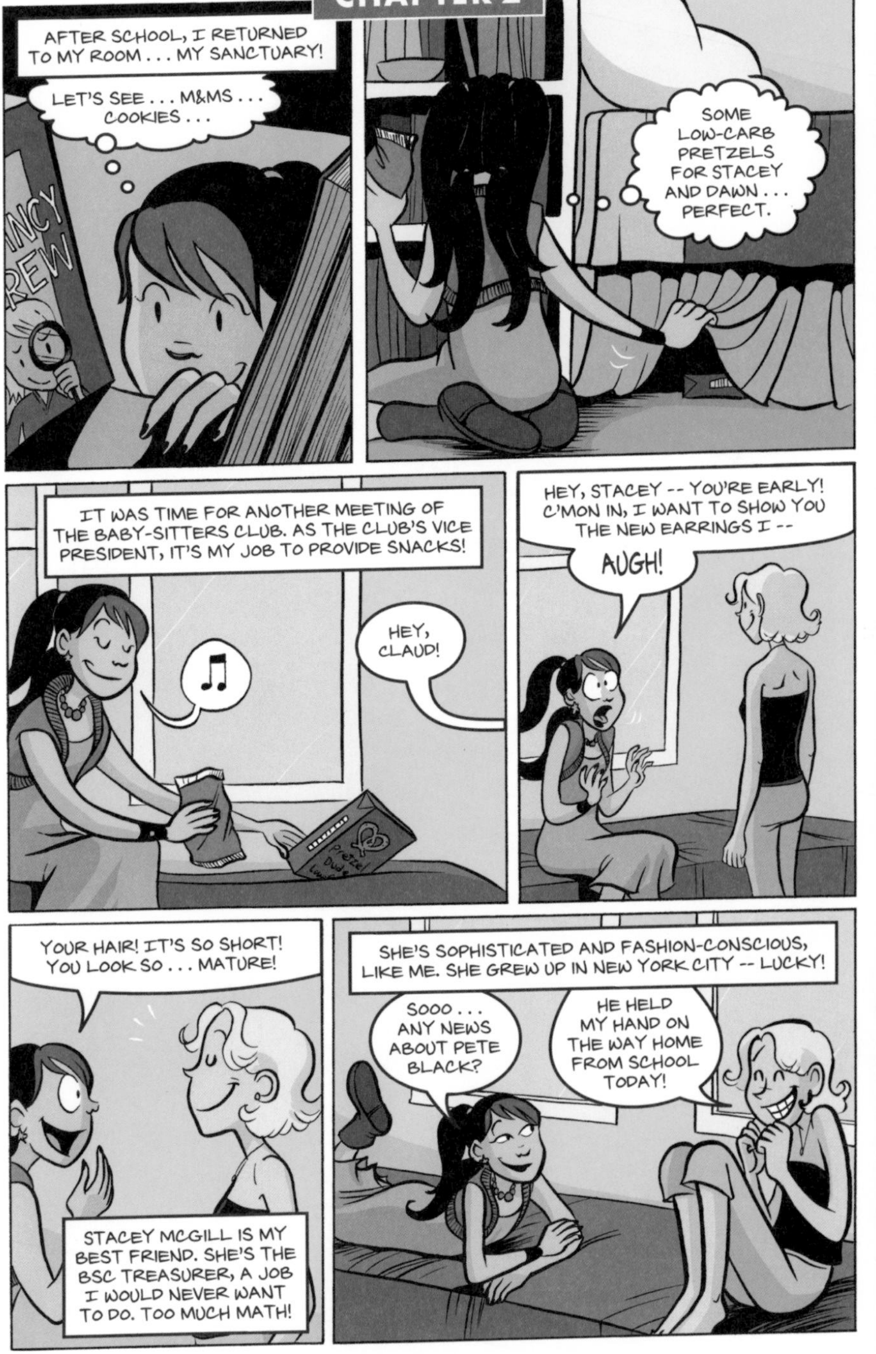

AFTER SCHOOL, I RETURNED TO MY ROOM . . . MY SANCTUARY!
LET'S SEE . . . M&MS . . . COOKIES . . .
SOME LOW-CARB PRETZELS FOR STACEY AND DAWN . . . PERFECT.
IT WAS TIME FOR ANOTHER MEETING OF THE BABY-SITTERS CLUB. AS THE CLUB'S VICE PRESIDENT, IT'S MY JOB TO PROVIDE SNACKS!
♫
HEY, CLAUD!
HEY, STACEY -- YOU'RE EARLY! C'MON IN, I WANT TO SHOW YOU THE NEW EARRINGS I --
AUGH!
YOUR HAIR! IT'S SO SHORT! YOU LOOK SO . . . MATURE!
STACEY MCGILL IS MY BEST FRIEND. SHE'S THE BSC TREASURER, A JOB I WOULD NEVER WANT TO DO. TOO MUCH MATH!
SHE'S SOPHISTICATED AND FASHION-CONSCIOUS, LIKE ME. SHE GREW UP IN NEW YORK CITY -- LUCKY!
SOOO . . . ANY NEWS ABOUT PETE BLACK?
HE HELD MY HAND ON THE WAY HOME FROM SCHOOL TODAY!

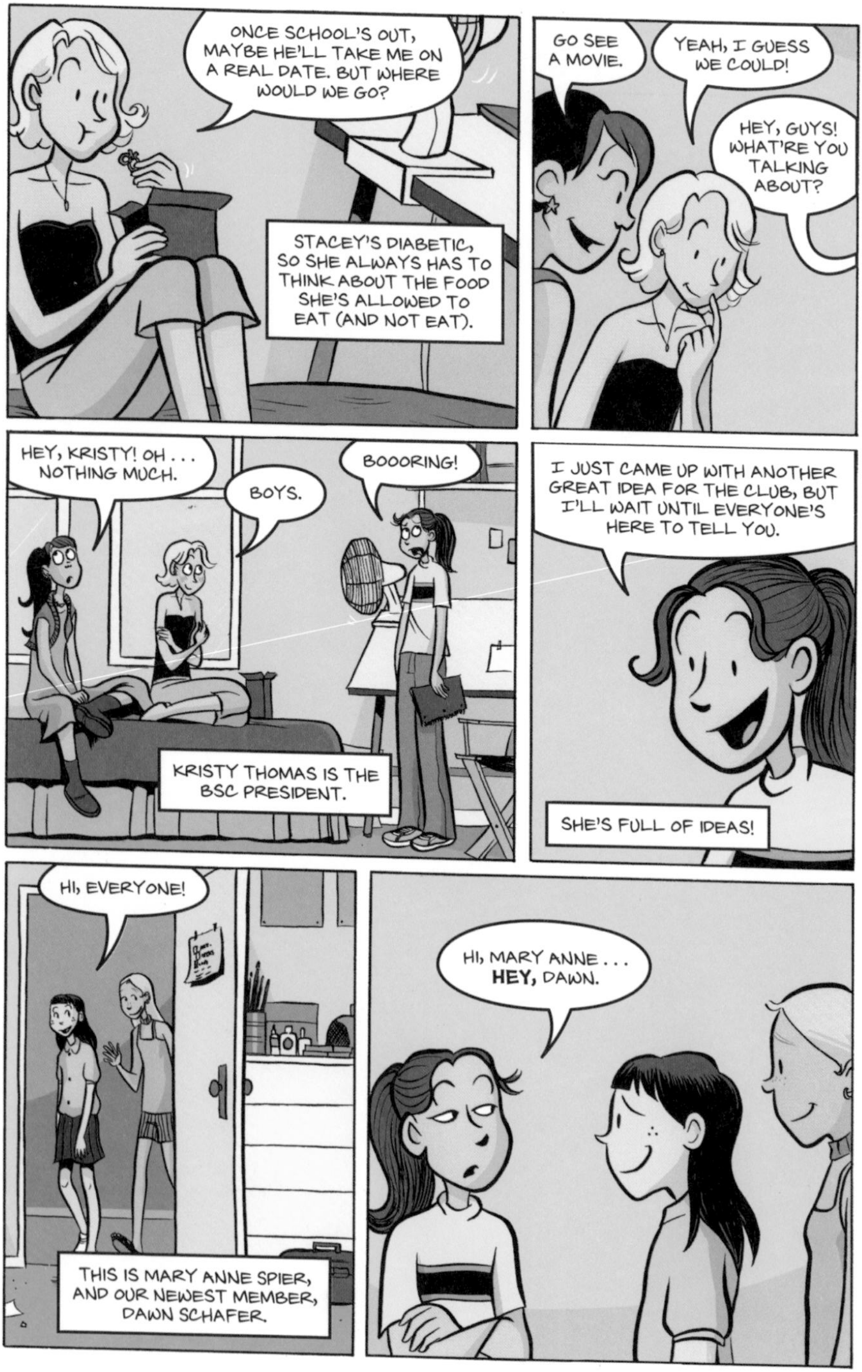
ONCE SCHOOL'S OUT, MAYBE HE'LL TAKE ME ON A REAL DATE. BUT WHERE WOULD WE GO?
STACEY'S DIABETIC, SO SHE ALWAYS HAS TO THINK ABOUT THE FOOD SHE'S ALLOWED TO EAT (AND NOT EAT).
GO SEE A MOVIE.
YEAH, I GUESS WE COULD!
HEY, GUYS! WHAT'RE YOU TALKING ABOUT?
HEY, KRISTY! OH . . . NOTHING MUCH.
BOYS.
BOOORING!
KRISTY THOMAS IS THE BSC PRESIDENT.
I JUST CAME UP WITH ANOTHER GREAT IDEA FOR THE CLUB, BUT I'LL WAIT UNTIL EVERYONE'S HERE TO TELL YOU.
SHE'S FULL OF IDEAS!
HI, EVERYONE!
THIS IS MARY ANNE SPIER, AND OUR NEWEST MEMBER, DAWN SCHAFER.
HI, MARY ANNE . . . **HEY,** DAWN.

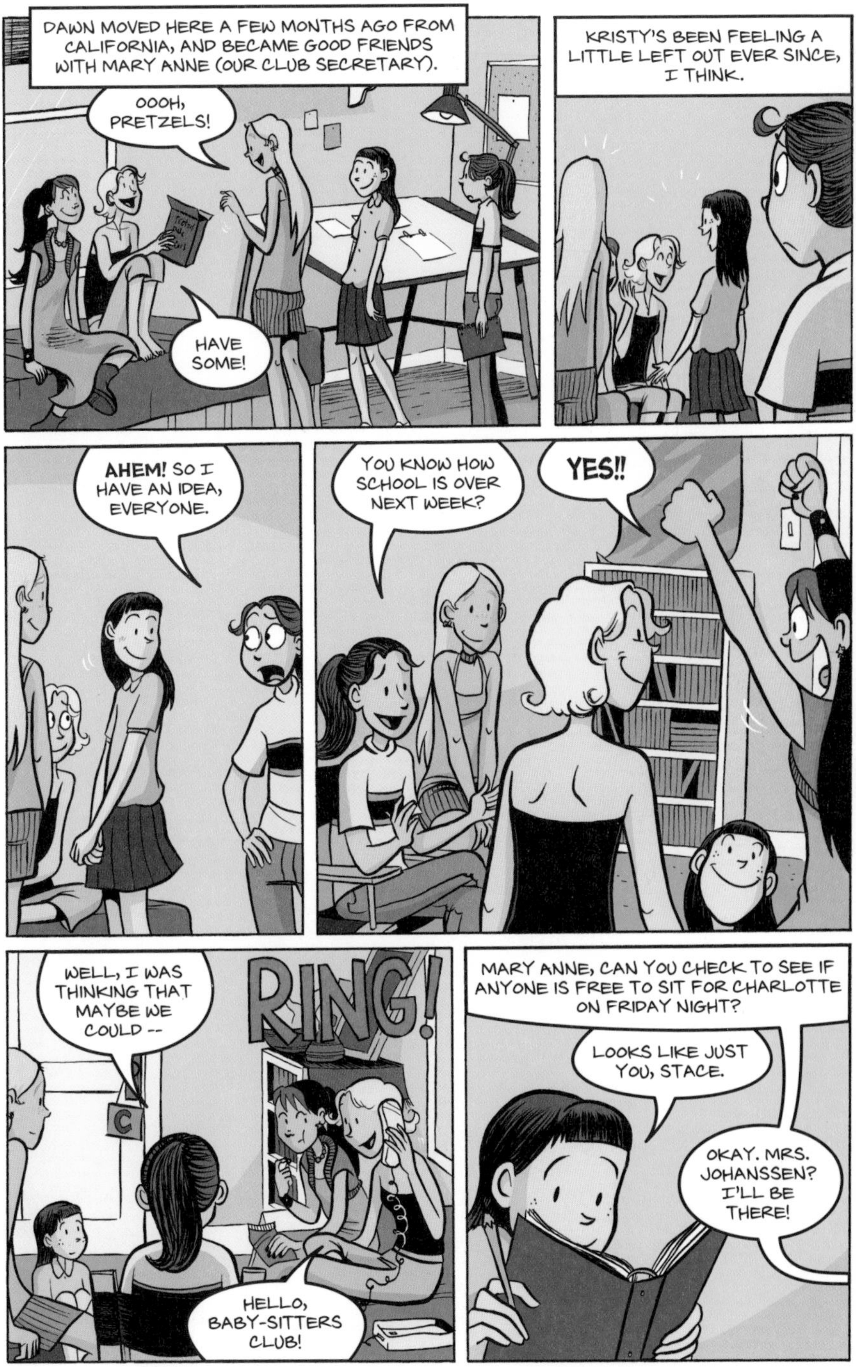
DAWN MOVED HERE A FEW MONTHS AGO FROM CALIFORNIA, AND BECAME GOOD FRIENDS WITH MARY ANNE (OUR CLUB SECRETARY).
OOOH, PRETZELS!
HAVE SOME!
KRISTY'S BEEN FEELING A LITTLE LEFT OUT EVER SINCE, I THINK.
AHEM! SO I HAVE AN IDEA, EVERYONE.
YOU KNOW HOW SCHOOL IS OVER NEXT WEEK?
YES!!
WELL, I WAS THINKING THAT MAYBE WE COULD --
RING!
HELLO, BABY-SITTERS CLUB!
MARY ANNE, CAN YOU CHECK TO SEE IF ANYONE IS FREE TO SIT FOR CHARLOTTE ON FRIDAY NIGHT?
LOOKS LIKE JUST YOU, STACE.
OKAY. MRS. JOHANSSEN? I'LL BE THERE!

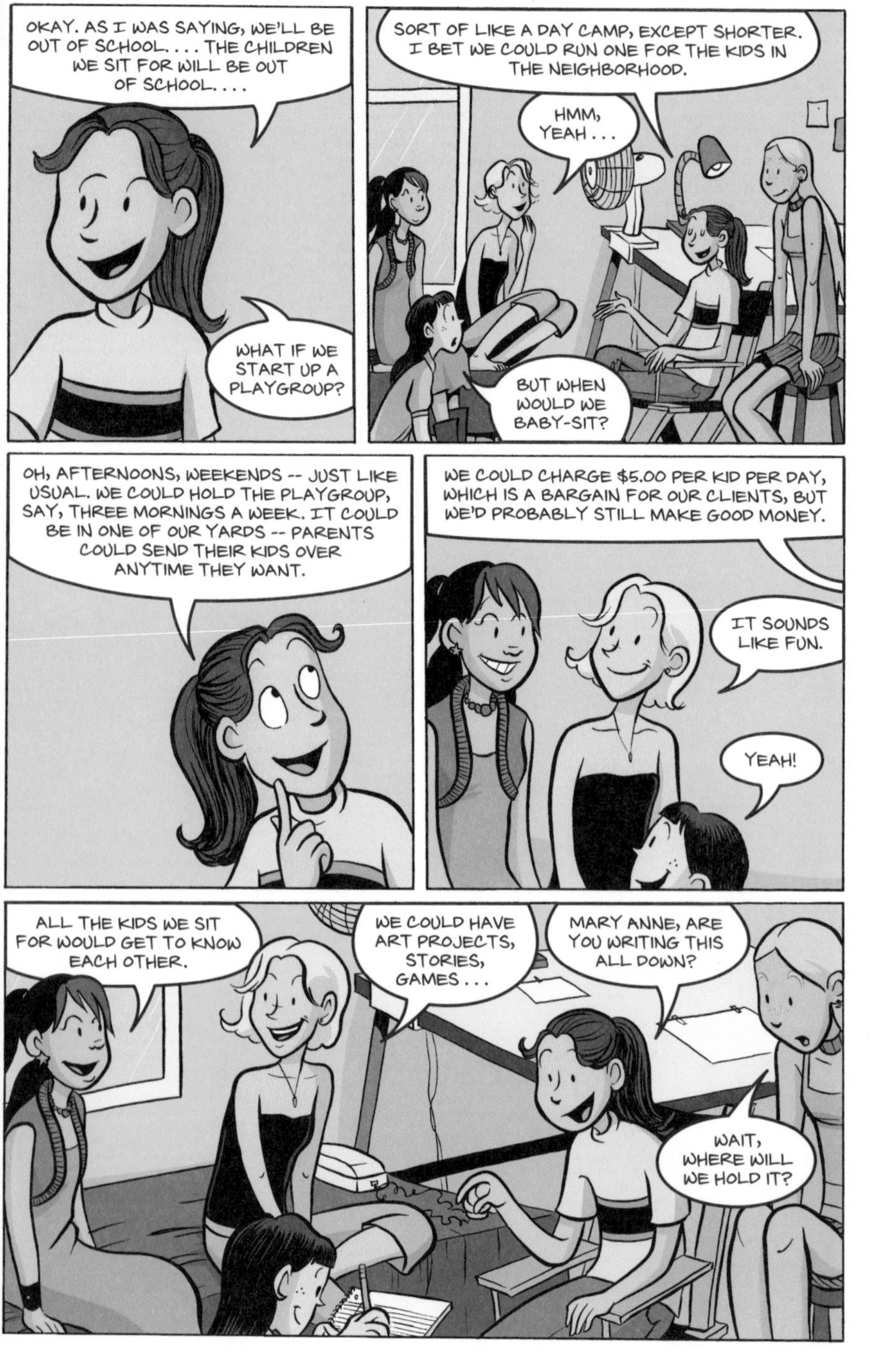
OKAY. AS I WAS SAYING, WE'LL BE OUT OF SCHOOL. . . . THE CHILDREN WE SIT FOR WILL BE OUT OF SCHOOL. . . .
WHAT IF WE START UP A PLAYGROUP?
SORT OF LIKE A DAY CAMP, EXCEPT SHORTER. I BET WE COULD RUN ONE FOR THE KIDS IN THE NEIGHBORHOOD.
HMM, YEAH . . .
BUT WHEN WOULD WE BABY-SIT?
OH, AFTERNOONS, WEEKENDS -- JUST LIKE USUAL. WE COULD HOLD THE PLAYGROUP, SAY, THREE MORNINGS A WEEK. IT COULD BE IN ONE OF OUR YARDS -- PARENTS COULD SEND THEIR KIDS OVER ANYTIME THEY WANT.
WE COULD CHARGE $5.00 PER KID PER DAY, WHICH IS A BARGAIN FOR OUR CLIENTS, BUT WE'D PROBABLY STILL MAKE GOOD MONEY.
IT SOUNDS LIKE FUN.
YEAH!
ALL THE KIDS WE SIT FOR WOULD GET TO KNOW EACH OTHER.
WE COULD HAVE ART PROJECTS, STORIES, GAMES . . .
MARY ANNE, ARE YOU WRITING THIS ALL DOWN?
WAIT, WHERE WILL WE HOLD IT?

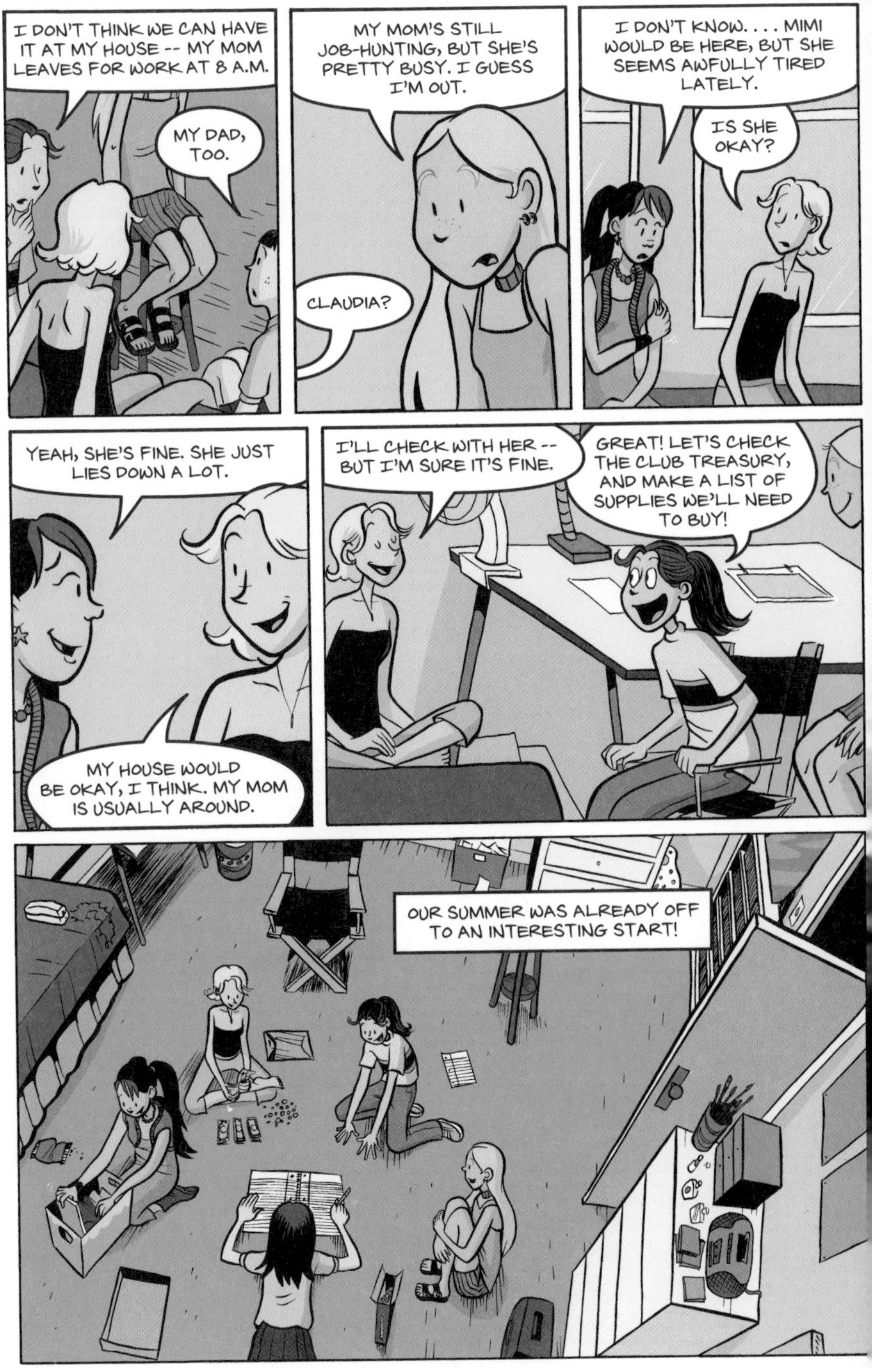
I DON'T THINK WE CAN HAVE IT AT MY HOUSE -- MY MOM LEAVES FOR WORK AT 8 A.M.
MY DAD, TOO.
MY MOM'S STILL JOB-HUNTING, BUT SHE'S PRETTY BUSY. I GUESS I'M OUT.
CLAUDIA?
I DON'T KNOW. . . . MIMI WOULD BE HERE, BUT SHE SEEMS AWFULLY TIRED LATELY.
IS SHE OKAY?
YEAH, SHE'S FINE. SHE JUST LIES DOWN A LOT.
MY HOUSE WOULD BE OKAY, I THINK. MY MOM IS USUALLY AROUND.
I'LL CHECK WITH HER -- BUT I'M SURE IT'S FINE.
GREAT! LET'S CHECK THE CLUB TREASURY, AND MAKE A LIST OF SUPPLIES WE'LL NEED TO BUY!
OUR SUMMER WAS ALREADY OFF TO AN INTERESTING START!

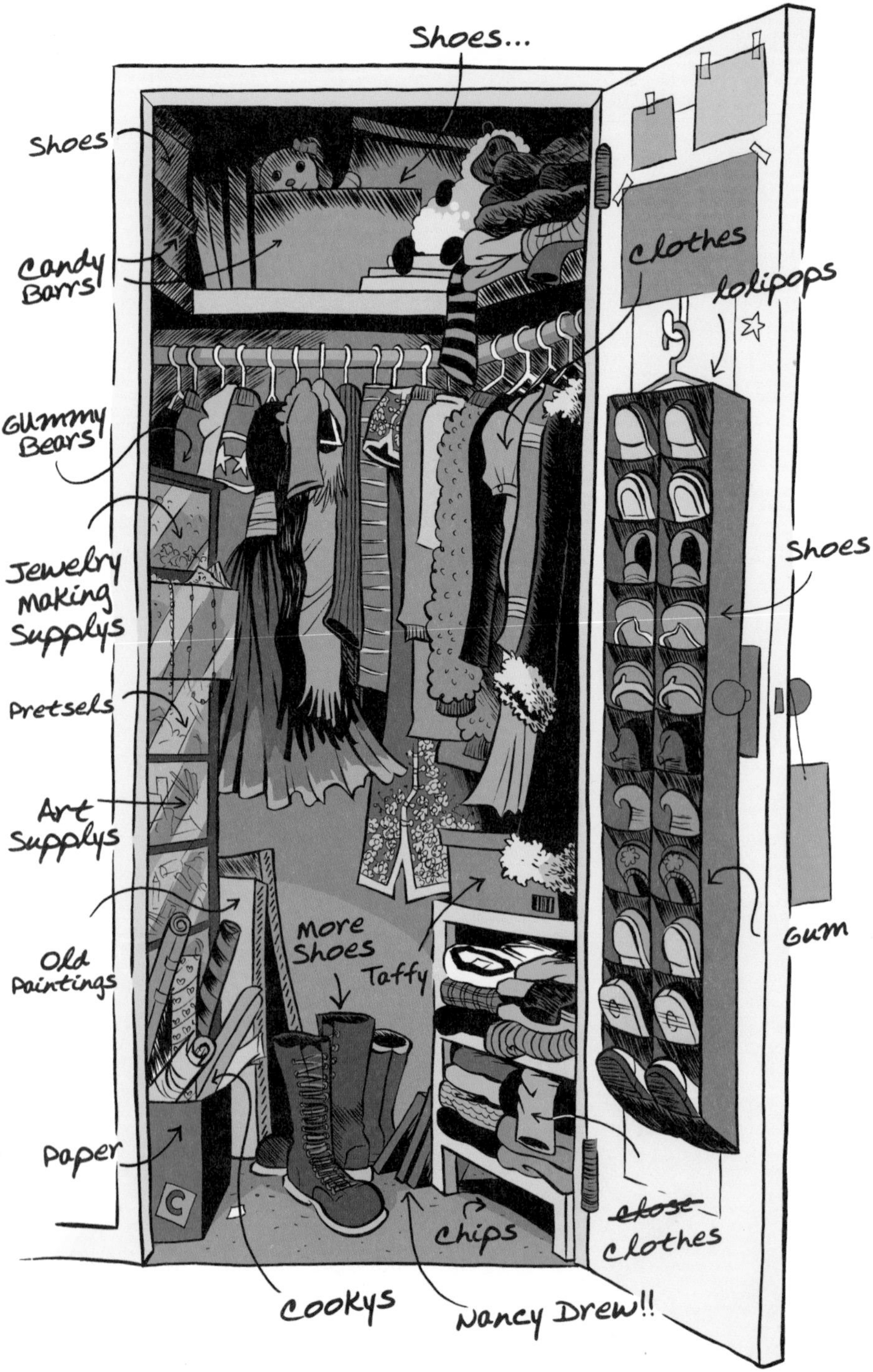
Shoes...
Shoes
Candy Barrs
Clothes
lolipops
Gummy Bears
Jewelry Making Supplys
Shoes
Pretsels
Art Supplys
Old Paintings
More Shoes
Taffy
Gum
Paper
close
Clothes
Chips
Cookys
Nancy Drew!!

CHAPTER 3

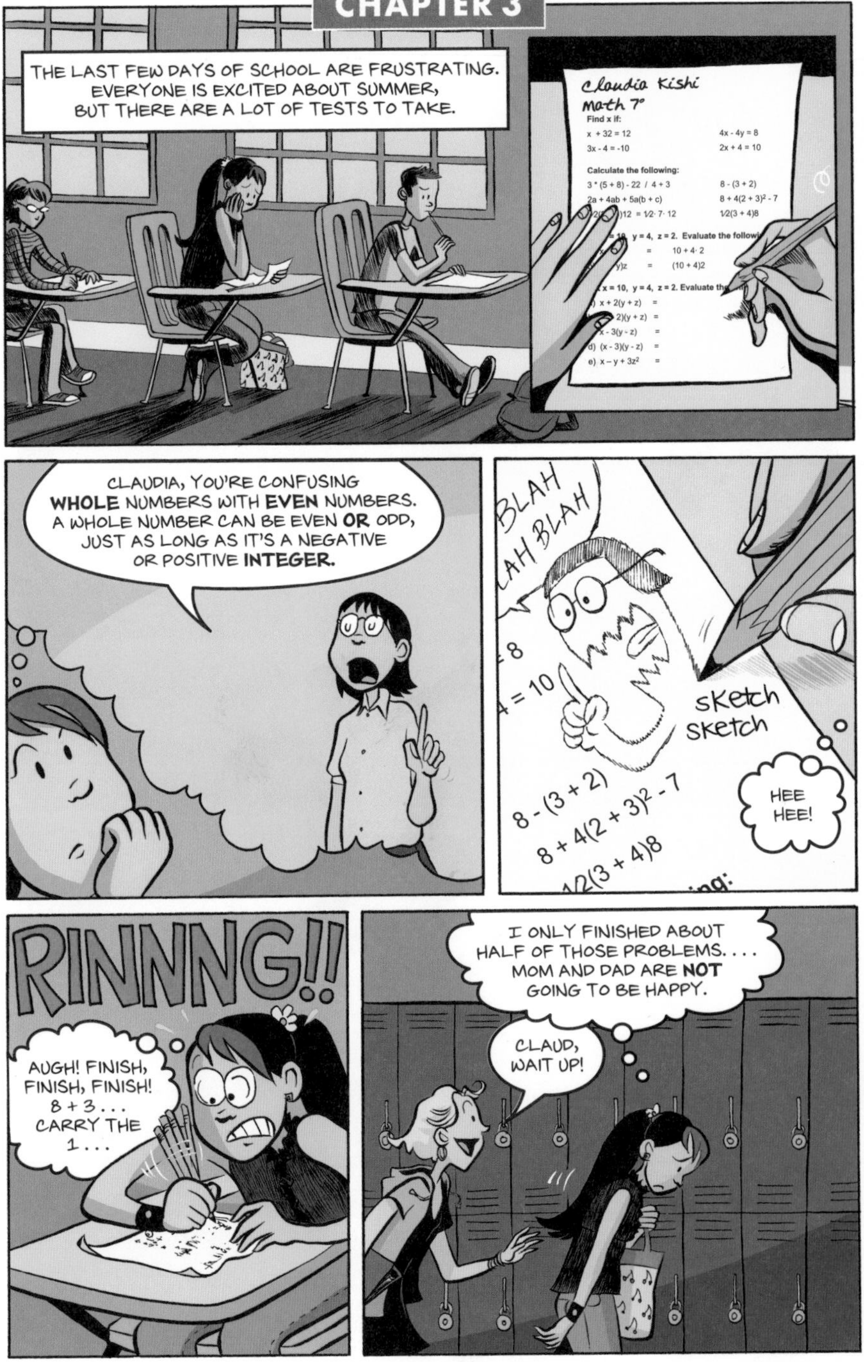
THE LAST FEW DAYS OF SCHOOL ARE FRUSTRATING. EVERYONE IS EXCITED ABOUT SUMMER, BUT THERE ARE A LOT OF TESTS TO TAKE.
Claudia Kishi
Math 7°
Find x if:
x + 32 = 12
4x - 4y = 8
3x - 4 = -10
2x + 4 = 10
Calculate the following:
3 * (5 + 8) - 22 / 4 + 3
8 - (3 + 2)
2a + 4ab + 5a(b + c)
8 + 4(2 + 3)² - 7
1/2(3 + 4)8
CLAUDIA, YOU'RE CONFUSING **WHOLE** NUMBERS WITH **EVEN** NUMBERS. A WHOLE NUMBER CAN BE EVEN **OR** ODD, JUST AS LONG AS IT'S A NEGATIVE OR POSITIVE **INTEGER.**
BLAH BLAH BLAH
sketch sketch
HEE HEE!
RINNNG!!
AUGH! FINISH, FINISH, FINISH! 8 + 3 . . . CARRY THE 1 . . .
I ONLY FINISHED ABOUT HALF OF THOSE PROBLEMS. . . . MOM AND DAD ARE **NOT** GOING TO BE HAPPY.
CLAUD, WAIT UP!

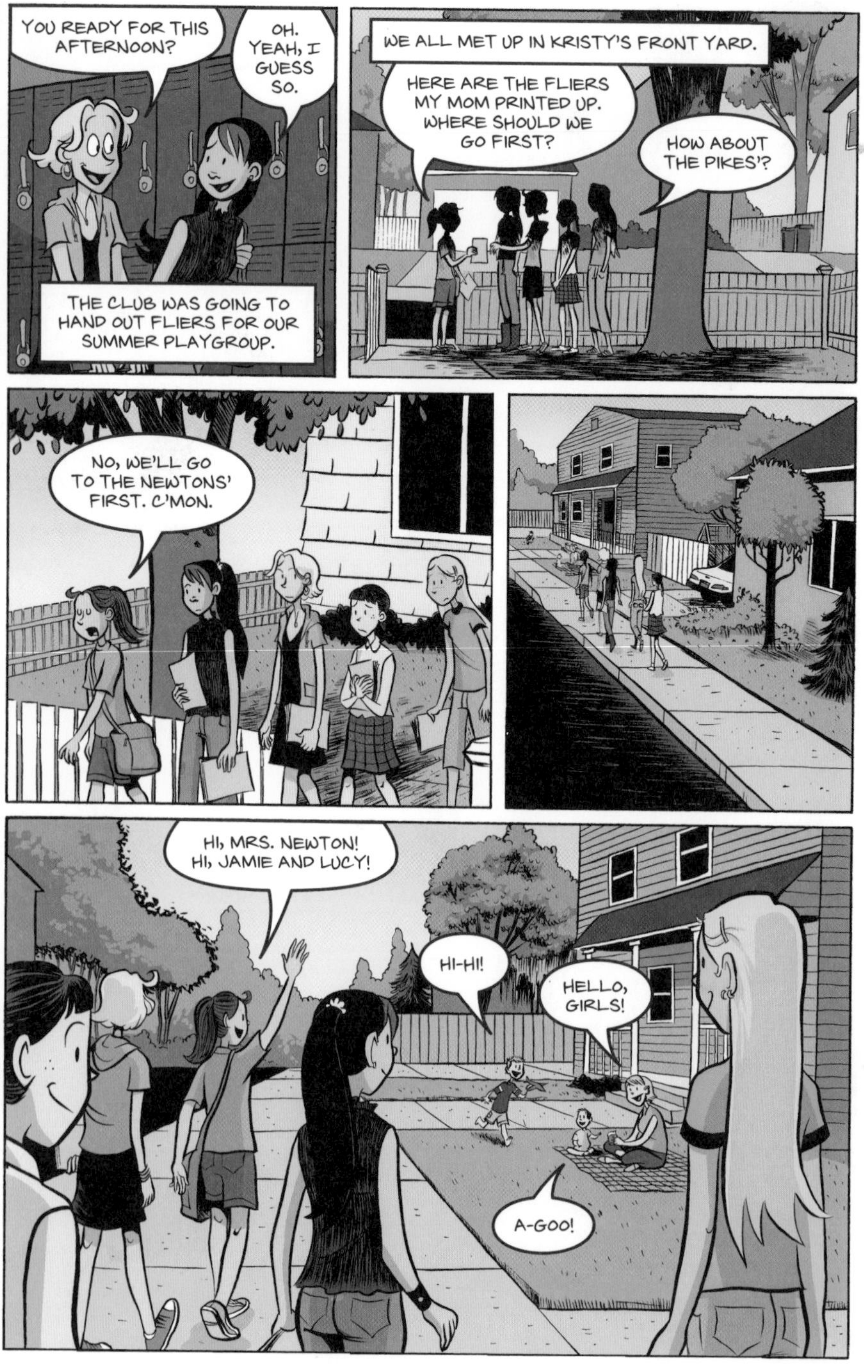
YOU READY FOR THIS AFTERNOON?
OH. YEAH, I GUESS SO.
THE CLUB WAS GOING TO HAND OUT FLIERS FOR OUR SUMMER PLAYGROUP.
WE ALL MET UP IN KRISTY'S FRONT YARD.
HERE ARE THE FLIERS MY MOM PRINTED UP. WHERE SHOULD WE GO FIRST?
HOW ABOUT THE PIKES'?
NO, WE'LL GO TO THE NEWTONS' FIRST. C'MON.
HI, MRS. NEWTON! HI, JAMIE AND LUCY!
HI-HI!
HELLO, GIRLS!
A-GOO!

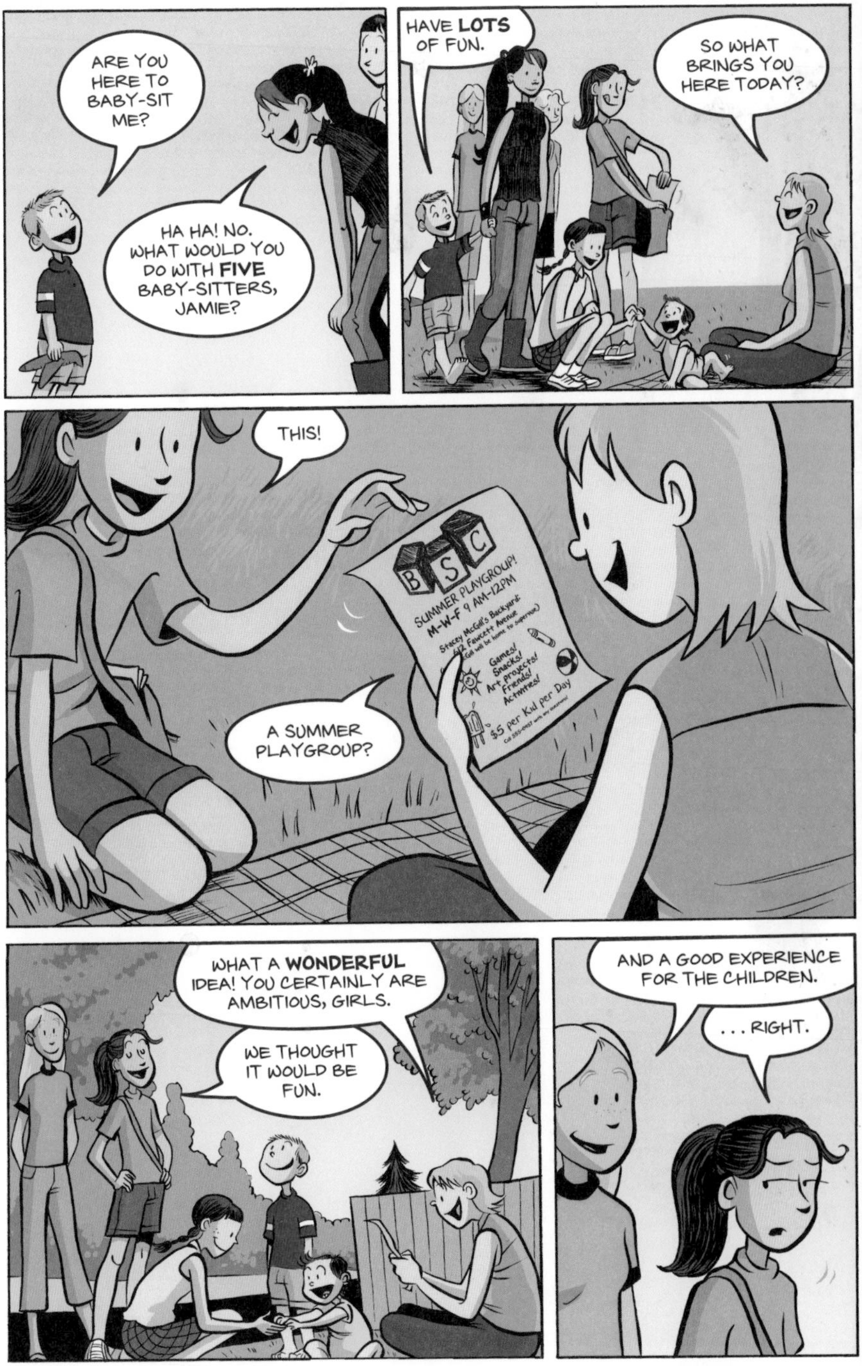
ARE YOU HERE TO BABY-SIT ME?
HA HA! NO. WHAT WOULD YOU DO WITH **FIVE** BABY-SITTERS, JAMIE?
HAVE **LOTS** OF FUN.
SO WHAT BRINGS YOU HERE TODAY?
THIS!
BSC
SUMMER PLAYGROUP!
M-W-F 9 AM-12PM
Stacey McGill's Backyard
612 Fawcett Avenue
Games!
Snacks!
Art projects!
Friends!
Activities!
$5 per Kid per Day
A SUMMER PLAYGROUP?
WHAT A **WONDERFUL** IDEA! YOU CERTAINLY ARE AMBITIOUS, GIRLS.
WE THOUGHT IT WOULD BE FUN.
AND A GOOD EXPERIENCE FOR THE CHILDREN.
. . . RIGHT.

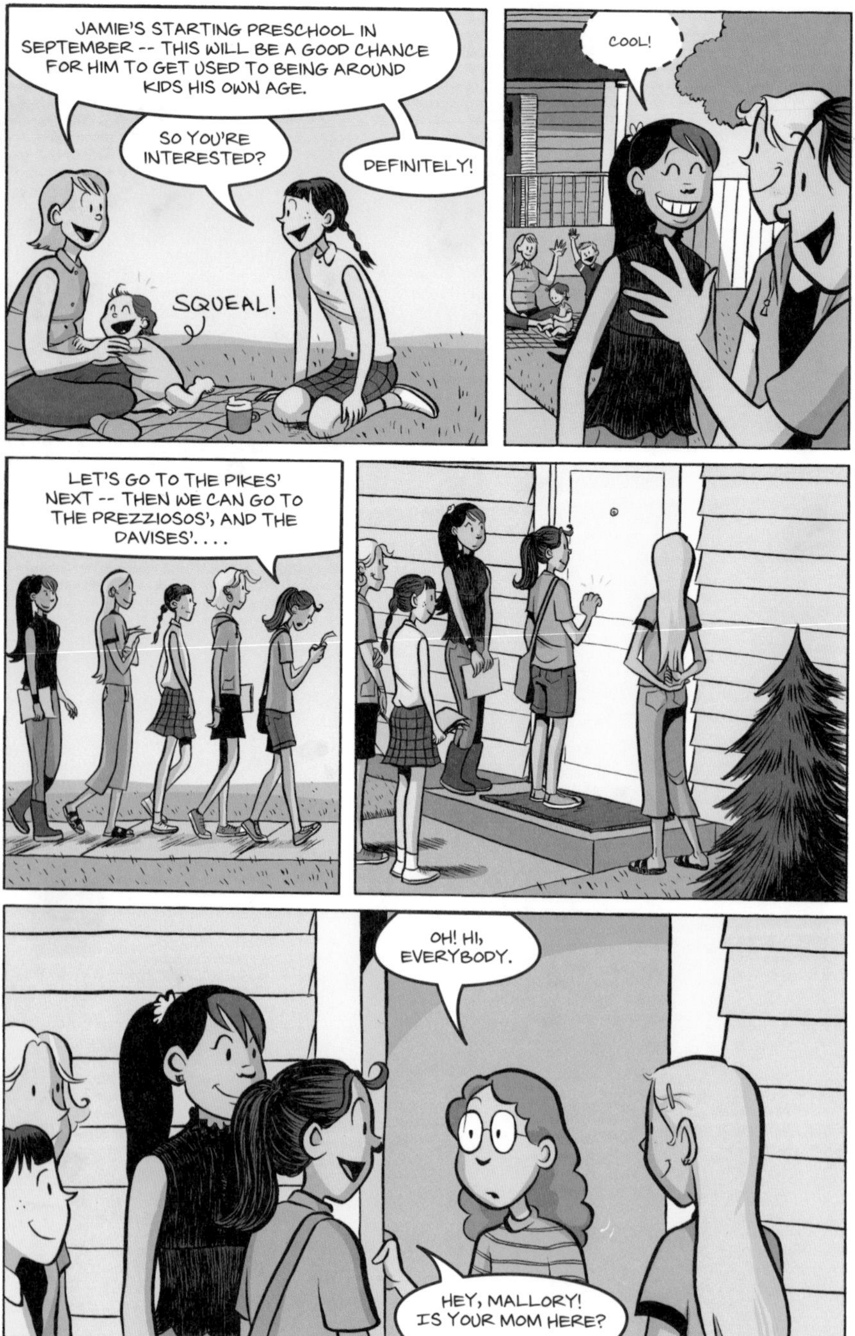
JAMIE'S STARTING PRESCHOOL IN SEPTEMBER -- THIS WILL BE A GOOD CHANCE FOR HIM TO GET USED TO BEING AROUND KIDS HIS OWN AGE.
SO YOU'RE INTERESTED?
DEFINITELY!
SQUEAL!
COOL!
LET'S GO TO THE PIKES' NEXT -- THEN WE CAN GO TO THE PREZZIOSOS', AND THE DAVISES'. . . .
OH! HI, EVERYBODY.
HEY, MALLORY! IS YOUR MOM HERE?

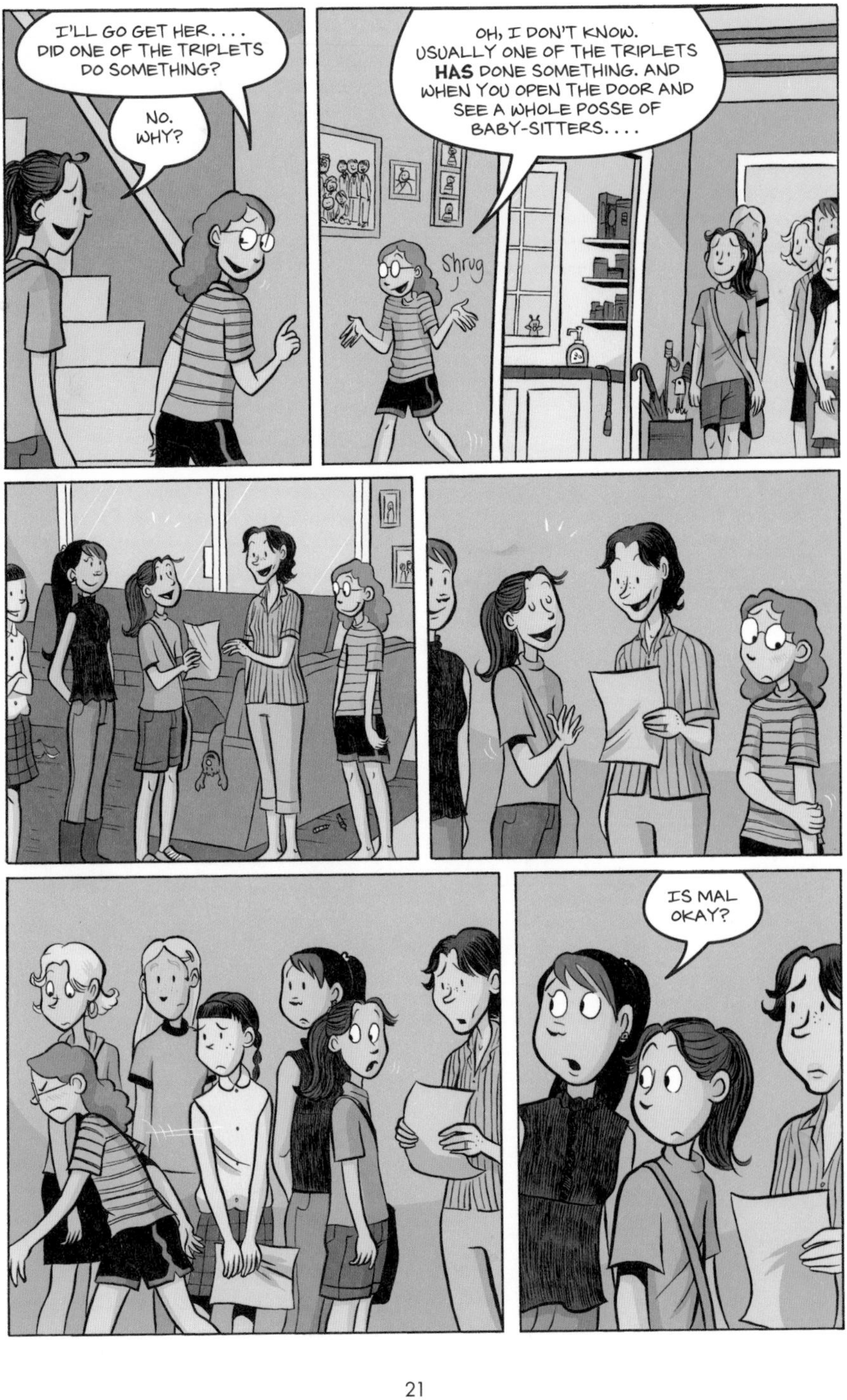
I'LL GO GET HER. . . .
DID ONE OF THE TRIPLETS DO SOMETHING?
NO. WHY?
OH, I DON'T KNOW. USUALLY ONE OF THE TRIPLETS **HAS** DONE SOMETHING. AND WHEN YOU OPEN THE DOOR AND SEE A WHOLE POSSE OF BABY-SITTERS. . . .
Shrug
IS MAL OKAY?

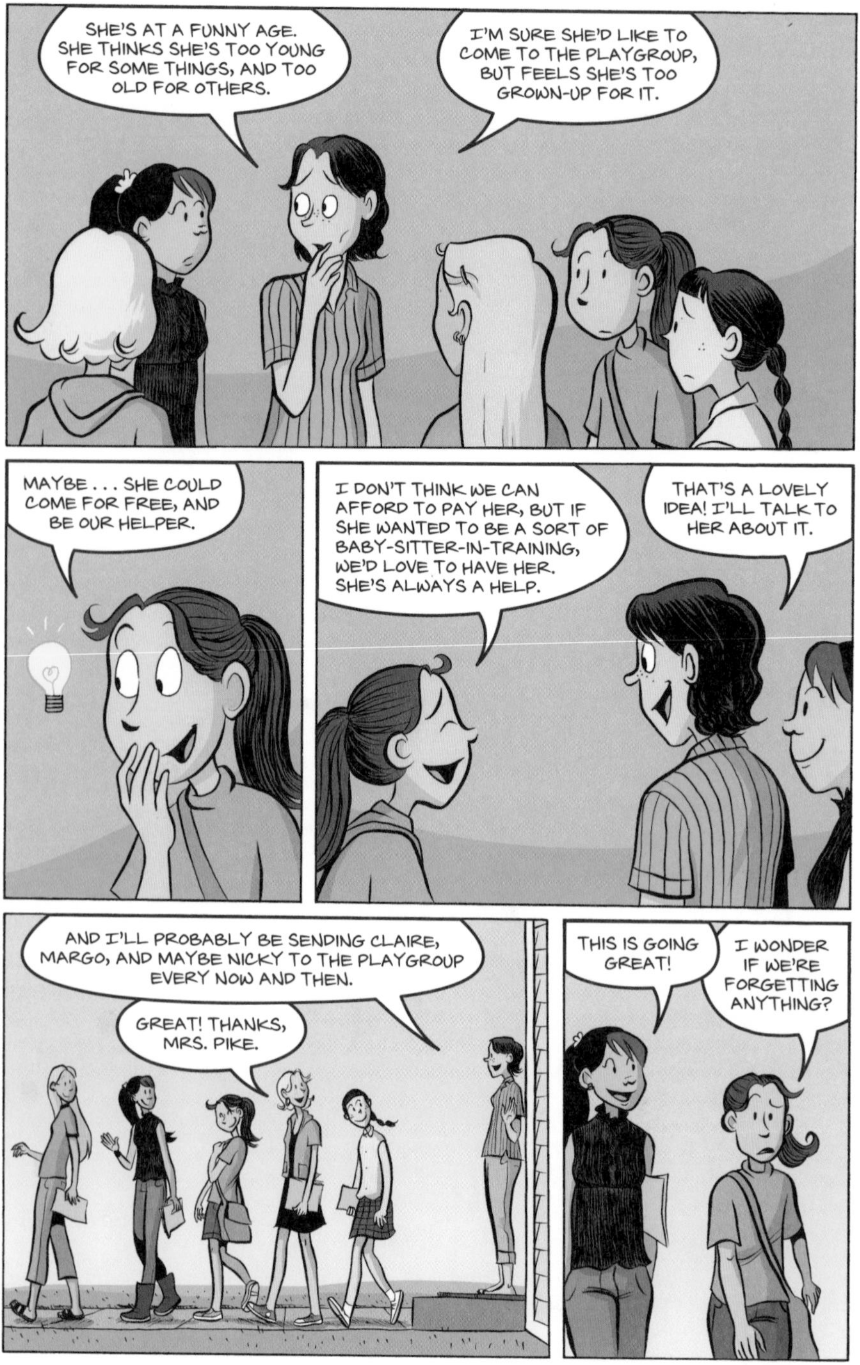
SHE'S AT A FUNNY AGE. SHE THINKS SHE'S TOO YOUNG FOR SOME THINGS, AND TOO OLD FOR OTHERS.
I'M SURE SHE'D LIKE TO COME TO THE PLAYGROUP, BUT FEELS SHE'S TOO GROWN-UP FOR IT.
MAYBE . . . SHE COULD COME FOR FREE, AND BE OUR HELPER.
I DON'T THINK WE CAN AFFORD TO PAY HER, BUT IF SHE WANTED TO BE A SORT OF BABY-SITTER-IN-TRAINING, WE'D LOVE TO HAVE HER. SHE'S ALWAYS A HELP.
THAT'S A LOVELY IDEA! I'LL TALK TO HER ABOUT IT.
AND I'LL PROBABLY BE SENDING CLAIRE, MARGO, AND MAYBE NICKY TO THE PLAYGROUP EVERY NOW AND THEN.
GREAT! THANKS, MRS. PIKE.
THIS IS GOING GREAT!
I WONDER IF WE'RE FORGETTING ANYTHING?

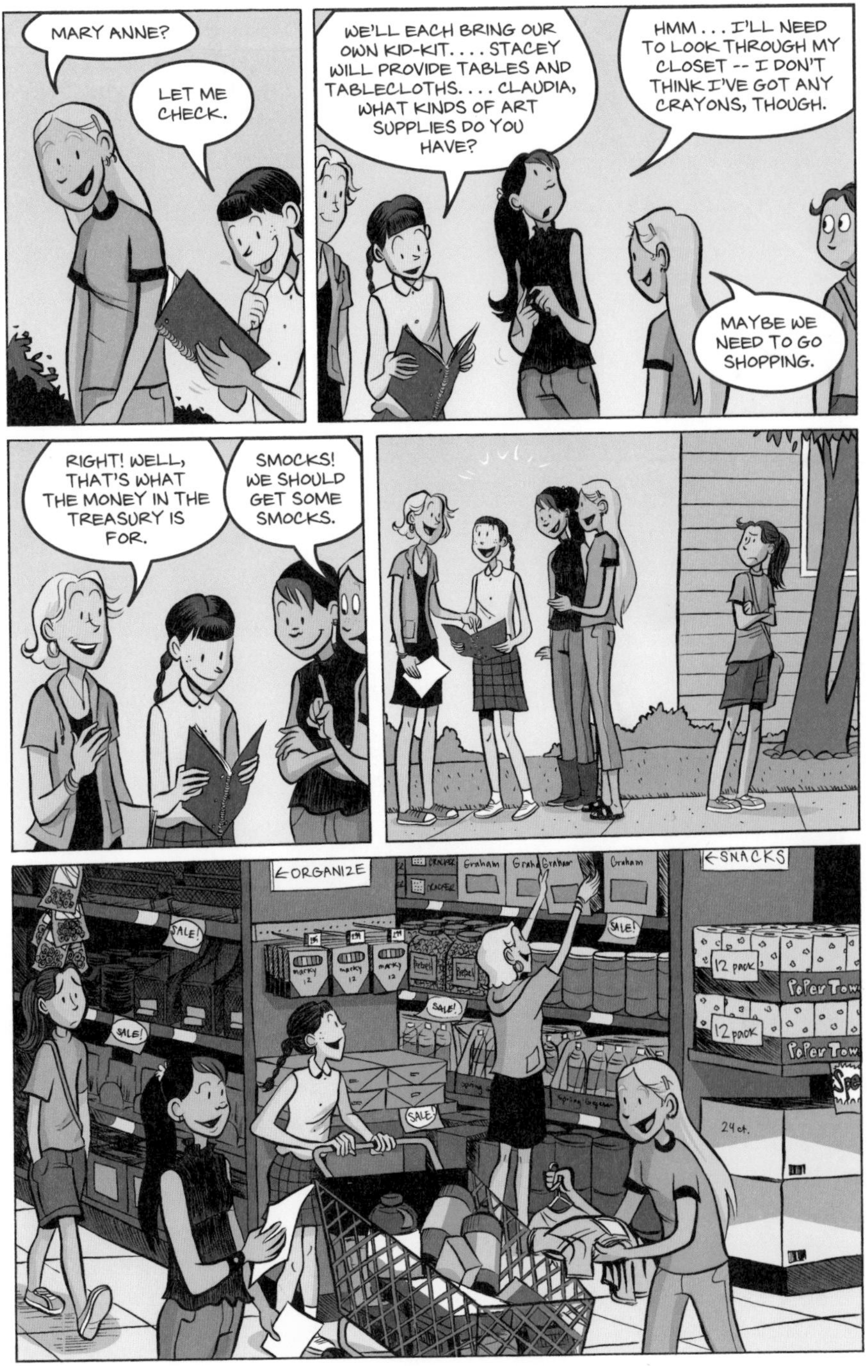
MARY ANNE?
LET ME CHECK.
WE'LL EACH BRING OUR OWN KID-KIT. . . . STACEY WILL PROVIDE TABLES AND TABLECLOTHS. . . . CLAUDIA, WHAT KINDS OF ART SUPPLIES DO YOU HAVE?
HMM . . . I'LL NEED TO LOOK THROUGH MY CLOSET -- I DON'T THINK I'VE GOT ANY CRAYONS, THOUGH.
MAYBE WE NEED TO GO SHOPPING.
RIGHT! WELL, THAT'S WHAT THE MONEY IN THE TREASURY IS FOR.
SMOCKS! WE SHOULD GET SOME SMOCKS.
←ORGANIZE
←SNACKS
Graham
SALE!
12 pack
24 ct.

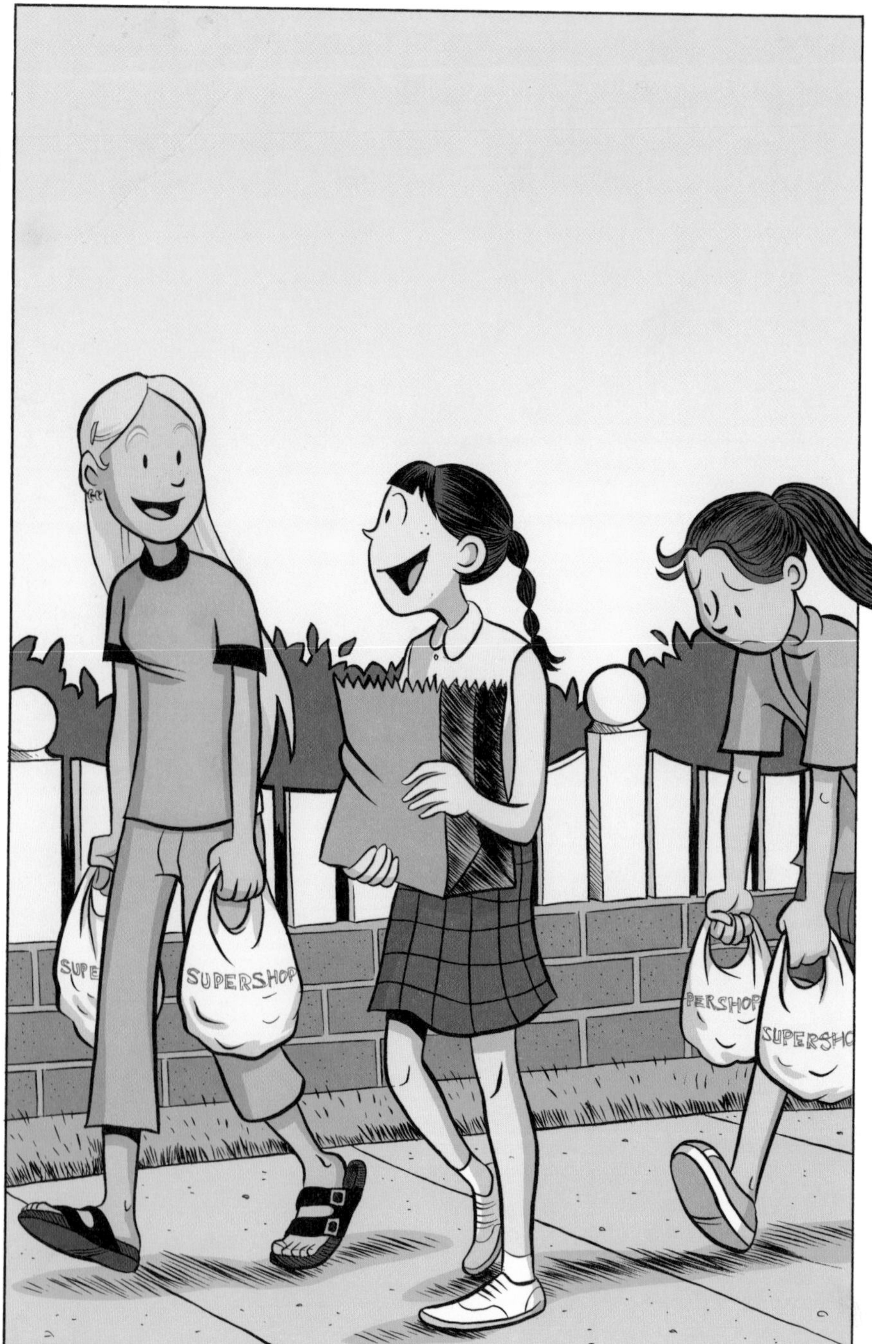
SUPE
SUPERSHOP
PERSHOP
SUPERSHO

CHAPTER 4

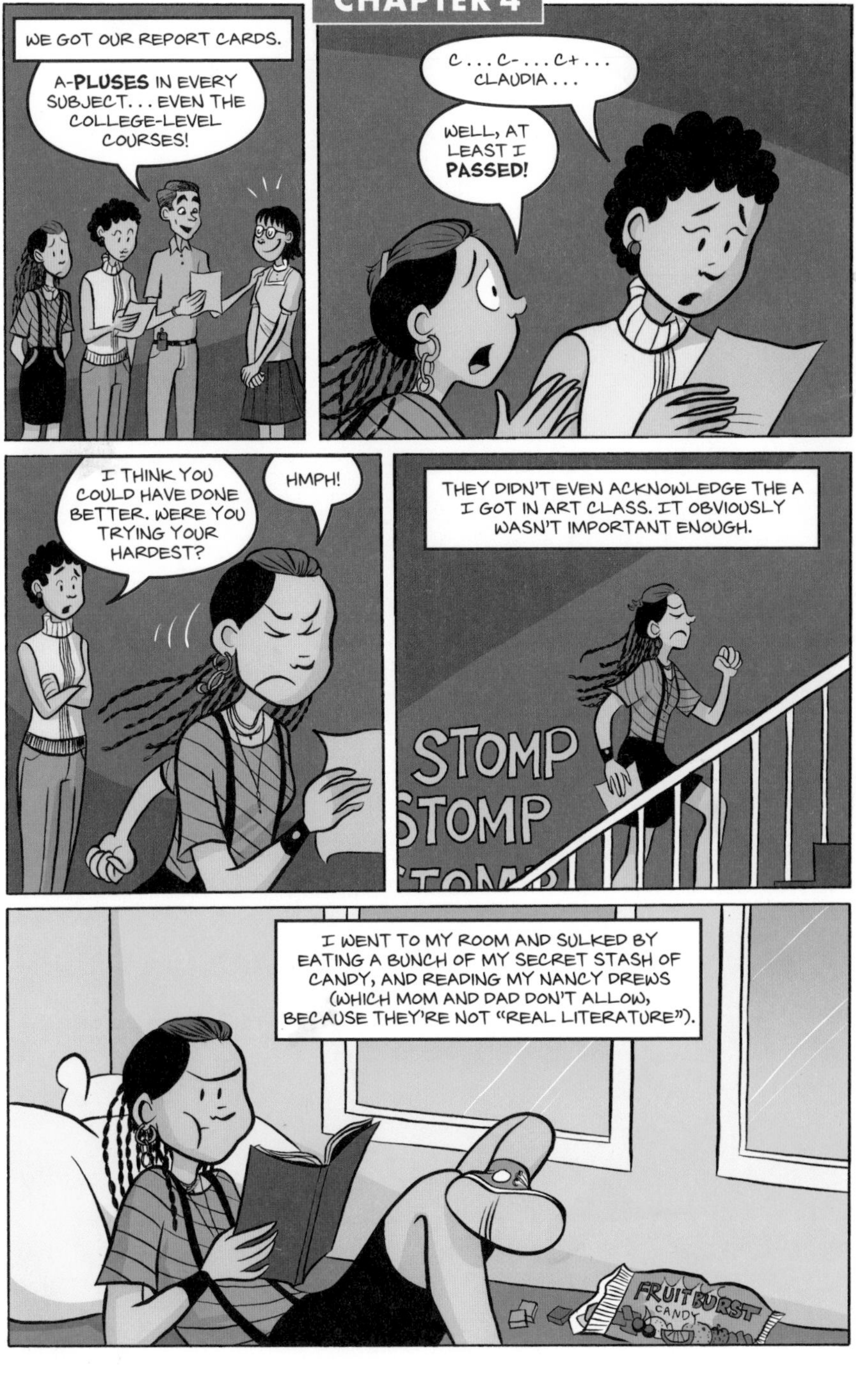

WE GOT OUR REPORT CARDS.
A-**PLUSES** IN EVERY SUBJECT... EVEN THE COLLEGE-LEVEL COURSES!
C... C-... C+... CLAUDIA...
WELL, AT LEAST I **PASSED!**
I THINK YOU COULD HAVE DONE BETTER. WERE YOU TRYING YOUR HARDEST?
HMPH!
THEY DIDN'T EVEN ACKNOWLEDGE THE A I GOT IN ART CLASS. IT OBVIOUSLY WASN'T IMPORTANT ENOUGH.
STOMP
STOMP
I WENT TO MY ROOM AND SULKED BY EATING A BUNCH OF MY SECRET STASH OF CANDY, AND READING MY NANCY DREWS (WHICH MOM AND DAD DON'T ALLOW, BECAUSE THEY'RE NOT "REAL LITERATURE").
FRUITBURST
CANDY

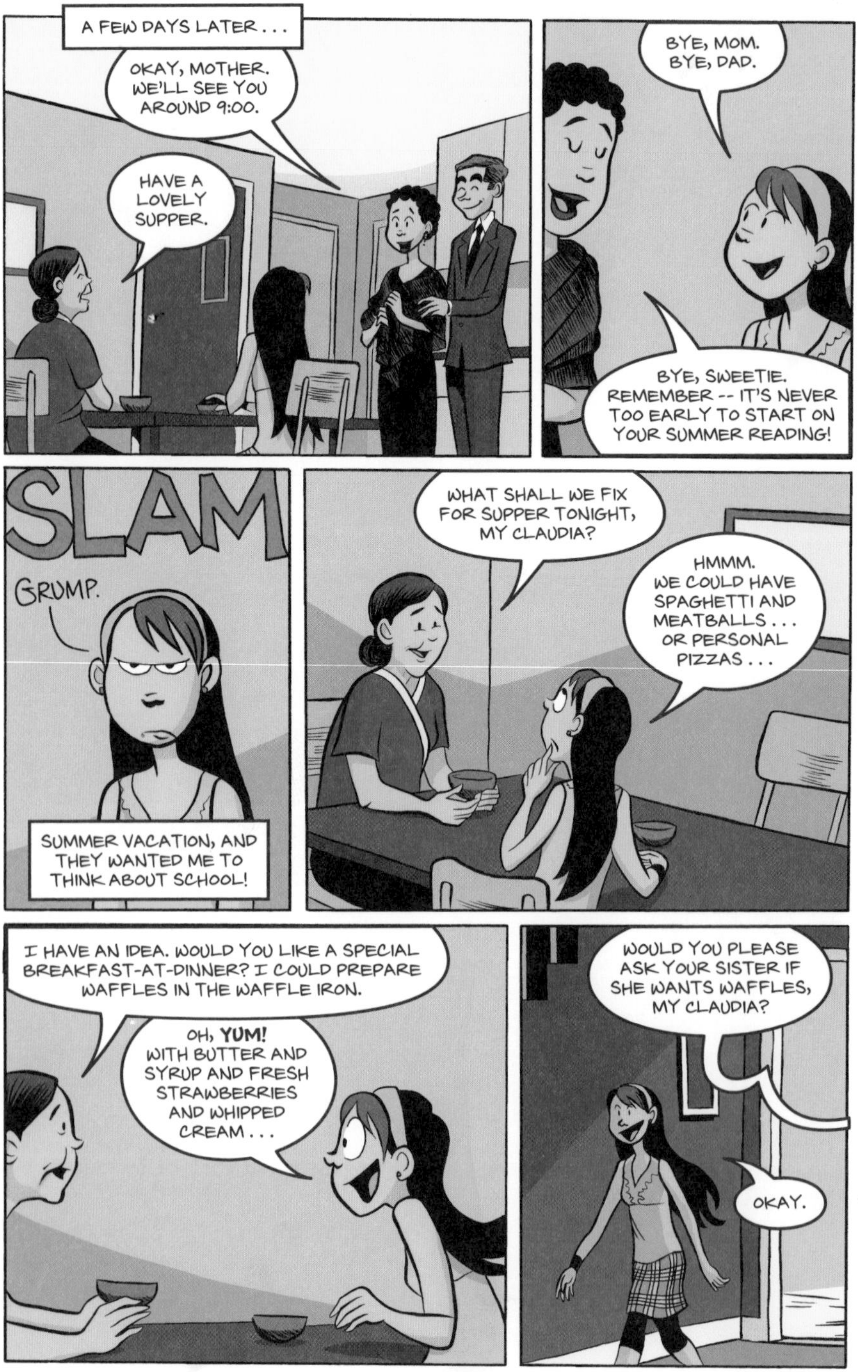
A FEW DAYS LATER . . .
OKAY, MOTHER. WE'LL SEE YOU AROUND 9:00.
HAVE A LOVELY SUPPER.
BYE, MOM. BYE, DAD.
BYE, SWEETIE. REMEMBER -- IT'S NEVER TOO EARLY TO START ON YOUR SUMMER READING!
SLAM
GRUMP.
SUMMER VACATION, AND THEY WANTED ME TO THINK ABOUT SCHOOL!
WHAT SHALL WE FIX FOR SUPPER TONIGHT, MY CLAUDIA?
HMMM. WE COULD HAVE SPAGHETTI AND MEATBALLS . . . OR PERSONAL PIZZAS . . .
I HAVE AN IDEA. WOULD YOU LIKE A SPECIAL BREAKFAST-AT-DINNER? I COULD PREPARE WAFFLES IN THE WAFFLE IRON.
OH, YUM! WITH BUTTER AND SYRUP AND FRESH STRAWBERRIES AND WHIPPED CREAM . . .
WOULD YOU PLEASE ASK YOUR SISTER IF SHE WANTS WAFFLES, MY CLAUDIA?
OKAY.

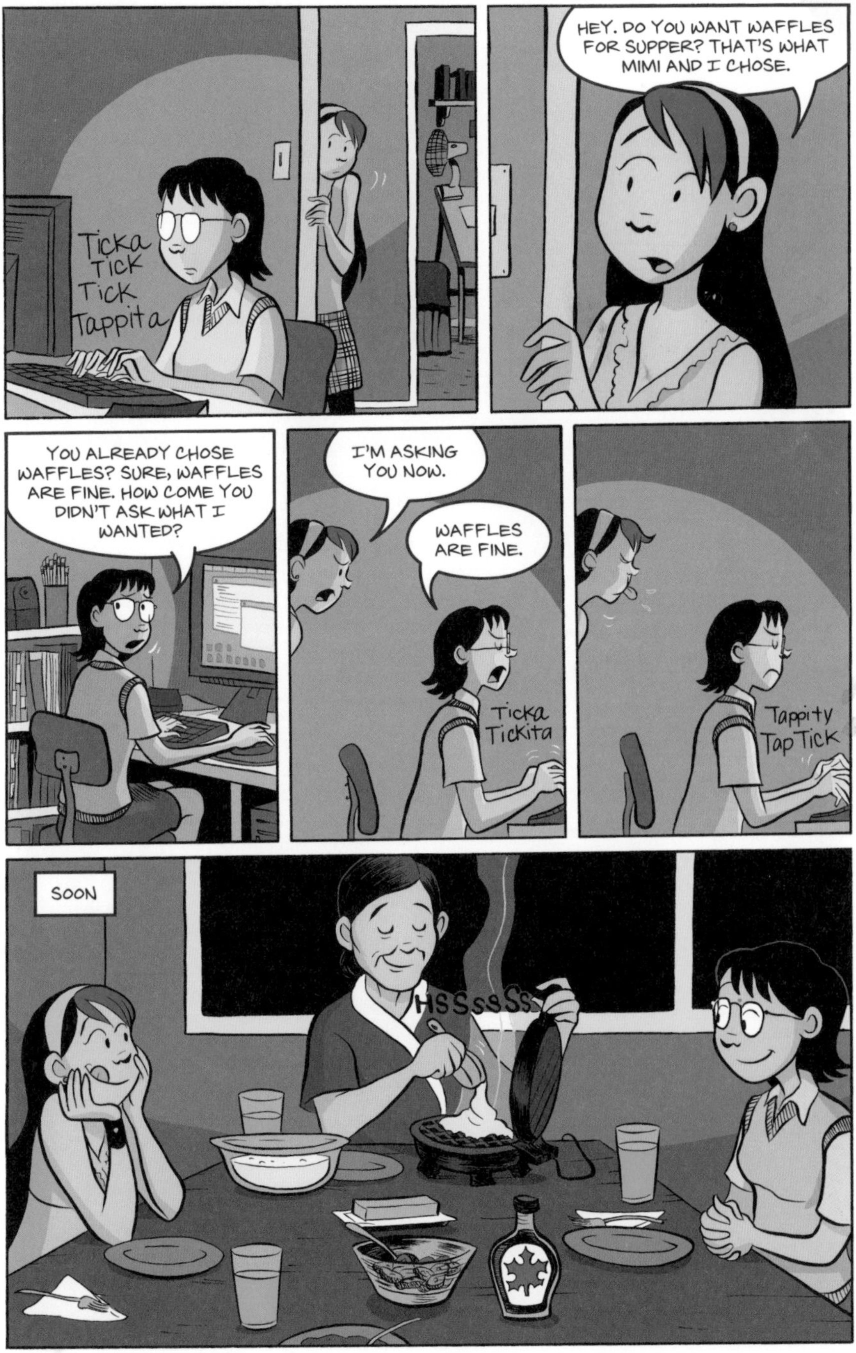

Ticka
Tick
Tick
Tappita
HEY. DO YOU WANT WAFFLES FOR SUPPER? THAT'S WHAT MIMI AND I CHOSE.
YOU ALREADY CHOSE WAFFLES? SURE, WAFFLES ARE FINE. HOW COME YOU DIDN'T ASK WHAT I WANTED?
I'M ASKING YOU NOW.
WAFFLES ARE FINE.
Ticka
Tickita
Tappity
Tap Tick
SOON
HSSssSS

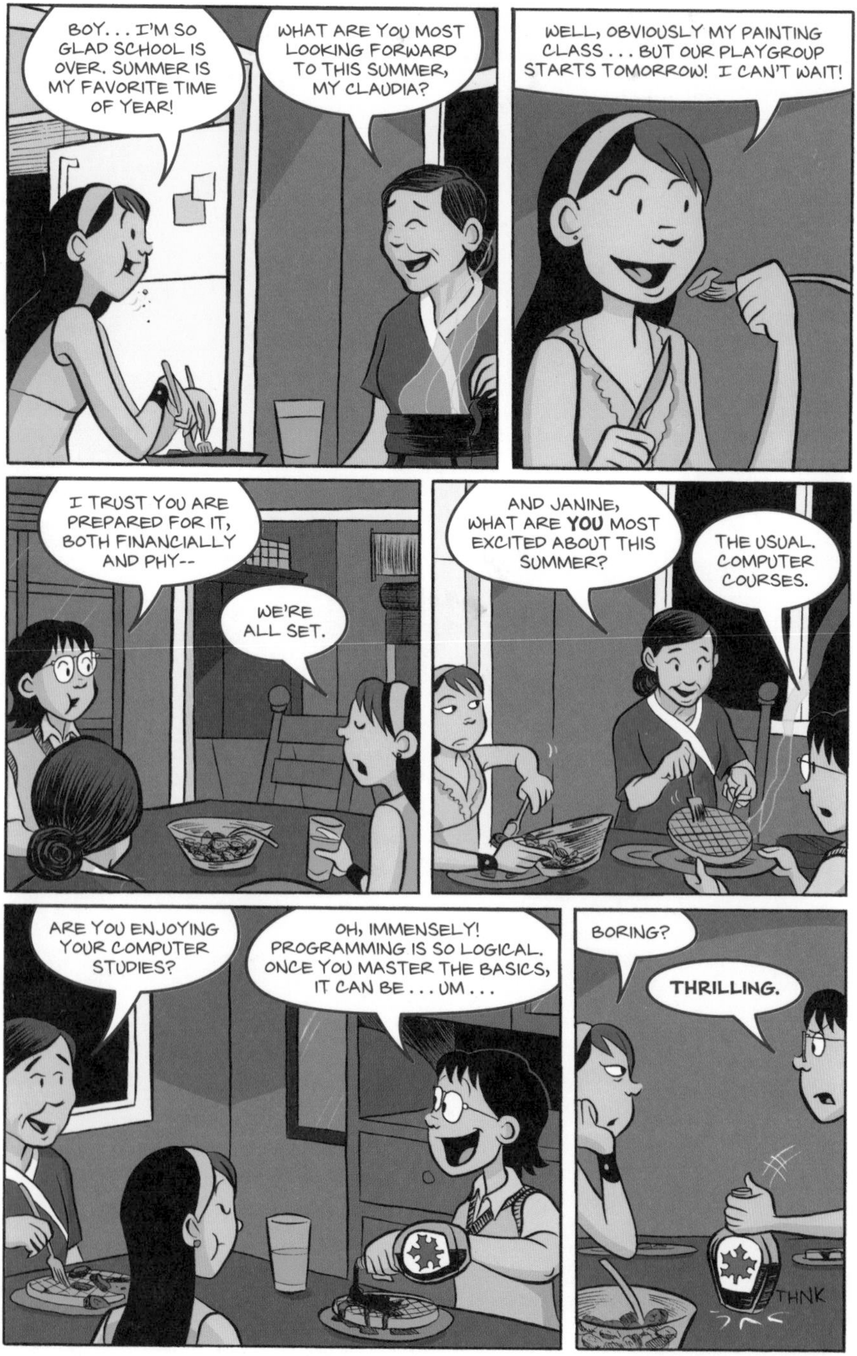
BOY. . . I'M SO GLAD SCHOOL IS OVER. SUMMER IS MY FAVORITE TIME OF YEAR!
WHAT ARE YOU MOST LOOKING FORWARD TO THIS SUMMER, MY CLAUDIA?
WELL, OBVIOUSLY MY PAINTING CLASS . . . BUT OUR PLAYGROUP STARTS TOMORROW! I CAN'T WAIT!
I TRUST YOU ARE PREPARED FOR IT, BOTH FINANCIALLY AND PHY--
WE'RE ALL SET.
AND JANINE, WHAT ARE **YOU** MOST EXCITED ABOUT THIS SUMMER?
THE USUAL. COMPUTER COURSES.
ARE YOU ENJOYING YOUR COMPUTER STUDIES?
OH, IMMENSELY! PROGRAMMING IS SO LOGICAL. ONCE YOU MASTER THE BASICS, IT CAN BE . . . UM . . .
BORING?
THRILLING.
THNK

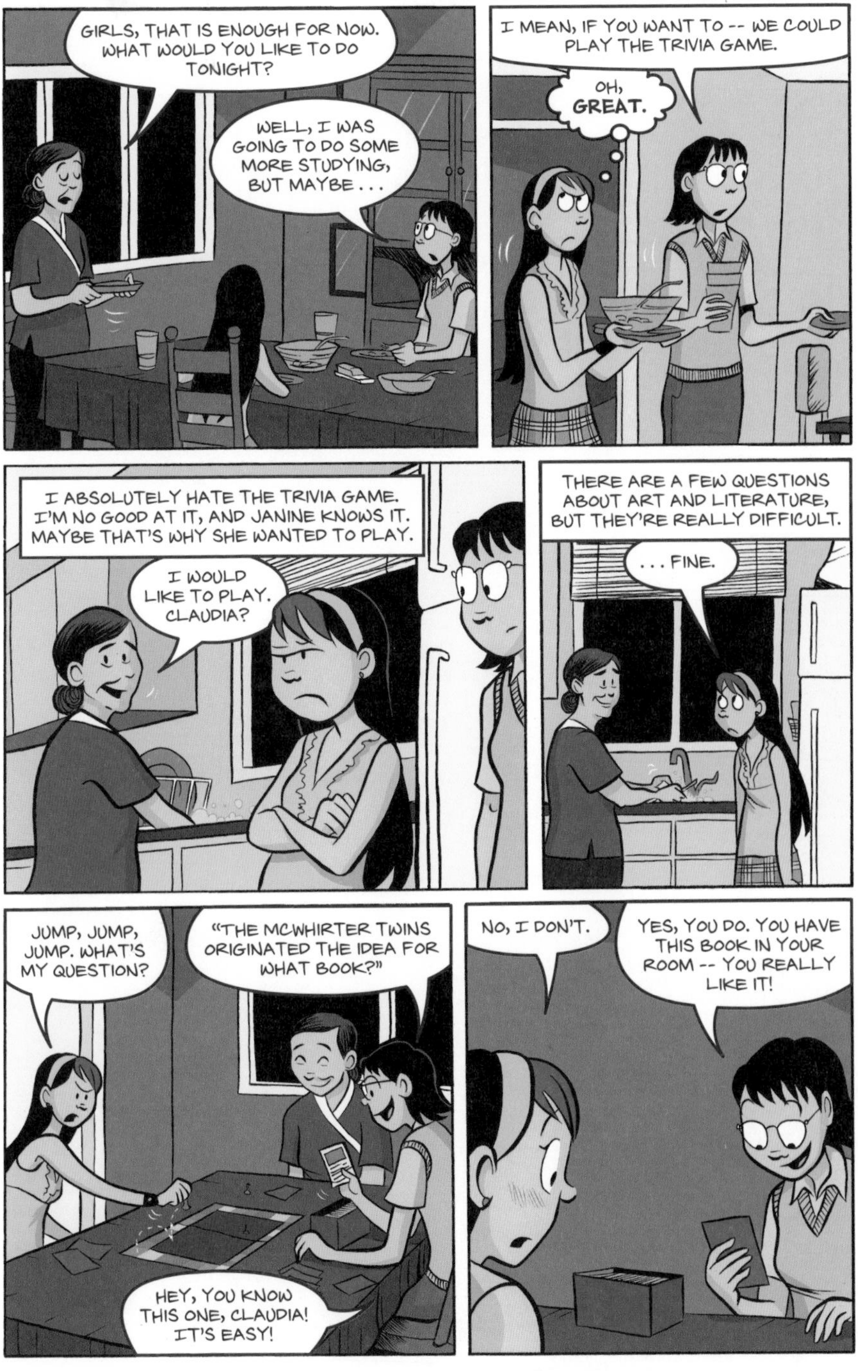
GIRLS, THAT IS ENOUGH FOR NOW. WHAT WOULD YOU LIKE TO DO TONIGHT?
WELL, I WAS GOING TO DO SOME MORE STUDYING, BUT MAYBE . . .
I MEAN, IF YOU WANT TO -- WE COULD PLAY THE TRIVIA GAME.
OH, GREAT.
I ABSOLUTELY HATE THE TRIVIA GAME. I'M NO GOOD AT IT, AND JANINE KNOWS IT. MAYBE THAT'S WHY SHE WANTED TO PLAY.
I WOULD LIKE TO PLAY. CLAUDIA?
THERE ARE A FEW QUESTIONS ABOUT ART AND LITERATURE, BUT THEY'RE REALLY DIFFICULT.
. . . FINE.
JUMP, JUMP, JUMP. WHAT'S MY QUESTION?
"THE MCWHIRTER TWINS ORIGINATED THE IDEA FOR WHAT BOOK?"
HEY, YOU KNOW THIS ONE, CLAUDIA! IT'S EASY!
NO, I DON'T.
YES, YOU DO. YOU HAVE THIS BOOK IN YOUR ROOM -- YOU REALLY LIKE IT!

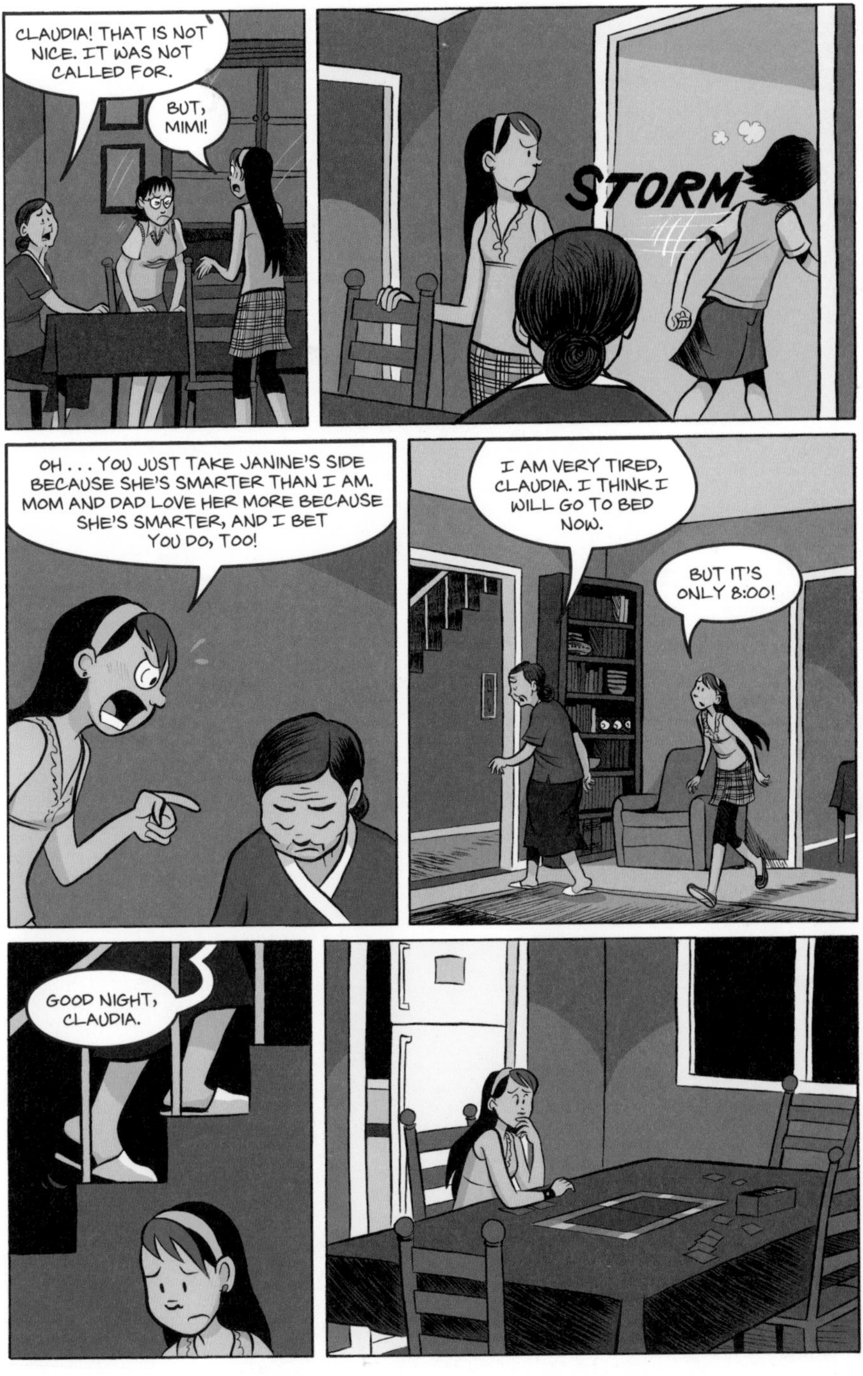
CLAUDIA! THAT IS NOT NICE. IT WAS NOT CALLED FOR.
BUT, MIMI!
STORM
OH . . . YOU JUST TAKE JANINE'S SIDE BECAUSE SHE'S SMARTER THAN I AM. MOM AND DAD LOVE HER MORE BECAUSE SHE'S SMARTER, AND I BET YOU DO, TOO!
I AM VERY TIRED, CLAUDIA. I THINK I WILL GO TO BED NOW.
BUT IT'S ONLY 8:00!
GOOD NIGHT, CLAUDIA.

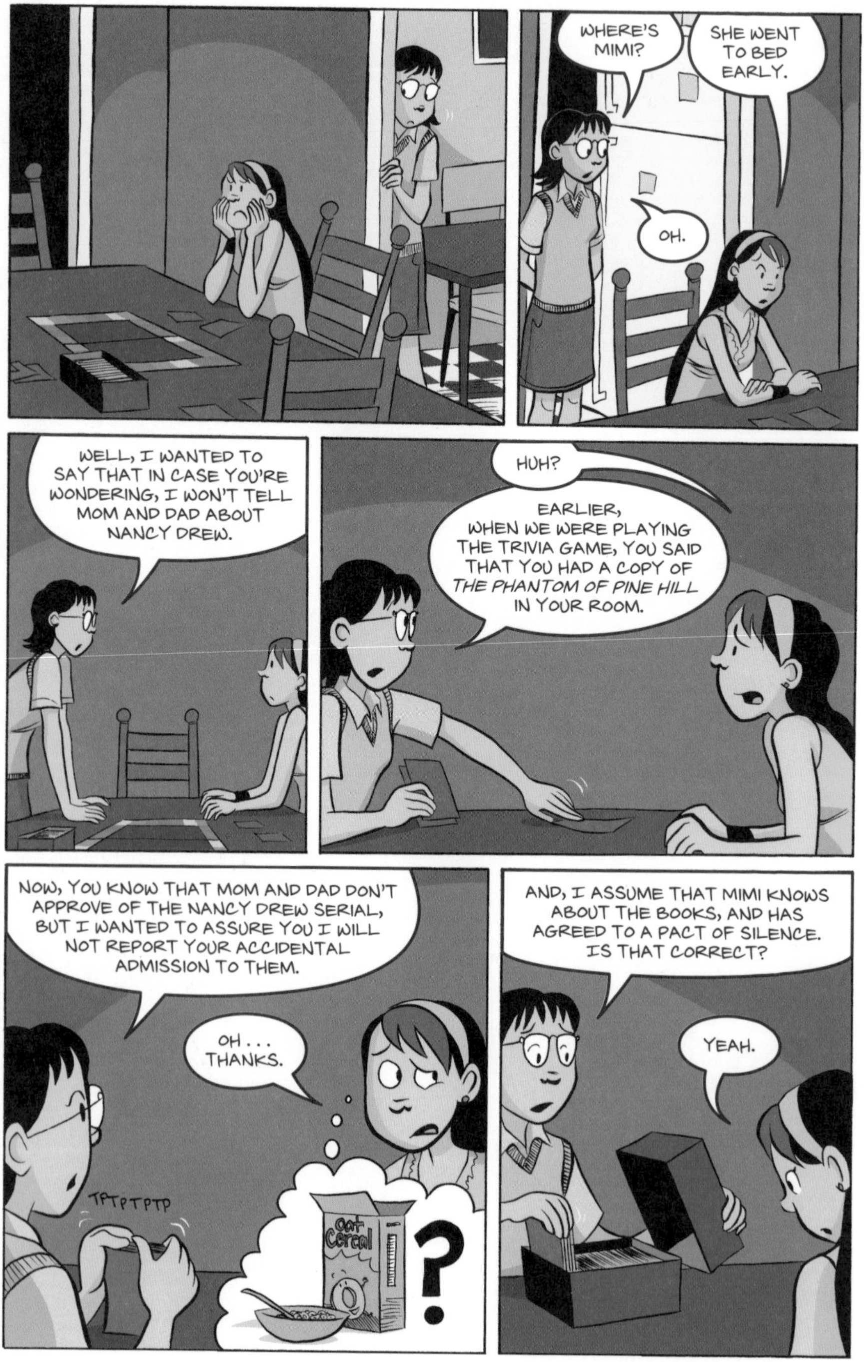
WHERE'S MIMI?
SHE WENT TO BED EARLY.
OH.
WELL, I WANTED TO SAY THAT IN CASE YOU'RE WONDERING, I WON'T TELL MOM AND DAD ABOUT NANCY DREW.
HUH?
EARLIER, WHEN WE WERE PLAYING THE TRIVIA GAME, YOU SAID THAT YOU HAD A COPY OF *THE PHANTOM OF PINE HILL* IN YOUR ROOM.
NOW, YOU KNOW THAT MOM AND DAD DON'T APPROVE OF THE NANCY DREW SERIAL, BUT I WANTED TO ASSURE YOU I WILL NOT REPORT YOUR ACCIDENTAL ADMISSION TO THEM.
OH . . . THANKS.
TPTPTPTP
Oat Cereal
?
AND, I ASSUME THAT MIMI KNOWS ABOUT THE BOOKS, AND HAS AGREED TO A PACT OF SILENCE. IS THAT CORRECT?
YEAH.

33

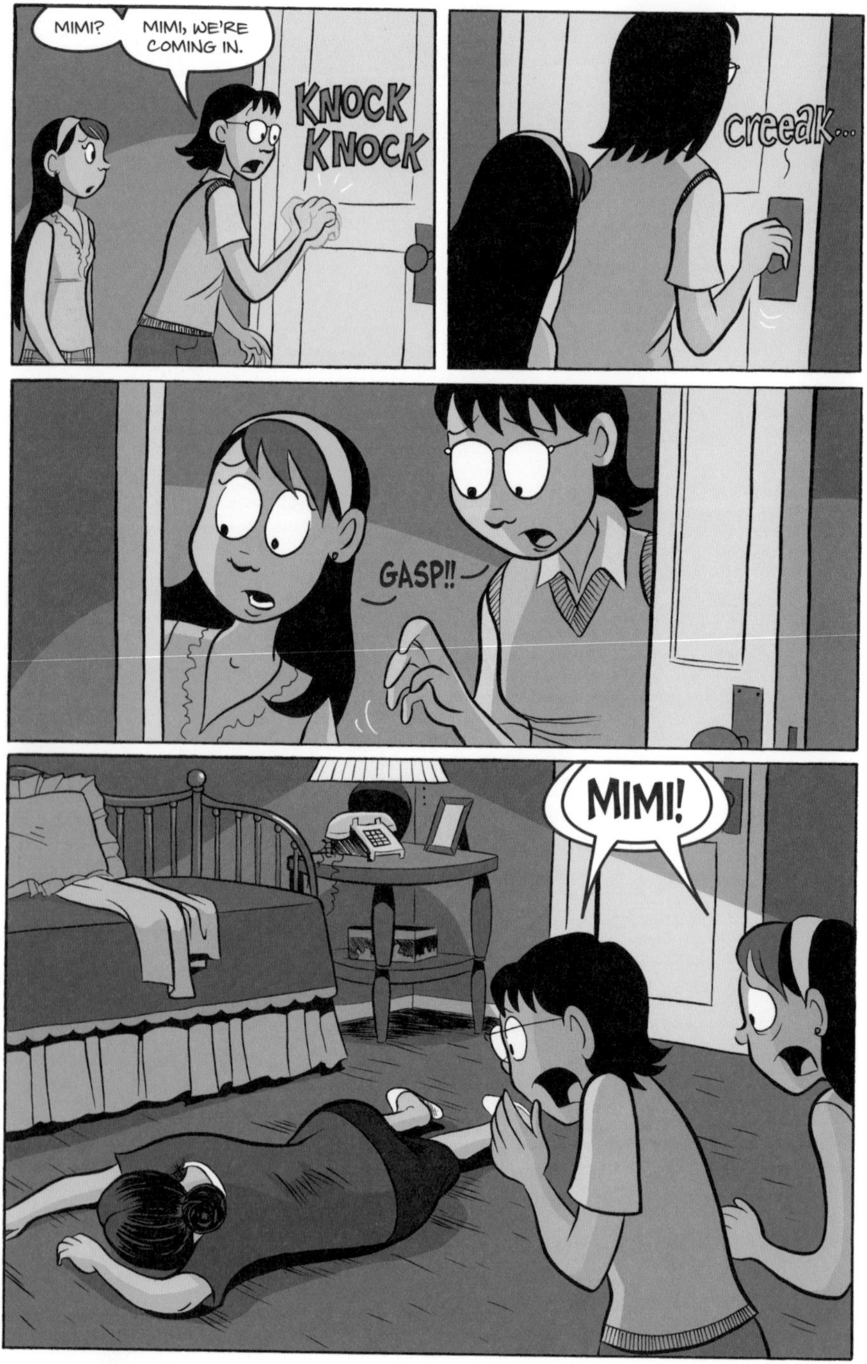
MIMI?
MIMI, WE'RE COMING IN.
KNOCK KNOCK
creeak...
GASP!!
MIMI!

CHAPTER 5

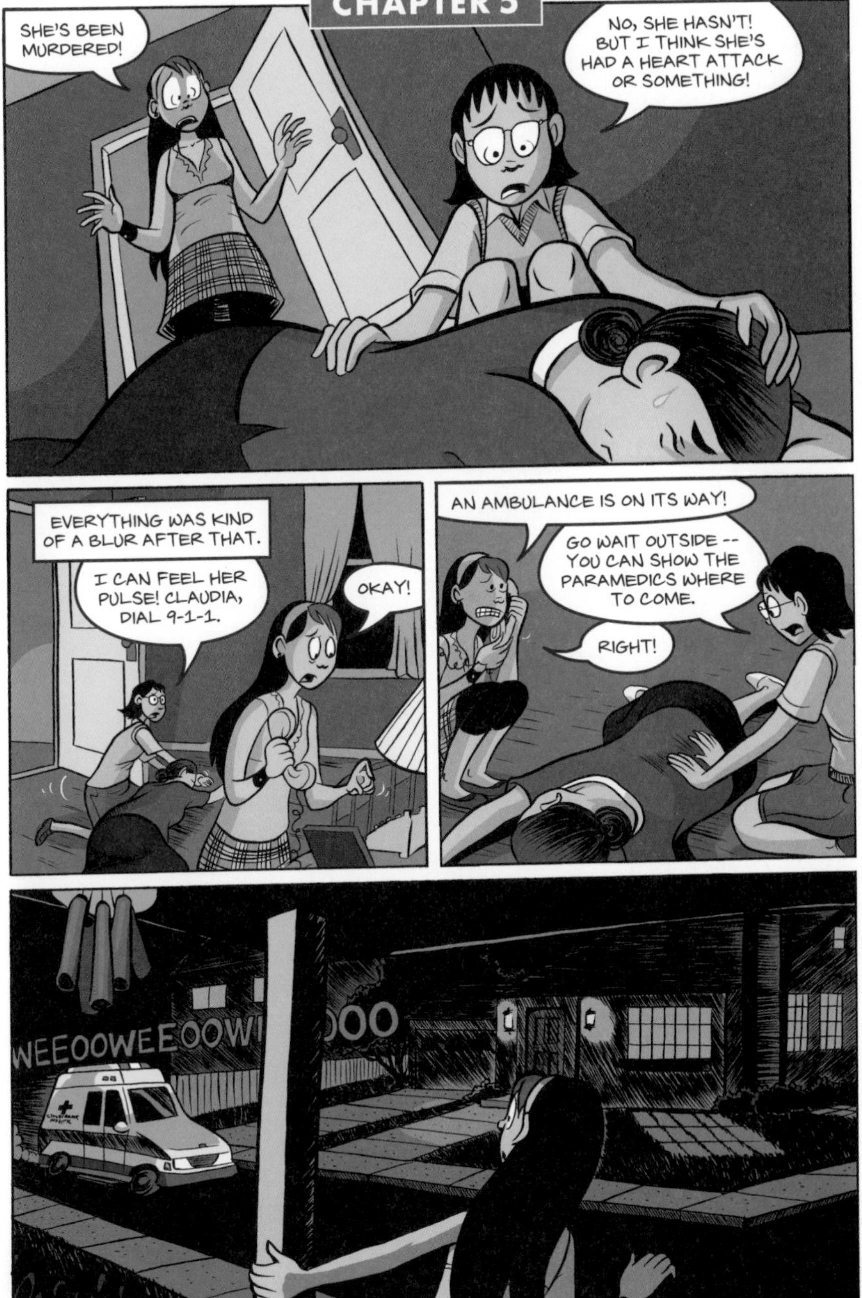
SHE'S BEEN MURDERED!
NO, SHE HASN'T! BUT I THINK SHE'S HAD A HEART ATTACK OR SOMETHING!
EVERYTHING WAS KIND OF A BLUR AFTER THAT.
I CAN FEEL HER PULSE! CLAUDIA, DIAL 9-1-1.
OKAY!
AN AMBULANCE IS ON ITS WAY!
GO WAIT OUTSIDE -- YOU CAN SHOW THE PARAMEDICS WHERE TO COME.
RIGHT!
WEEOOWEEOOWI
OOO

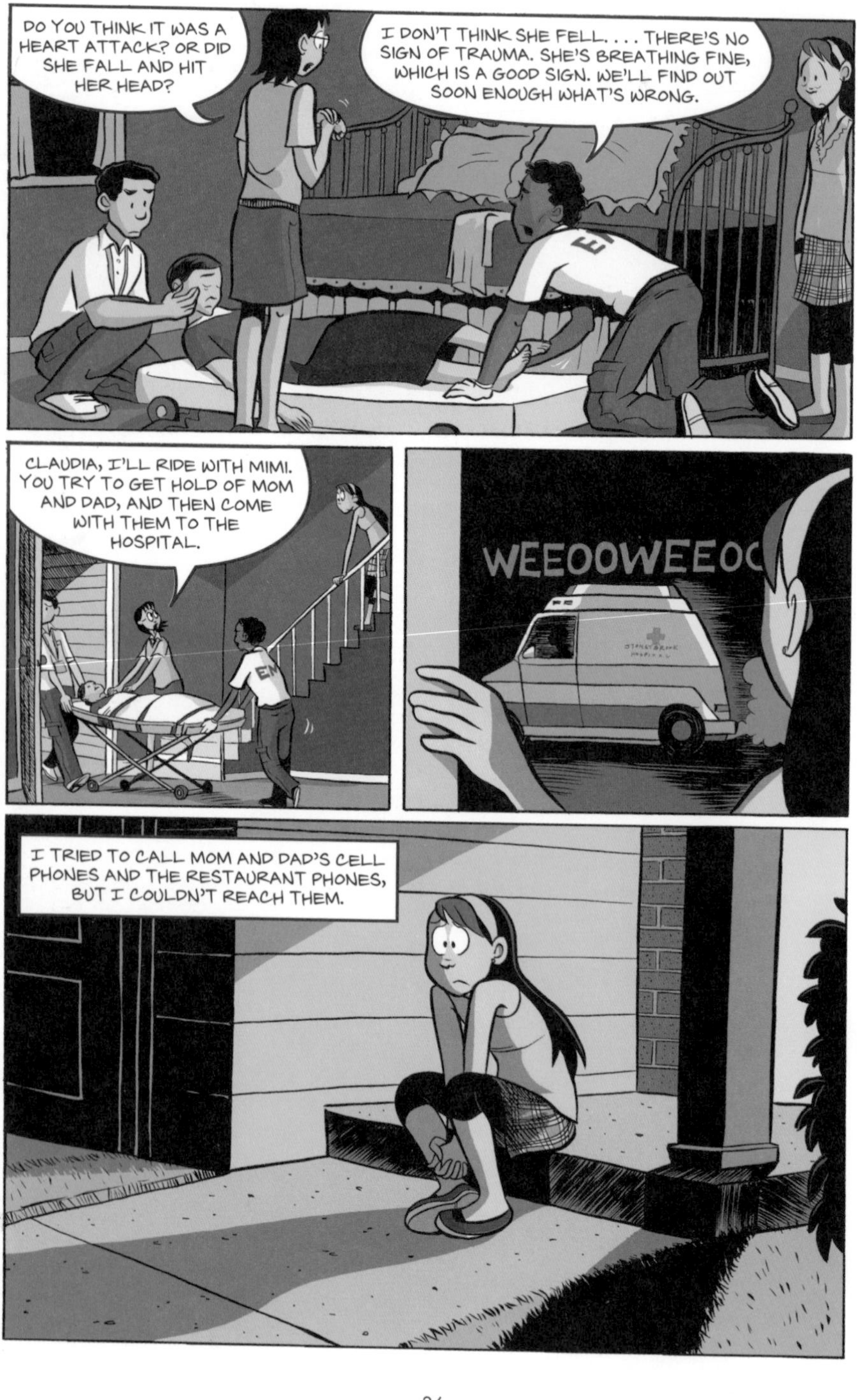
DO YOU THINK IT WAS A HEART ATTACK? OR DID SHE FALL AND HIT HER HEAD?
I DON'T THINK SHE FELL. . . . THERE'S NO SIGN OF TRAUMA. SHE'S BREATHING FINE, WHICH IS A GOOD SIGN. WE'LL FIND OUT SOON ENOUGH WHAT'S WRONG.
CLAUDIA, I'LL RIDE WITH MIMI. YOU TRY TO GET HOLD OF MOM AND DAD, AND THEN COME WITH THEM TO THE HOSPITAL.
WEEOOWEEOO
I TRIED TO CALL MOM AND DAD'S CELL PHONES AND THE RESTAURANT PHONES, BUT I COULDN'T REACH THEM.

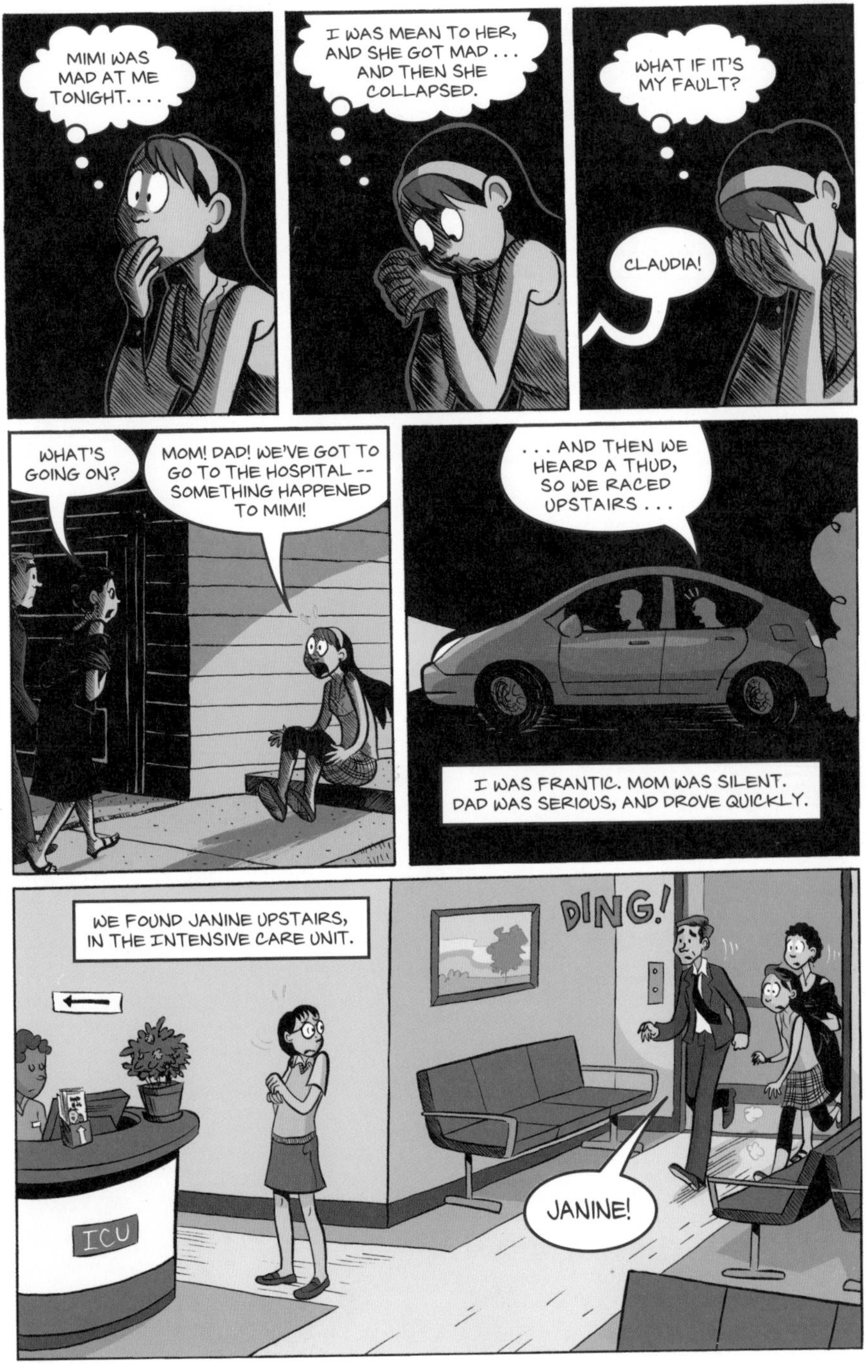
MIMI WAS MAD AT ME TONIGHT. . . .
I WAS MEAN TO HER, AND SHE GOT MAD . . . AND THEN SHE COLLAPSED.
WHAT IF IT'S MY FAULT?
CLAUDIA!
WHAT'S GOING ON?
MOM! DAD! WE'VE GOT TO GO TO THE HOSPITAL -- SOMETHING HAPPENED TO MIMI!
. . . AND THEN WE HEARD A THUD, SO WE RACED UPSTAIRS . . .
I WAS FRANTIC. MOM WAS SILENT. DAD WAS SERIOUS, AND DROVE QUICKLY.
WE FOUND JANINE UPSTAIRS, IN THE INTENSIVE CARE UNIT.
DING!
ICU
JANINE!

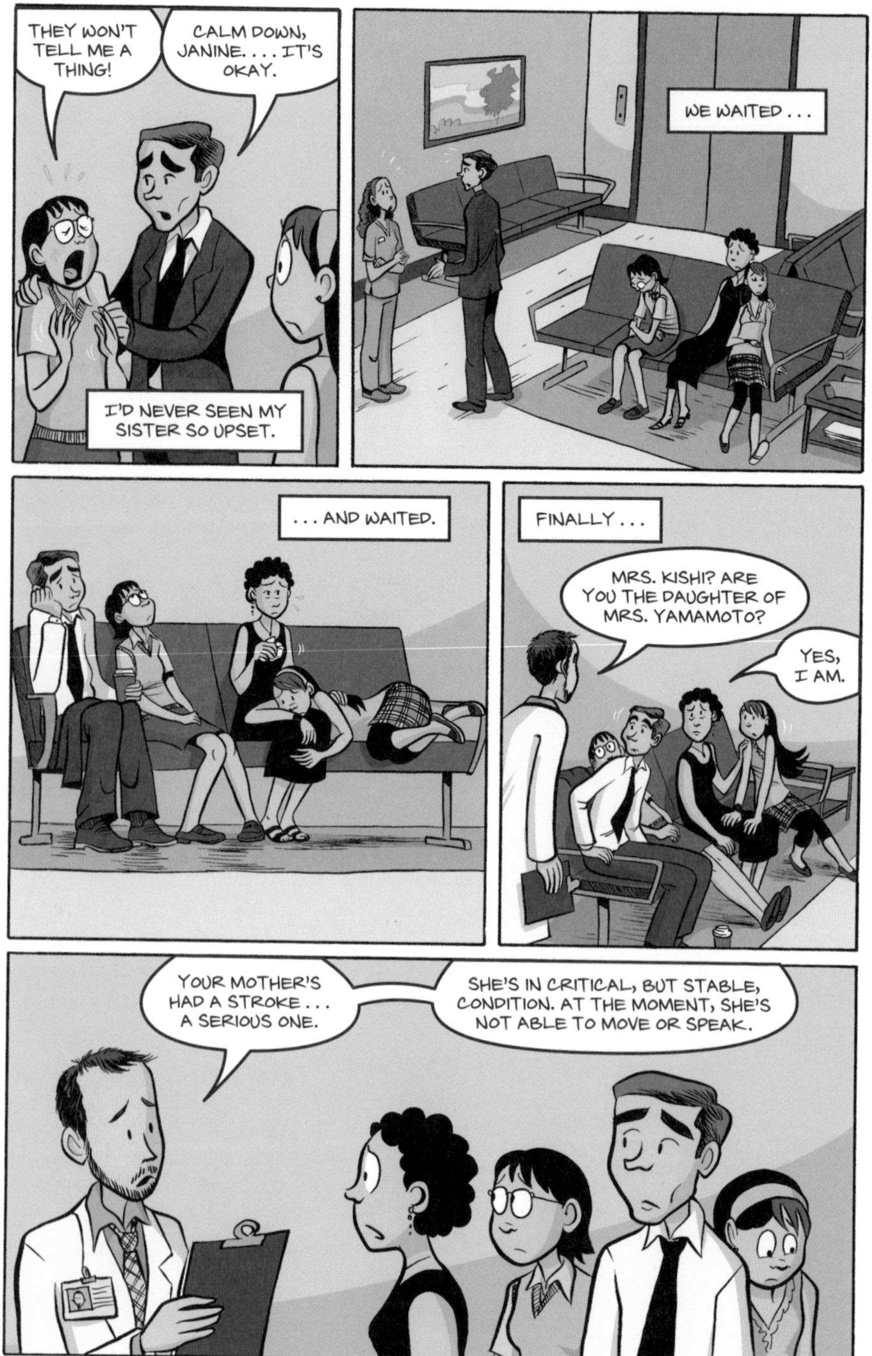
THEY WON'T TELL ME A THING!
CALM DOWN, JANINE. . . . IT'S OKAY.
I'D NEVER SEEN MY SISTER SO UPSET.
WE WAITED . . .
. . . AND WAITED.
FINALLY . . .
MRS. KISHI? ARE YOU THE DAUGHTER OF MRS. YAMAMOTO?
YES, I AM.
YOUR MOTHER'S HAD A STROKE . . . A SERIOUS ONE.
SHE'S IN CRITICAL, BUT STABLE, CONDITION. AT THE MOMENT, SHE'S NOT ABLE TO MOVE OR SPEAK.

MONDAY, JUNE 16

TODAY WAS A GOOD NEWS - BAD NEWS DAY FOR US

BABY-SITTERS. THE GOOD NEWS WAS THAT NINE CHILDREN

CAME TO THE FIRST SESSION OF OUR PLAYGROUP AND

IT WENT REALLY WELL. DAVID MICHAEL, NICKY, AND

MARCUS ARE KIND OF WILD WHEN THEY GET TOGETHER,

BUT THEY'RE MANAGEABLE. AND WE'RE GOING TO HAVE

TO DO SOMETHING ABOUT JENNY PREZZIOSO... SHE'S

A PAIN. GOT ANY IDEAS, MARY ANNE?

THE BAD NEWS WAS ABOUT CLAUDIA'S GRANDMOTHER, MIMI.

IT TURNS OUT THAT SHE HAD A STROKE LAST NIGHT AND

IS IN THE HOSPITAL. THE NEWS KIND OF UPSET US, BUT

WE WERE ABLE TO PUT OUR WORRIES ASIDE AND RUN

THE PLAYGROUP OKAY, WHICH I GUESS PROVES

WE'RE PROFESSIONALS.
                                    -DAWN

CHAPTER 6

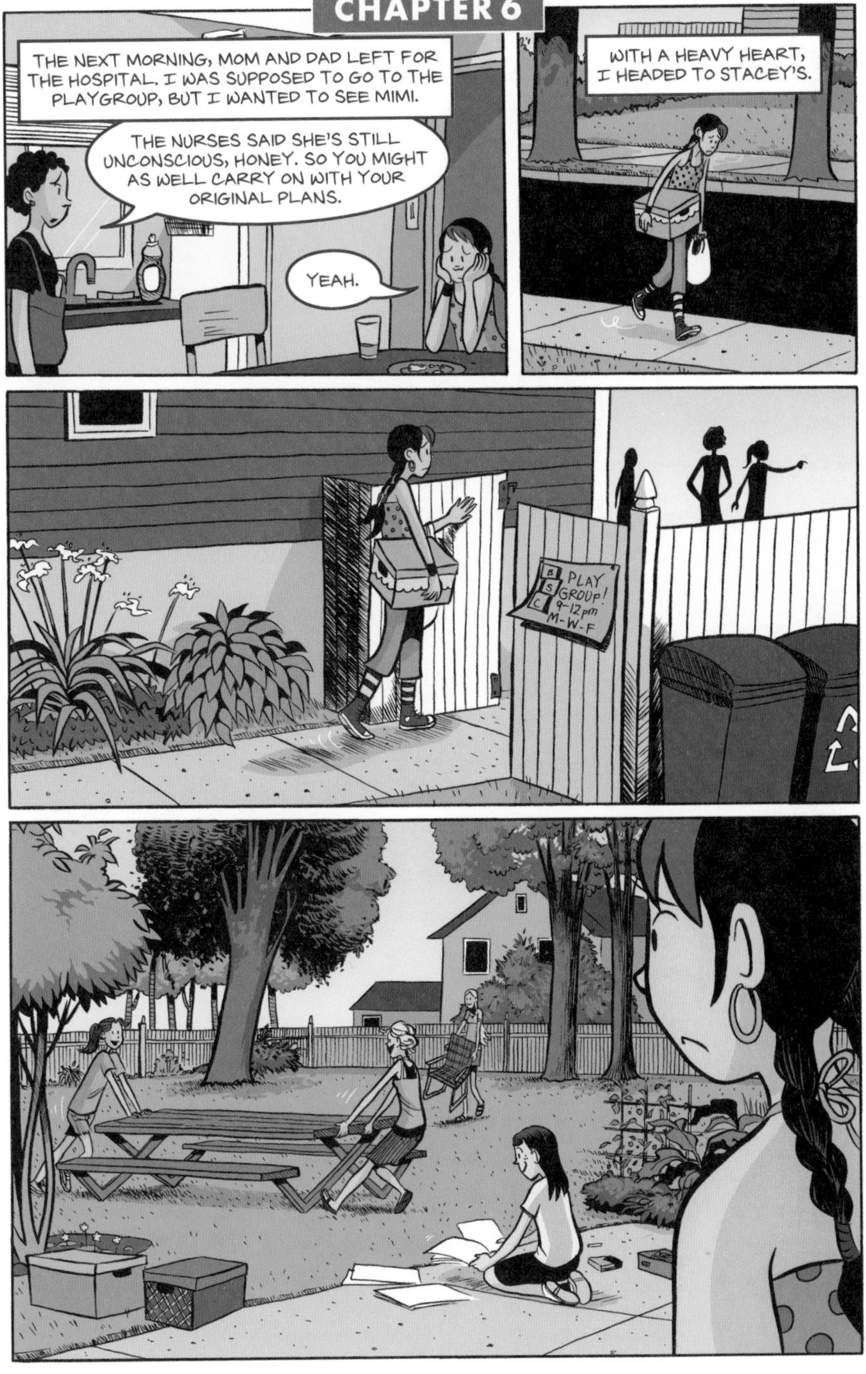
THE NEXT MORNING, MOM AND DAD LEFT FOR THE HOSPITAL. I WAS SUPPOSED TO GO TO THE PLAYGROUP, BUT I WANTED TO SEE MIMI.
THE NURSES SAID SHE'S STILL UNCONSCIOUS, HONEY. SO YOU MIGHT AS WELL CARRY ON WITH YOUR ORIGINAL PLANS.
YEAH.
WITH A HEAVY HEART, I HEADED TO STACEY'S.
B
S
C
PLAY GROUP!
9-12pm
M-W-F

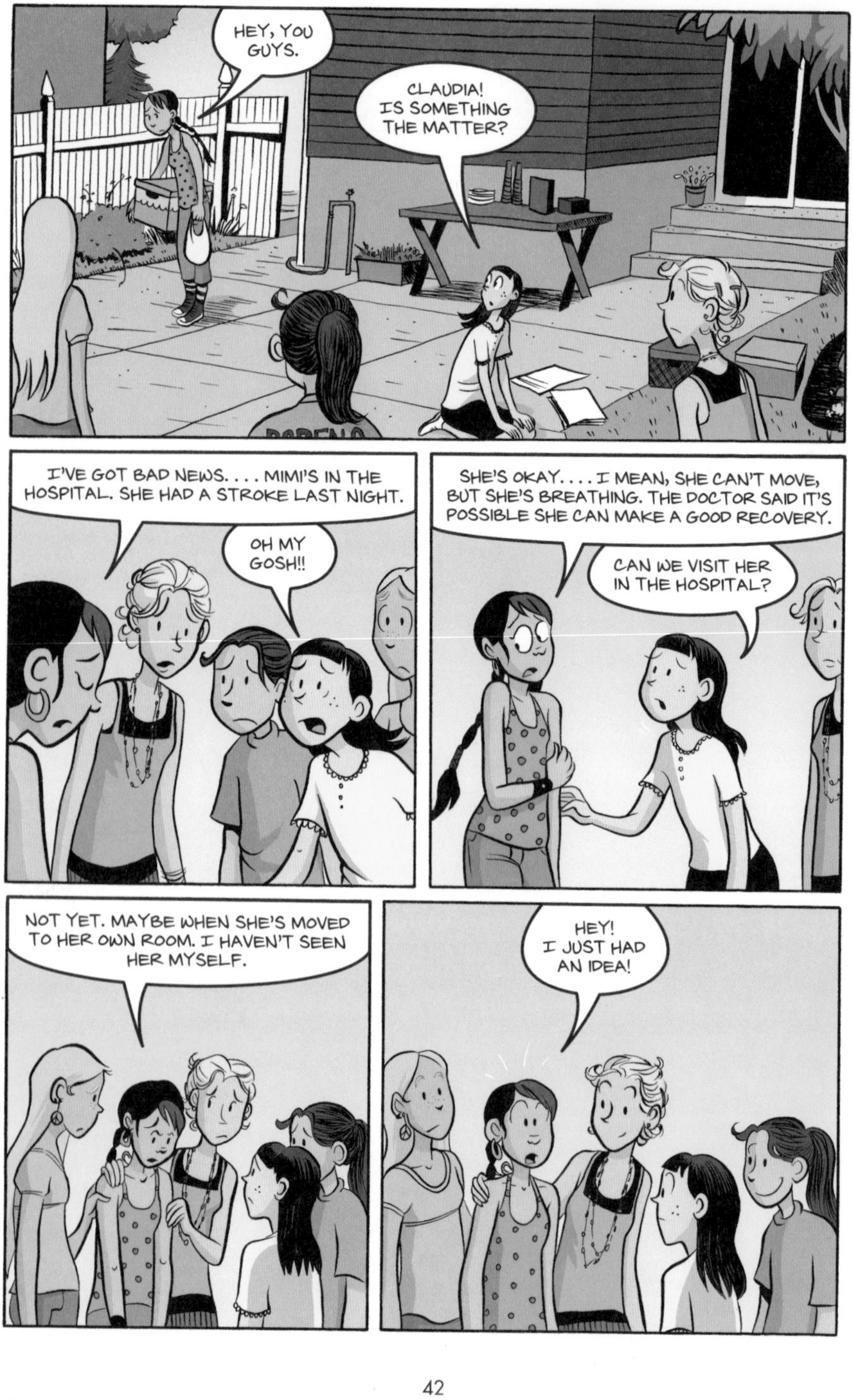
HEY, YOU GUYS.
CLAUDIA! IS SOMETHING THE MATTER?
I'VE GOT BAD NEWS. . . . MIMI'S IN THE HOSPITAL. SHE HAD A STROKE LAST NIGHT.
OH MY GOSH!!
SHE'S OKAY. . . . I MEAN, SHE CAN'T MOVE, BUT SHE'S BREATHING. THE DOCTOR SAID IT'S POSSIBLE SHE CAN MAKE A GOOD RECOVERY.
CAN WE VISIT HER IN THE HOSPITAL?
NOT YET. MAYBE WHEN SHE'S MOVED TO HER OWN ROOM. I HAVEN'T SEEN HER MYSELF.
HEY! I JUST HAD AN IDEA!

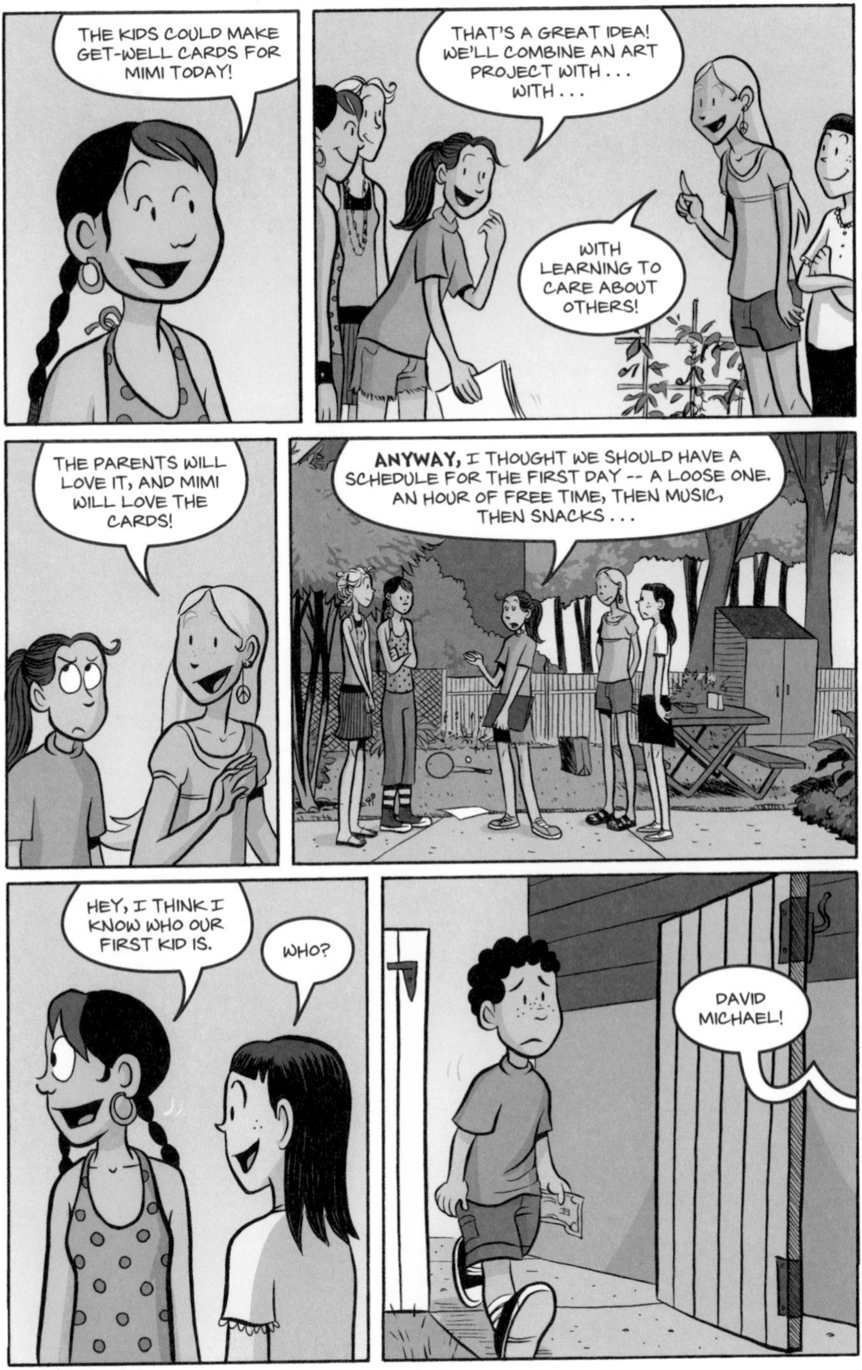
THE KIDS COULD MAKE GET-WELL CARDS FOR MIMI TODAY!
THAT'S A GREAT IDEA! WE'LL COMBINE AN ART PROJECT WITH . . . WITH . . .
WITH LEARNING TO CARE ABOUT OTHERS!
THE PARENTS WILL LOVE IT, AND MIMI WILL LOVE THE CARDS!
ANYWAY, I THOUGHT WE SHOULD HAVE A SCHEDULE FOR THE FIRST DAY -- A LOOSE ONE. AN HOUR OF FREE TIME, THEN MUSIC, THEN SNACKS . . .
HEY, I THINK I KNOW WHO OUR FIRST KID IS.
WHO?
DAVID MICHAEL!

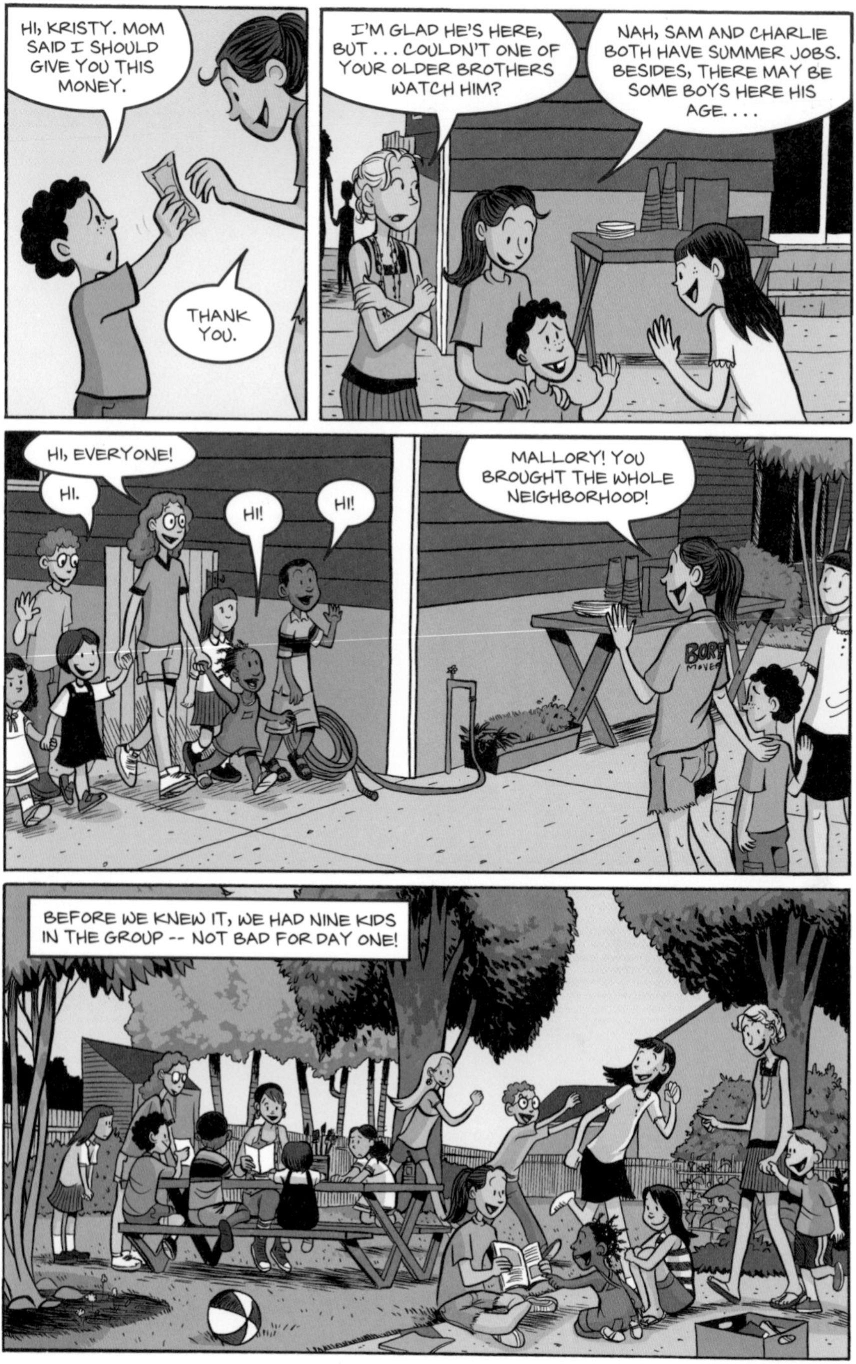
HI, KRISTY. MOM SAID I SHOULD GIVE YOU THIS MONEY.
THANK YOU.
I'M GLAD HE'S HERE, BUT . . . COULDN'T ONE OF YOUR OLDER BROTHERS WATCH HIM?
NAH, SAM AND CHARLIE BOTH HAVE SUMMER JOBS. BESIDES, THERE MAY BE SOME BOYS HERE HIS AGE. . . .
HI, EVERYONE!
HI.
HI!
HI!
MALLORY! YOU BROUGHT THE WHOLE NEIGHBORHOOD!
BEFORE WE KNEW IT, WE HAD NINE KIDS IN THE GROUP -- NOT BAD FOR DAY ONE!

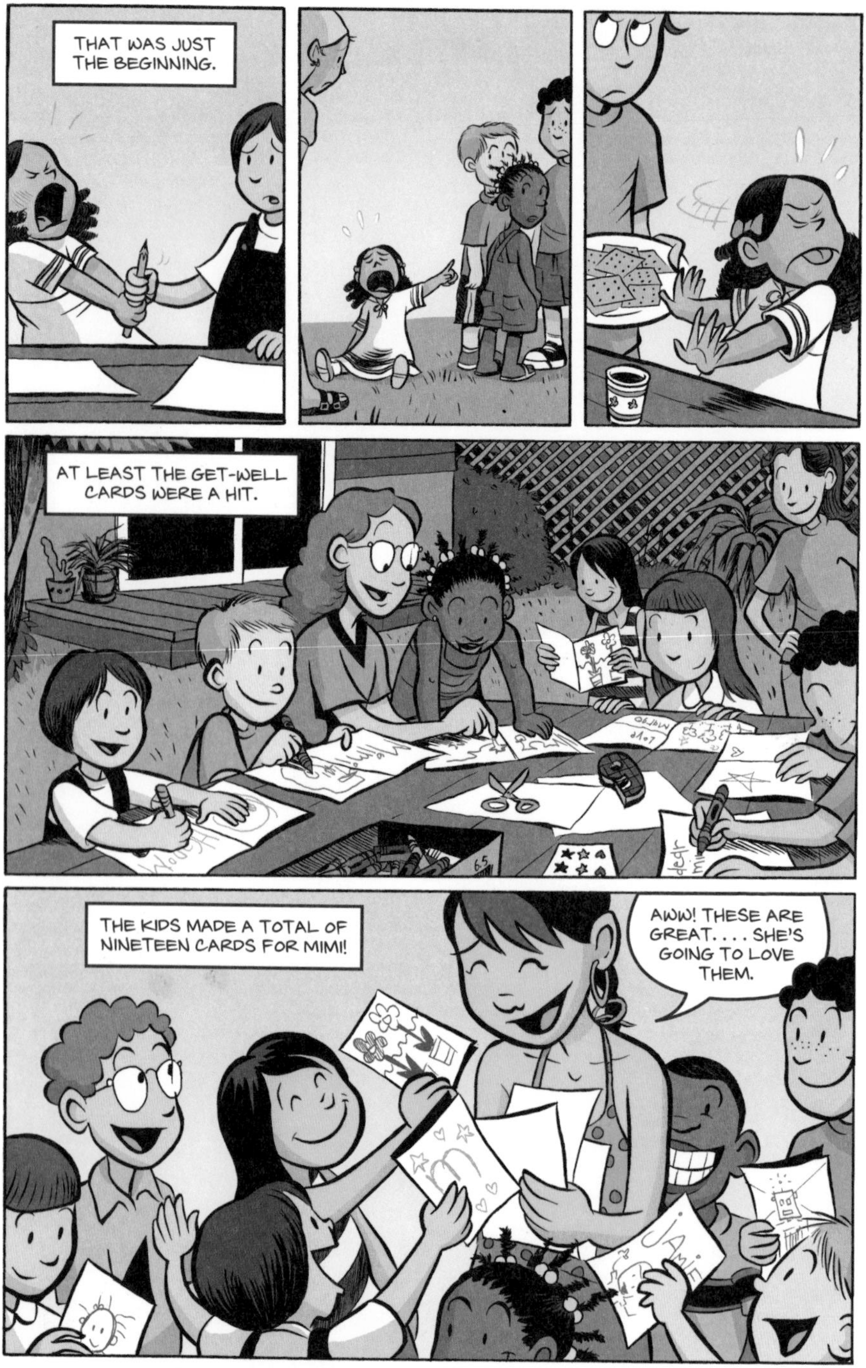
THAT WAS JUST THE BEGINNING.
AT LEAST THE GET-WELL CARDS WERE A HIT.
THE KIDS MADE A TOTAL OF NINETEEN CARDS FOR MIMI!
AWW! THESE ARE GREAT. . . . SHE'S GOING TO LOVE THEM.
JAMIE

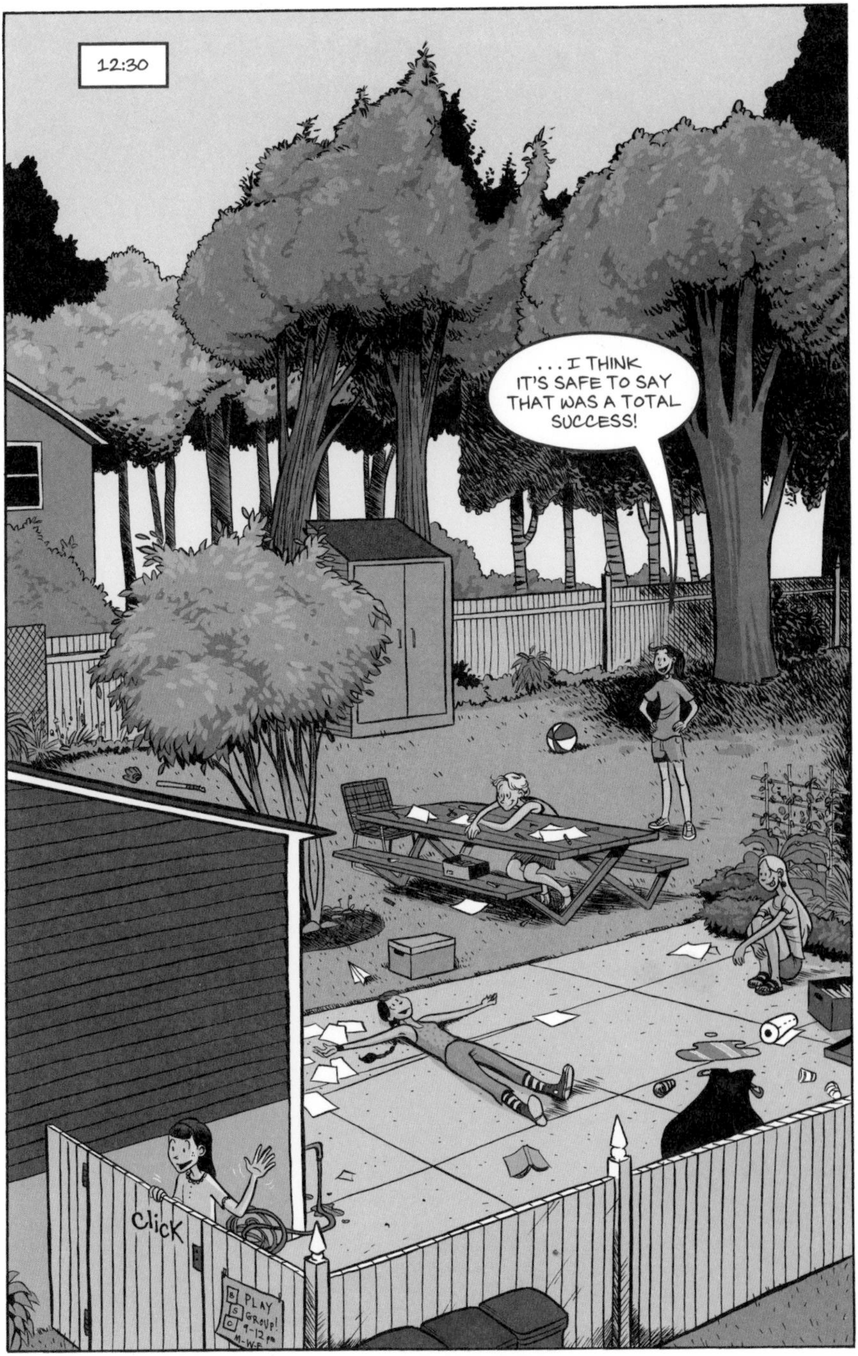
12:30
. . . I THINK IT'S SAFE TO SAY THAT WAS A TOTAL SUCCESS!
CLICK
B
S
C
PLAY GROUP! 9-12 pm M-W-F

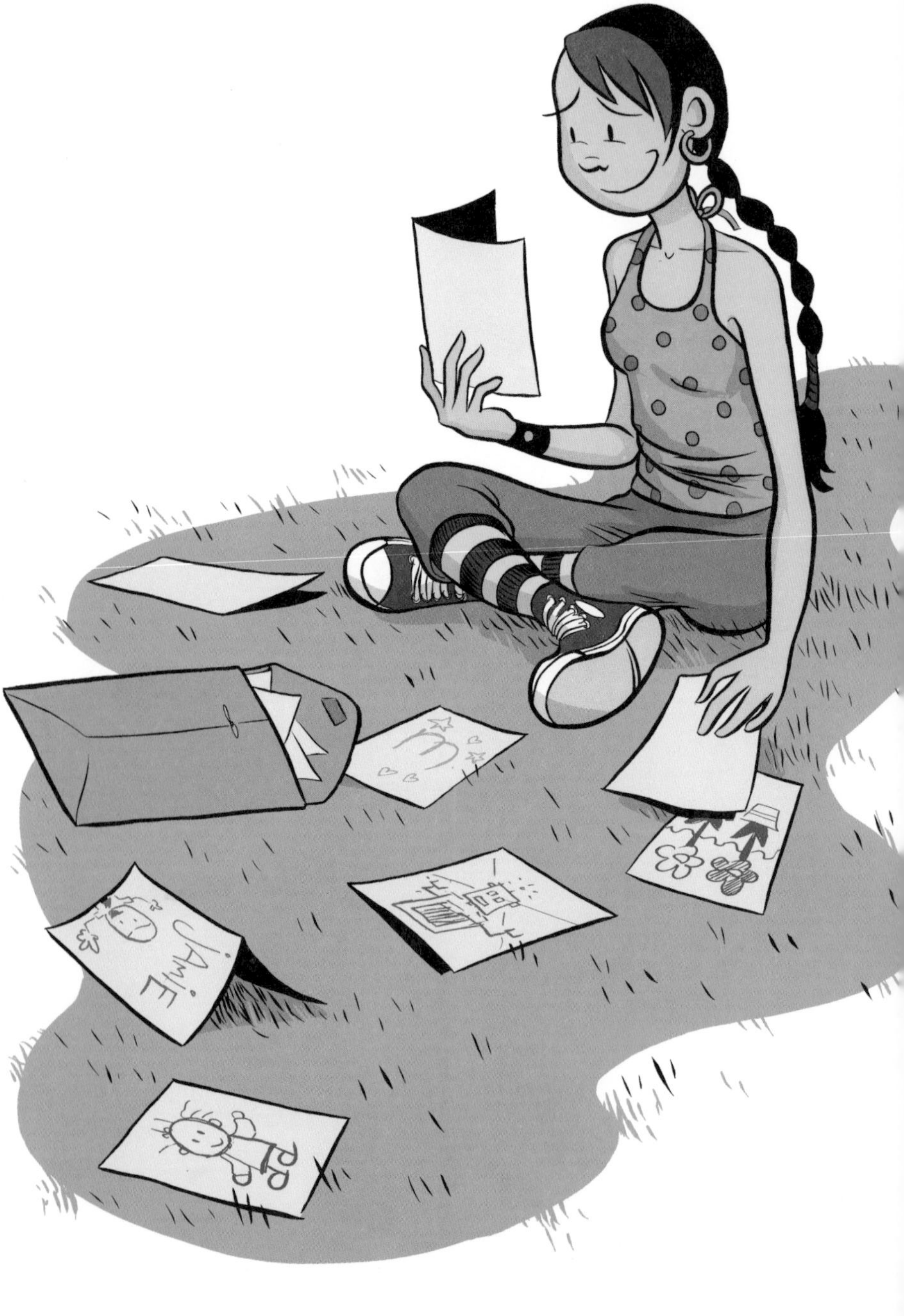
JAMiE

CHAPTER 7

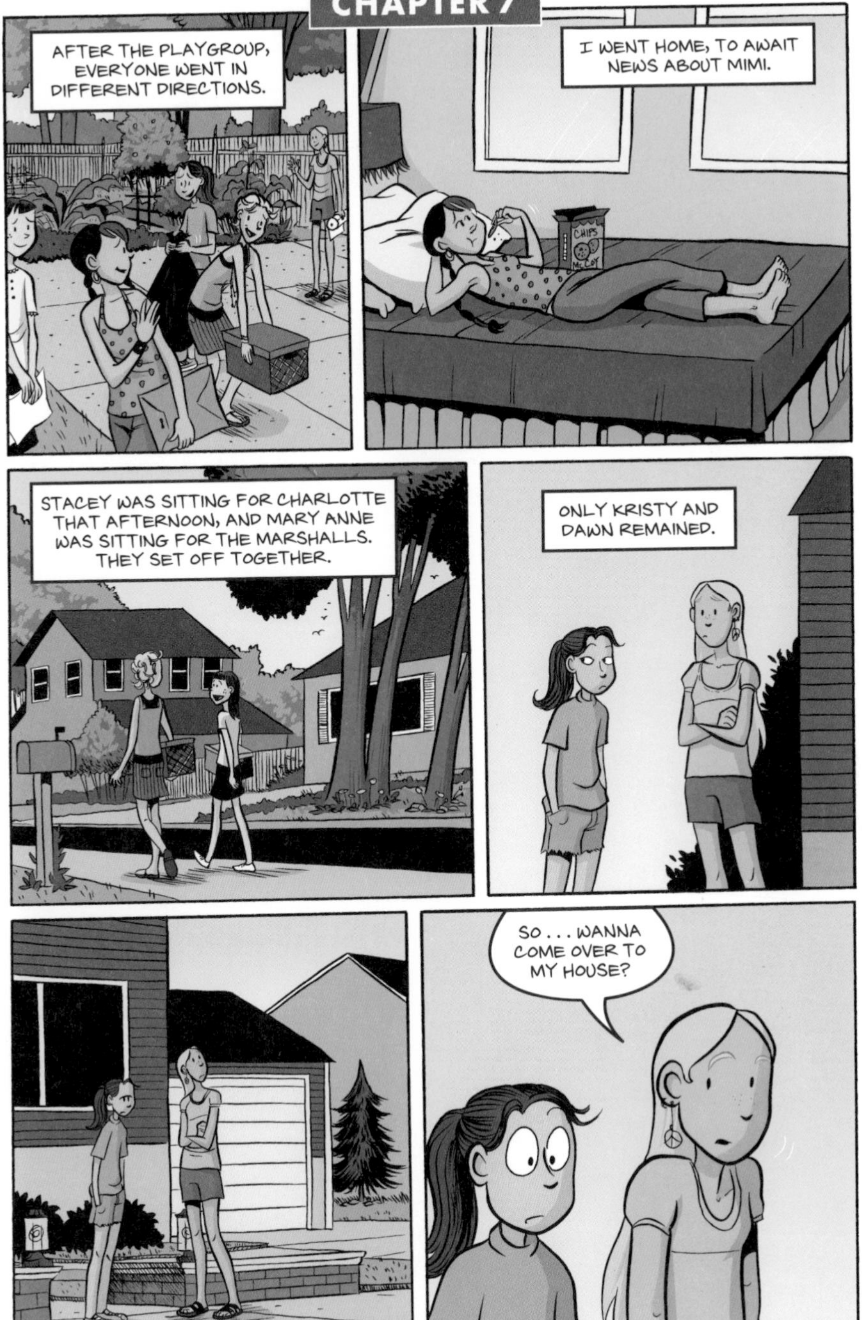
AFTER THE PLAYGROUP, EVERYONE WENT IN DIFFERENT DIRECTIONS.
I WENT HOME, TO AWAIT NEWS ABOUT MIMI.
STACEY WAS SITTING FOR CHARLOTTE THAT AFTERNOON, AND MARY ANNE WAS SITTING FOR THE MARSHALLS. THEY SET OFF TOGETHER.
ONLY KRISTY AND DAWN REMAINED.
SO . . . WANNA COME OVER TO MY HOUSE?

52

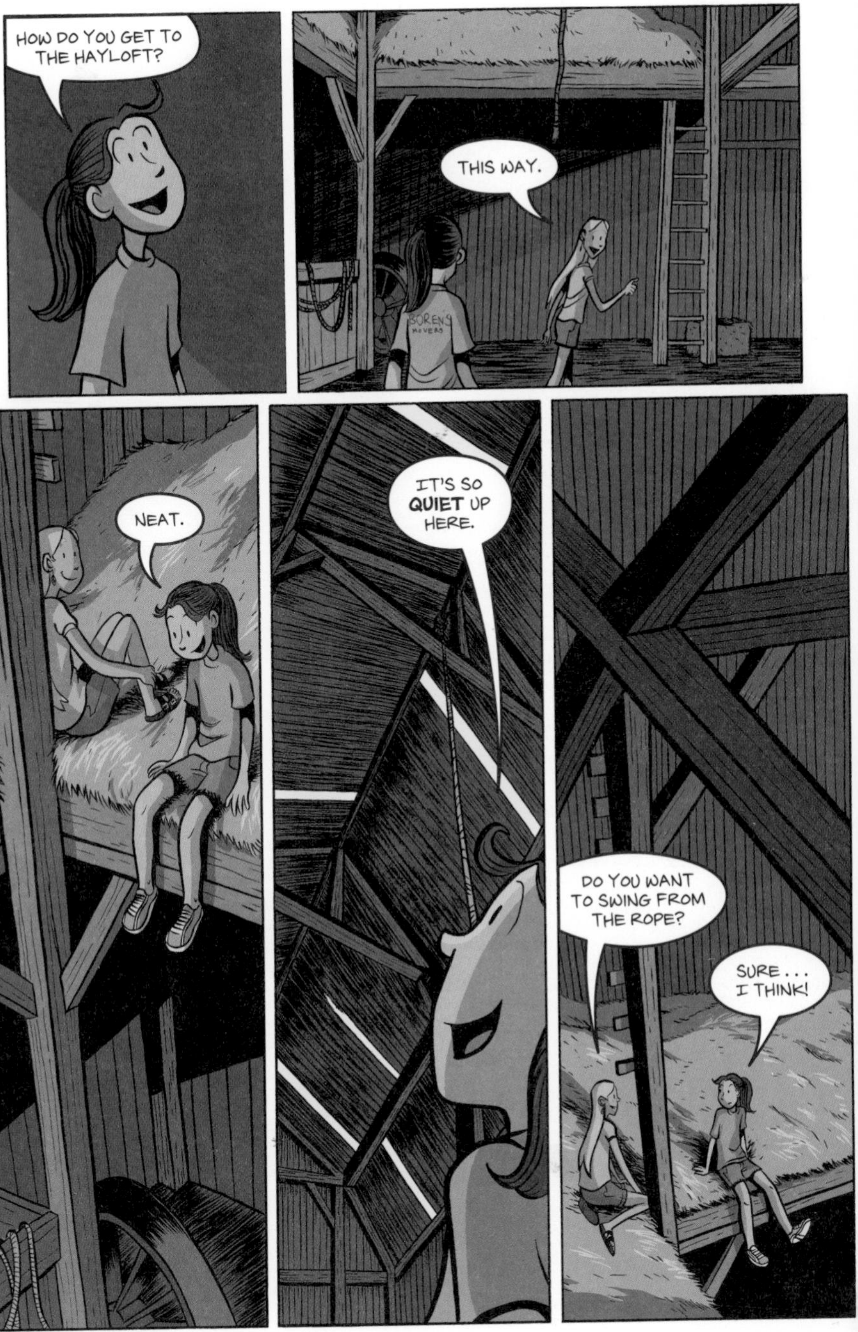
HOW DO YOU GET TO THE HAYLOFT?
THIS WAY.
BOREN'S MOVERS
NEAT.
IT'S SO **QUIET** UP HERE.
DO YOU WANT TO SWING FROM THE ROPE?
SURE . . . I THINK!

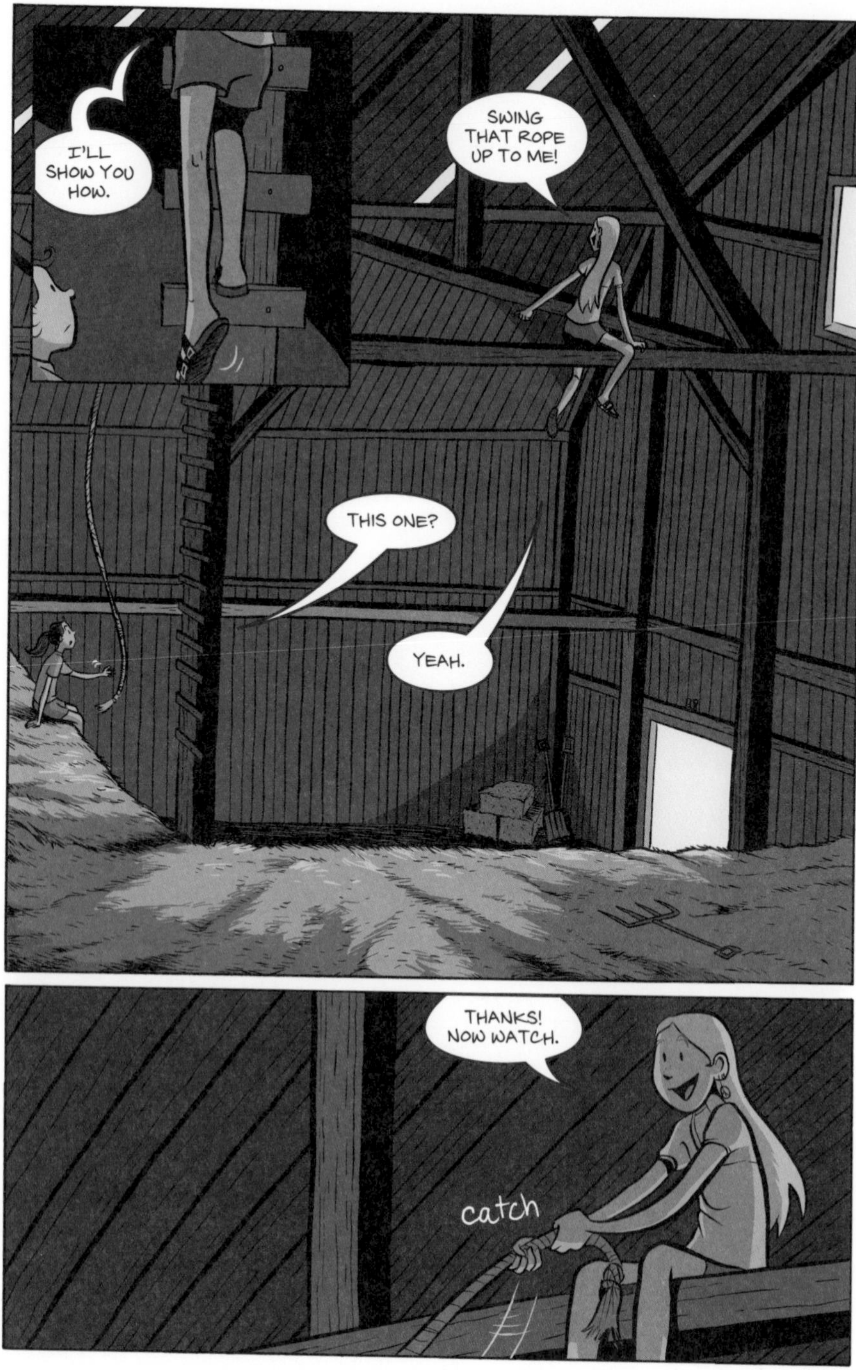
I'LL SHOW YOU HOW.
SWING THAT ROPE UP TO ME!
THIS ONE?
YEAH.
THANKS! NOW WATCH.
catch

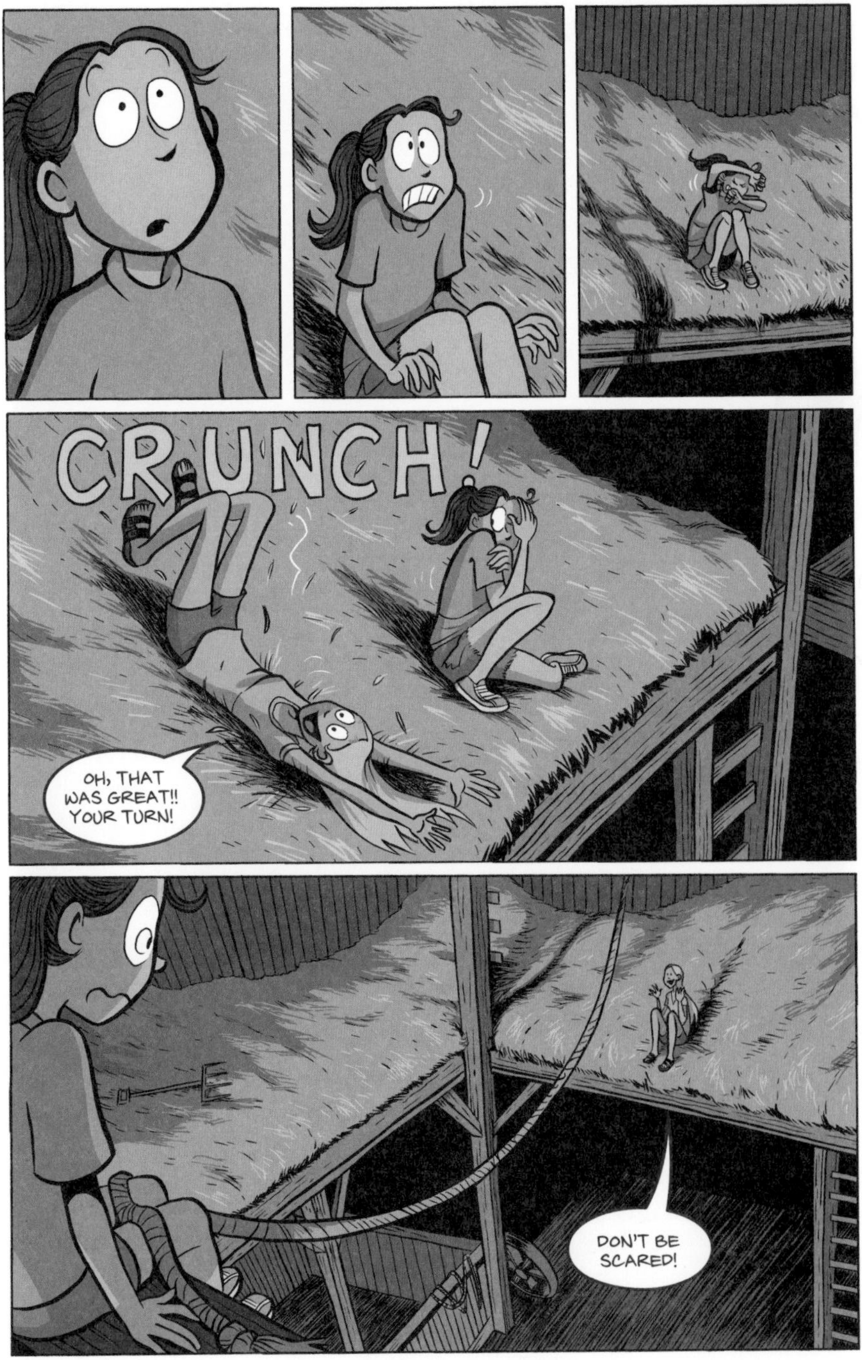
CRUNCH!
OH, THAT WAS GREAT!! YOUR TURN!
DON'T BE SCARED!

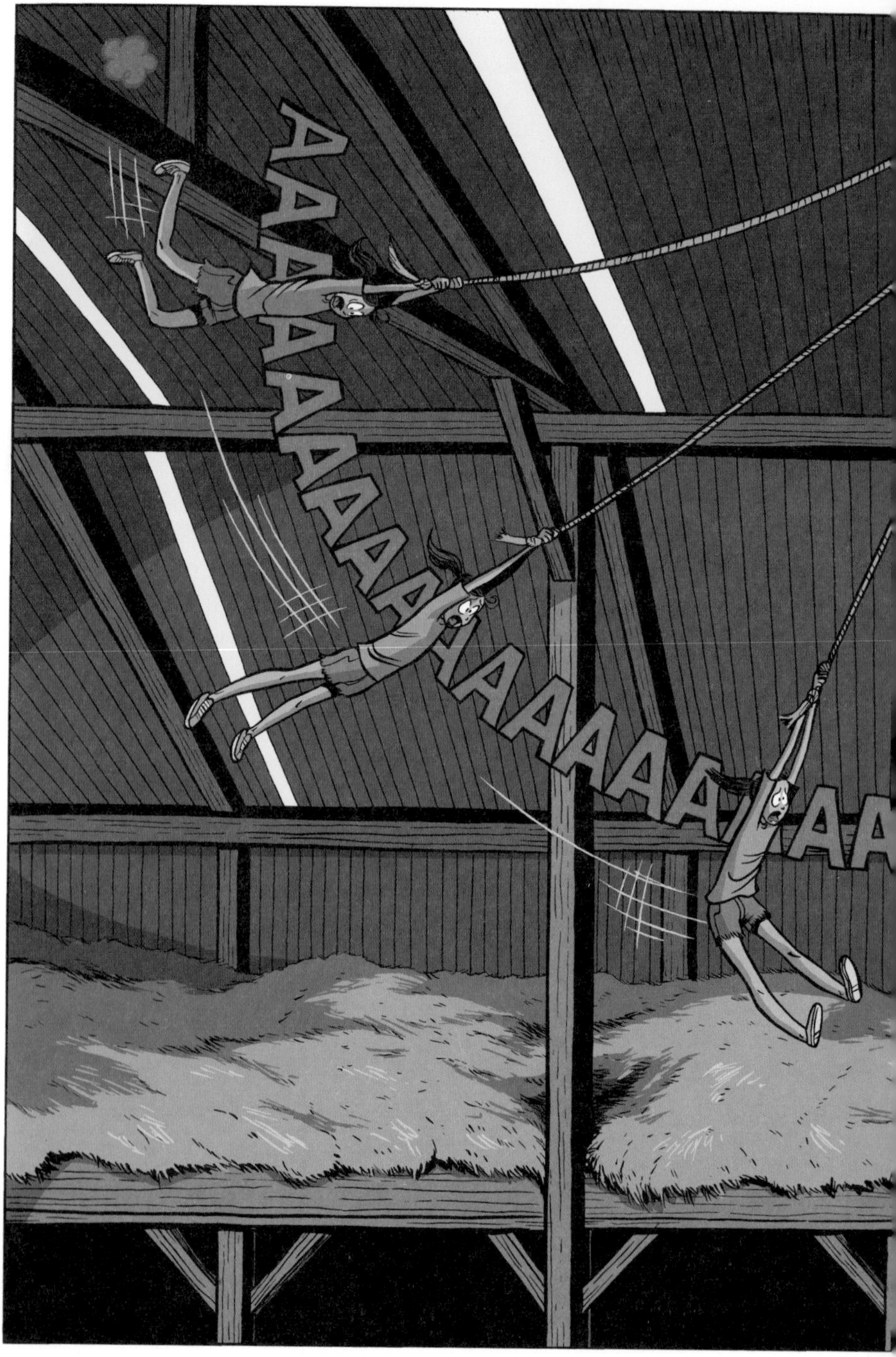
AAAAAAAAAAAAAAAAAAA

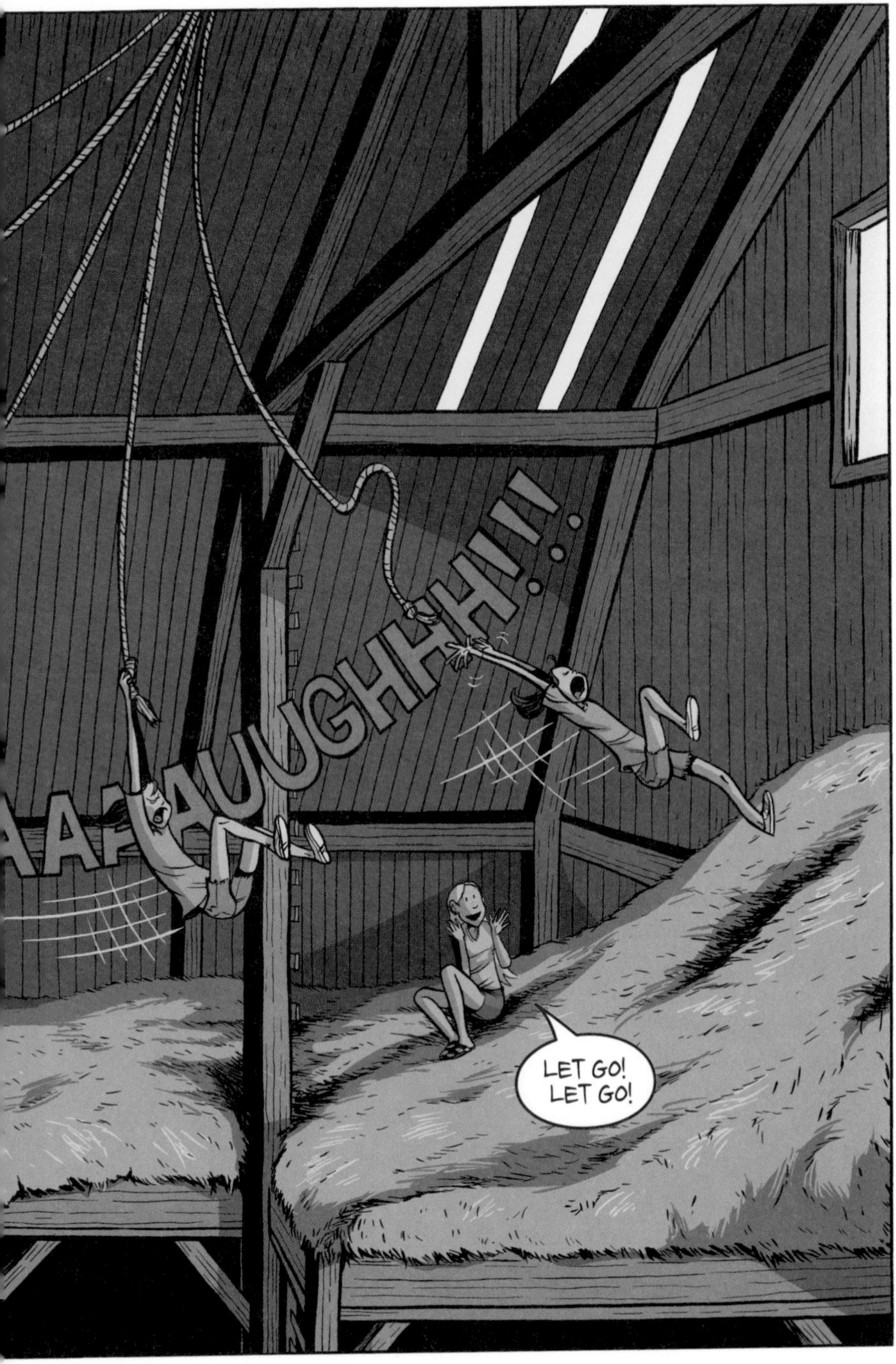
AAAAUUGHHH!!!...
LET GO! LET GO!

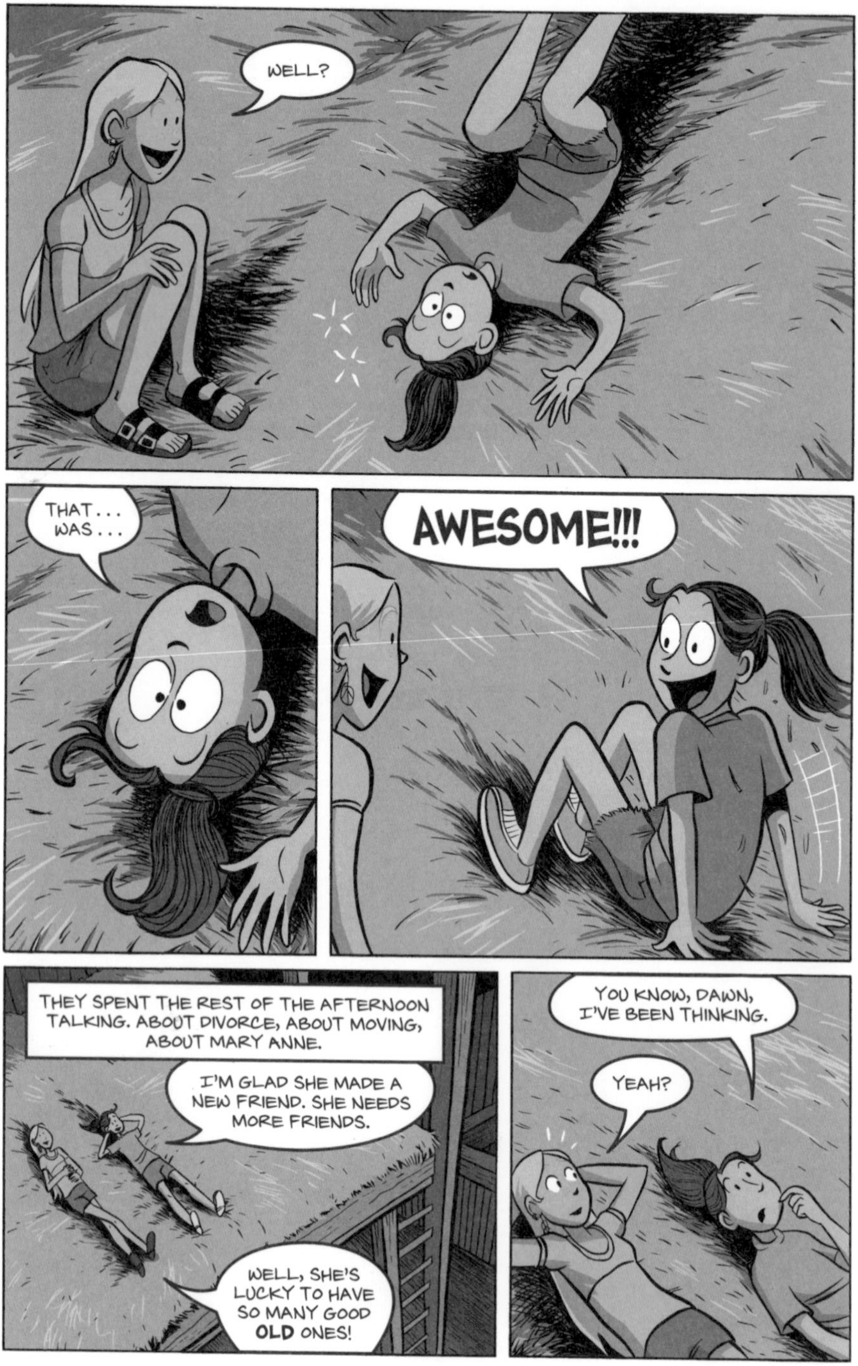
WELL?
THAT... WAS...
AWESOME!!!
THEY SPENT THE REST OF THE AFTERNOON TALKING. ABOUT DIVORCE, ABOUT MOVING, ABOUT MARY ANNE.
I'M GLAD SHE MADE A NEW FRIEND. SHE NEEDS MORE FRIENDS.
WELL, SHE'S LUCKY TO HAVE SO MANY GOOD **OLD** ONES!
YOU KNOW, DAWN, I'VE BEEN THINKING.
YEAH?

59

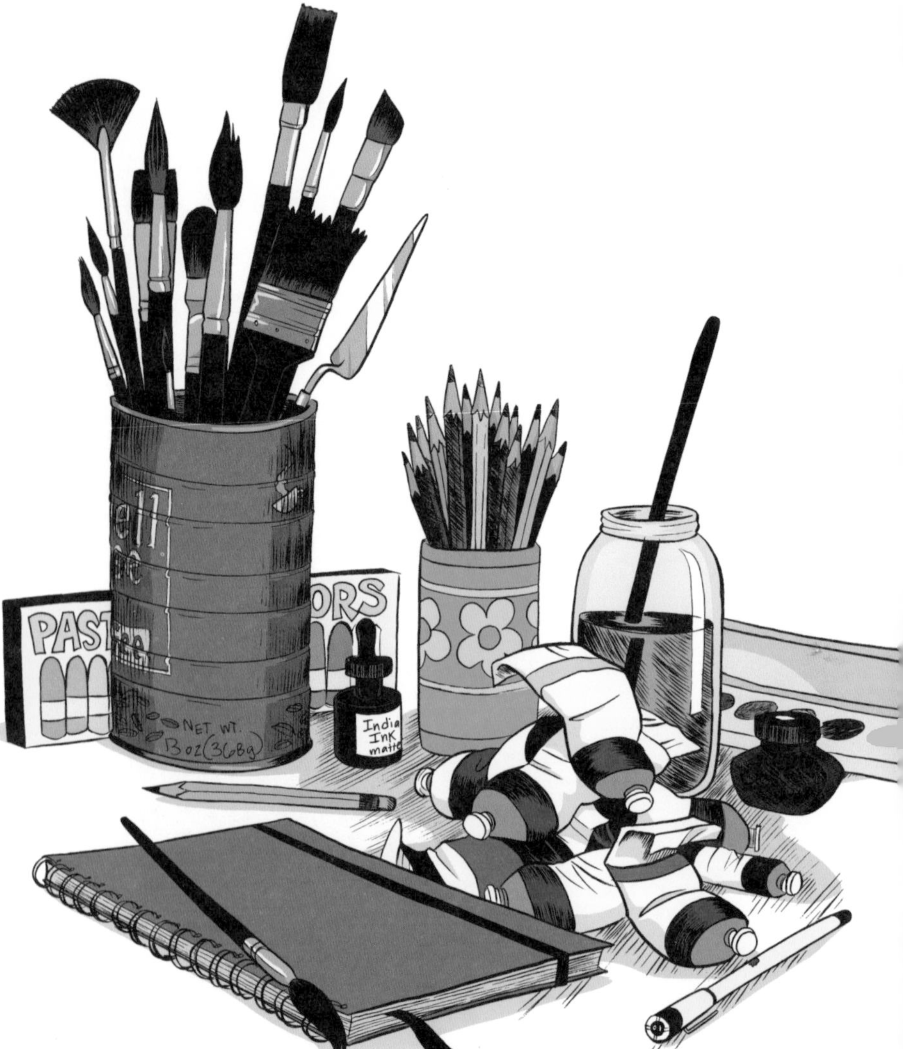
PAST
ORS
NET. WT.
India
Ink
matte

CHAPTER 8

THE MAIN THING WE TALKED ABOUT AT OUR MEETING THAT DAY WAS JENNY PREZZIOSO.

SHE STARTED THAT FIGHT WITH CLAIRE PIKE....

SHE WON'T SHARE WITH THE OTHER KIDS, SHE'S GOT A BAD ATTITUDE...

WE'LL DEFINITELY NEED TO DO SOMETHING.

BUT WHAT?

HELLO, GIRLS.

MOM! YOU'RE HOME! HOW'S MIMI?

GOOD NEWS: SHE JUST WOKE UP. SHE CAN'T MOVE OR SPEAK YET, BUT SHE'S AWAKE.

ALL RIGHT!

CAN I SEE HER?

YES -- FAMILY MEMBERS CAN SEE HER ONE AT A TIME, FOR ABOUT TEN MINUTES EACH.

WE'LL GO BACK TO THE HOSPITAL AFTER SUPPER. SPEAKING OF WHICH, CLAUDIA, I'LL NEED YOUR HELP IN THE KITCHEN.

I'LL BE RIGHT THERE.

61

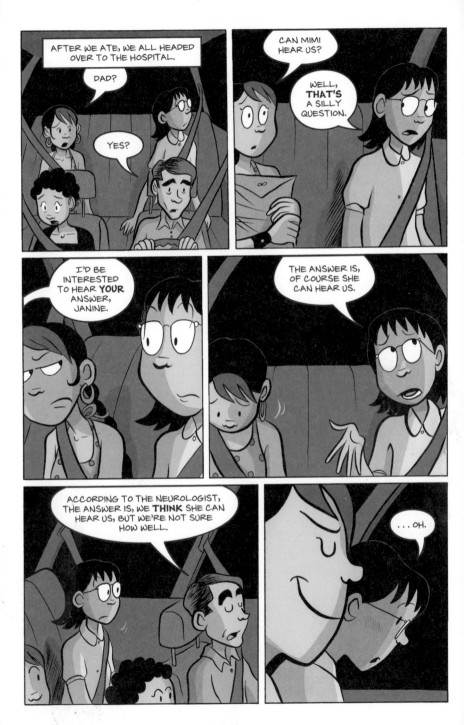

AFTER WE ATE, WE ALL HEADED OVER TO THE HOSPITAL.

DAD?

YES?

CAN MIMI HEAR US?

WELL, **THAT'S** A SILLY QUESTION.

I'D BE INTERESTED TO HEAR **YOUR** ANSWER, JANINE.

THE ANSWER IS, OF COURSE SHE CAN HEAR US.

ACCORDING TO THE NEUROLOGIST, THE ANSWER IS, WE **THINK** SHE CAN HEAR US, BUT WE'RE NOT SURE HOW WELL.

...OH.

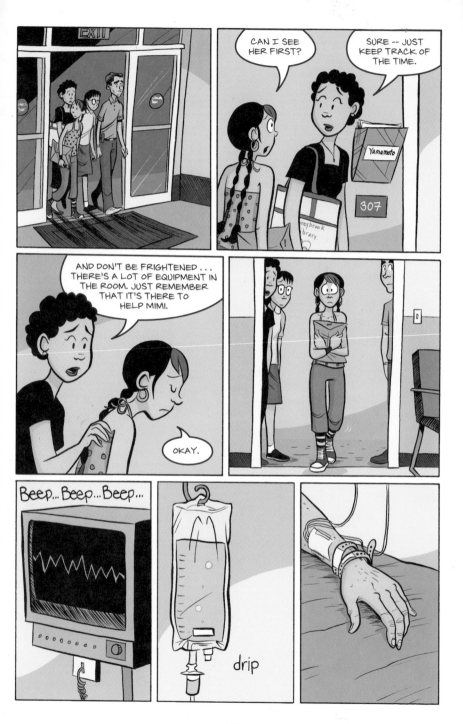

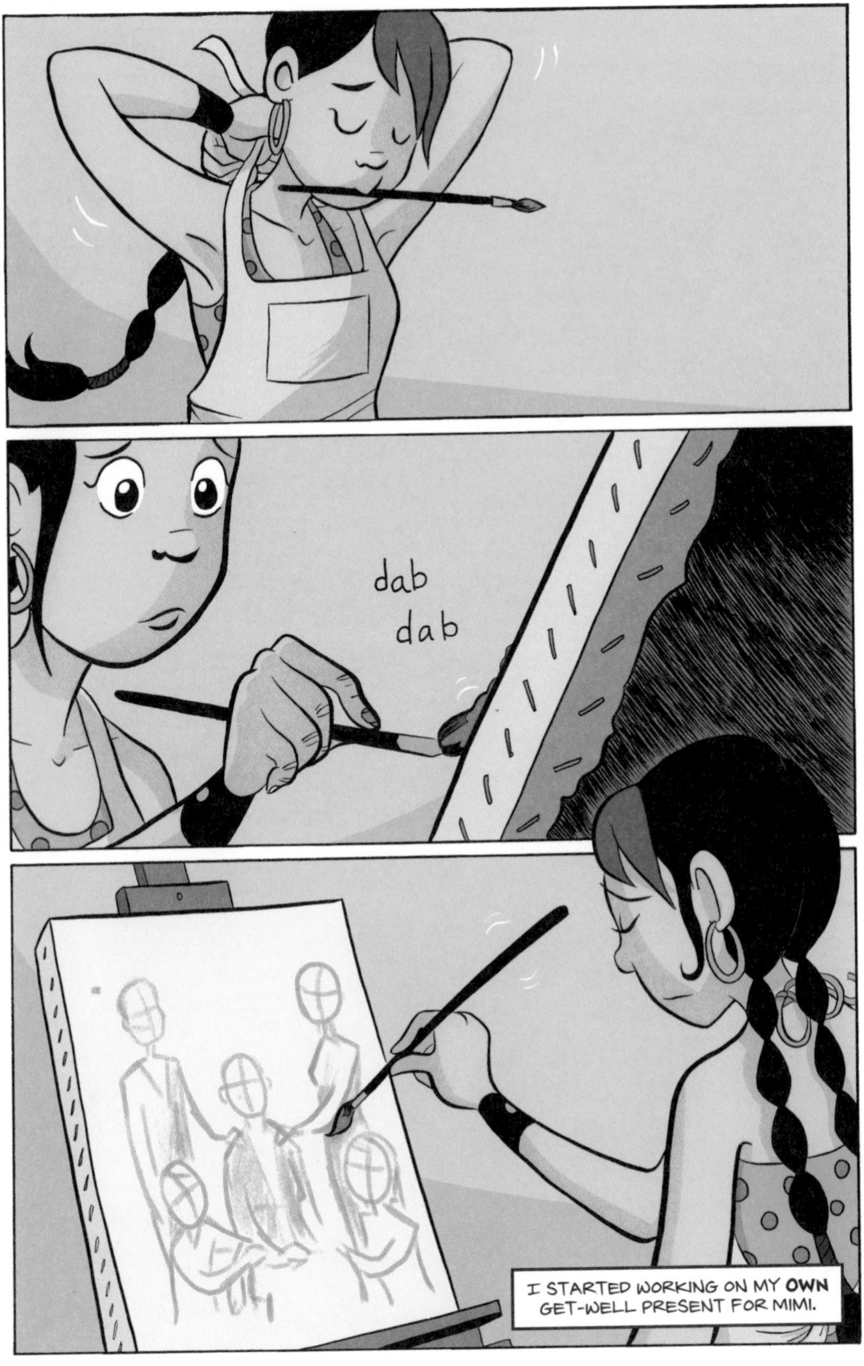
dab
dab
I STARTED WORKING ON MY **OWN** GET-WELL PRESENT FOR MIMI.

Wednesday, June 18

Well, Karen Brewer strikes again. When she's around, things are never dull. Today was the second session of our playgroup and Andrew and Karen came to it. Watson's ex-wife needed a last-minute sitter for them, so she called Watson and he decided to drop them off at Stacey's.

In the past, Karen has scared other kids with stories of witches, ghosts, and Martians. Today, she had a new one — a monster tale. But it was a monster tale with a twist, as you guys know. I'm not sure there's anything we can do about Karen. The thing is, she usually doesn't mean to scare people. She just has a wild imagination.

But, oh boy, when Karen and Jenny got together . . .

— Kristy

CHAPTER 9

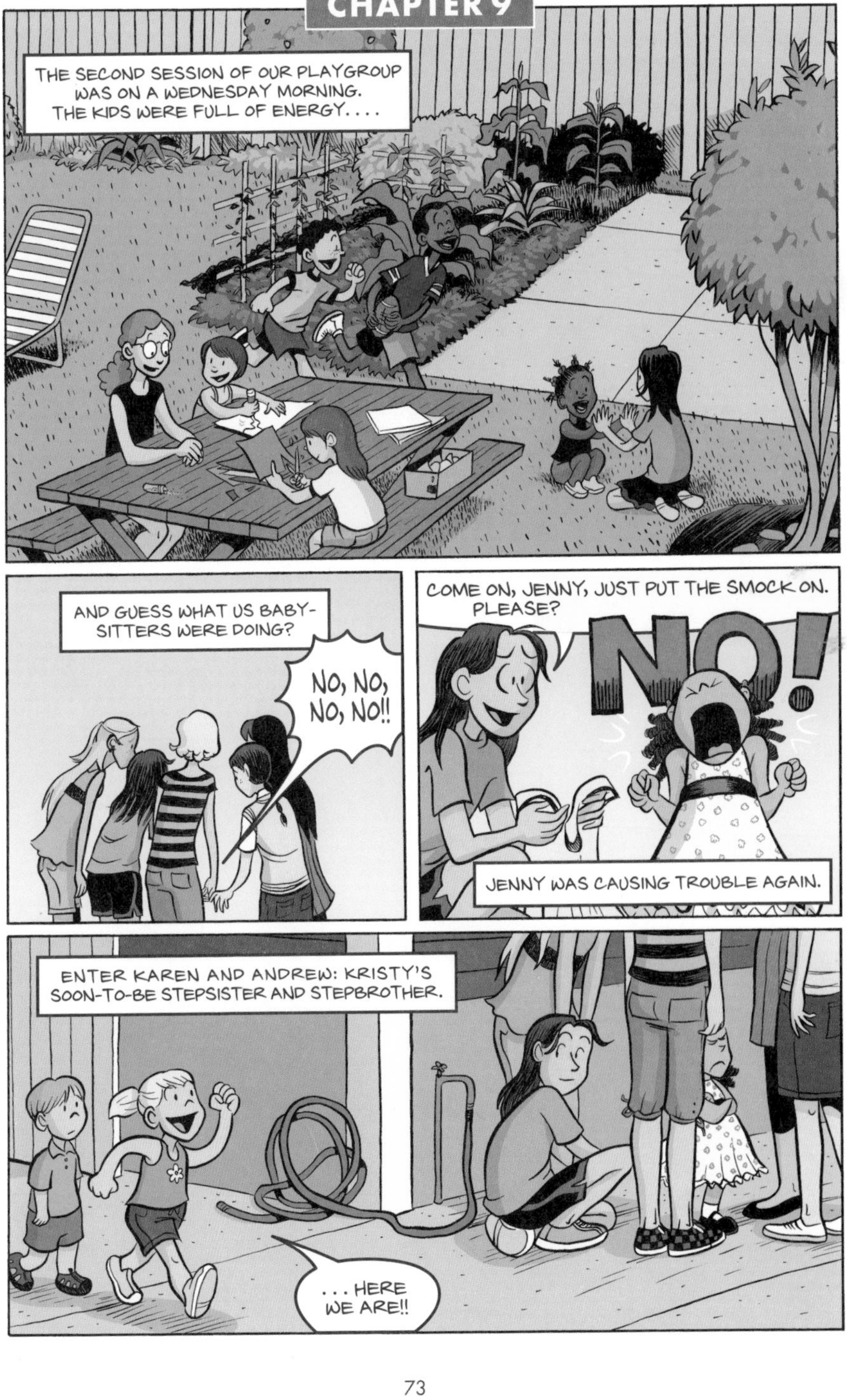

THE SECOND SESSION OF OUR PLAYGROUP WAS ON A WEDNESDAY MORNING. THE KIDS WERE FULL OF ENERGY. . . .
AND GUESS WHAT US BABY-SITTERS WERE DOING?
NO, NO, NO, NO!!
COME ON, JENNY, JUST PUT THE SMOCK ON. PLEASE?
NO!
JENNY WAS CAUSING TROUBLE AGAIN.
ENTER KAREN AND ANDREW: KRISTY'S SOON-TO-BE STEPSISTER AND STEPBROTHER.
. . . HERE WE ARE!!

75

CHAPTER 10

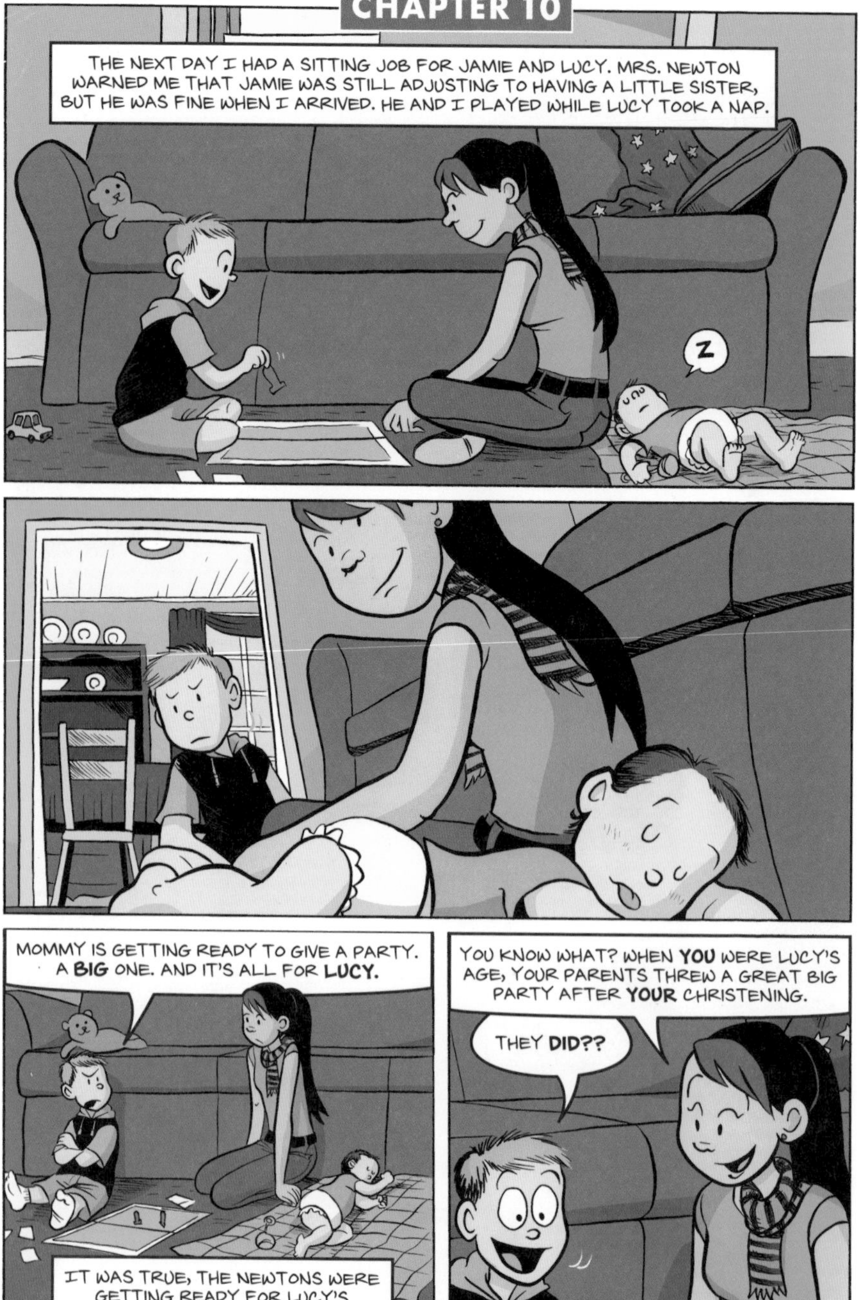

THE NEXT DAY I HAD A SITTING JOB FOR JAMIE AND LUCY. MRS. NEWTON WARNED ME THAT JAMIE WAS STILL ADJUSTING TO HAVING A LITTLE SISTER, BUT HE WAS FINE WHEN I ARRIVED. HE AND I PLAYED WHILE LUCY TOOK A NAP.
Z
MOMMY IS GETTING READY TO GIVE A PARTY. A **BIG** ONE. AND IT'S ALL FOR **LUCY.**
IT WAS TRUE, THE NEWTONS WERE GETTING READY FOR LUCY'S CHRISTENING IN A FEW WEEKS.
YOU KNOW WHAT? WHEN **YOU** WERE LUCY'S AGE, YOUR PARENTS THREW A GREAT BIG PARTY AFTER **YOUR** CHRISTENING.
THEY **DID??**

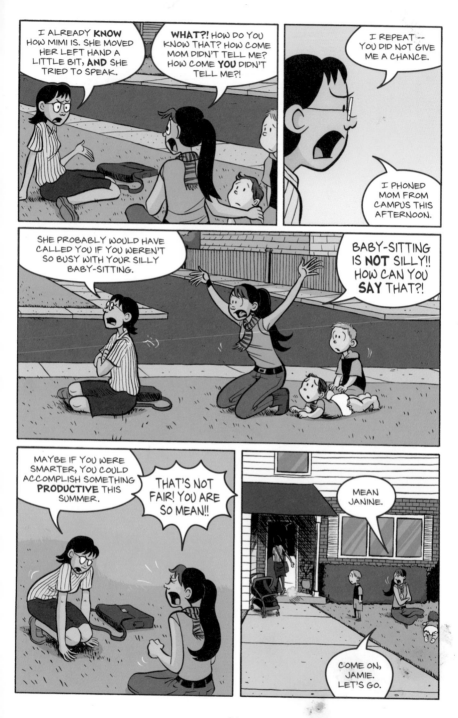

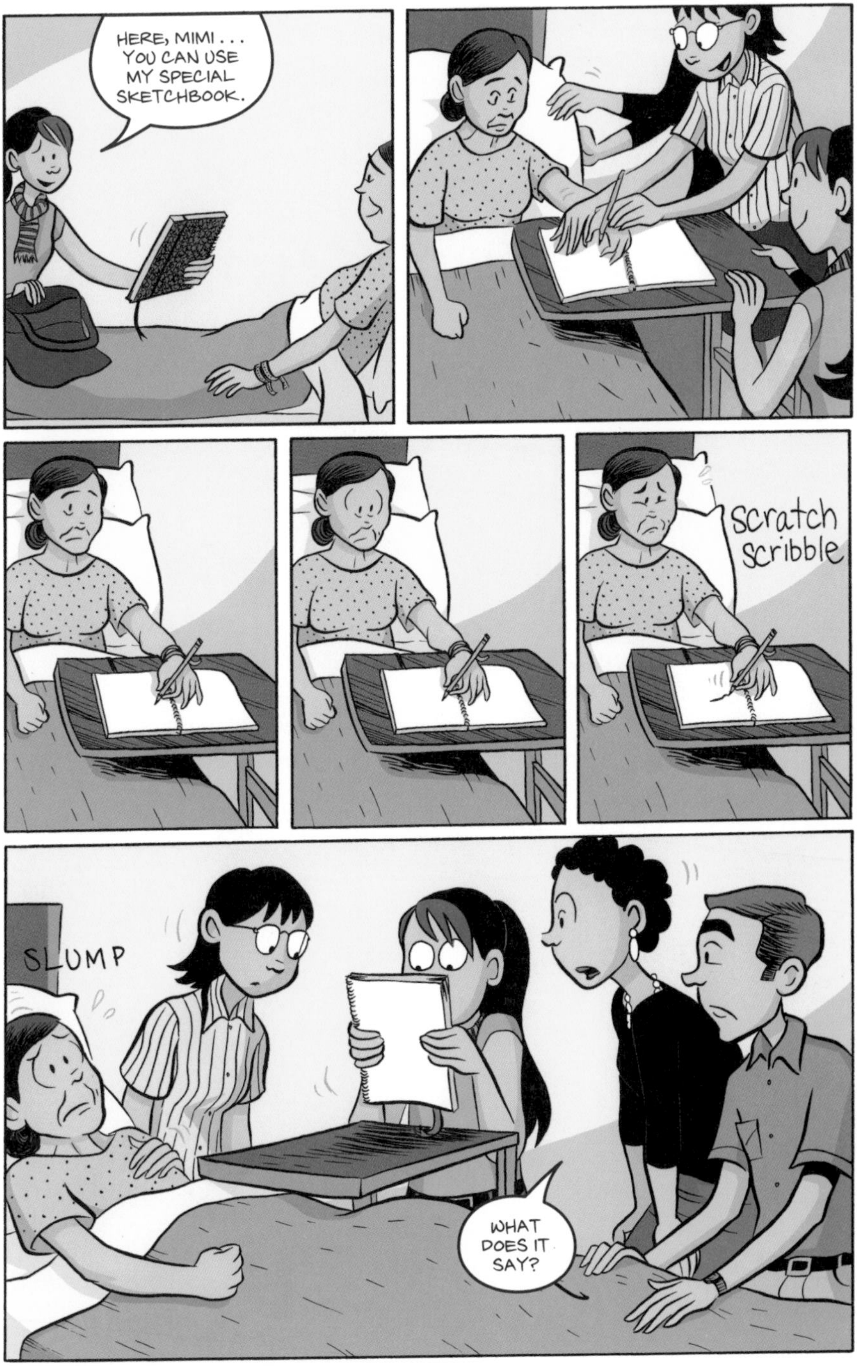
HERE, MIMI . . . YOU CAN USE MY SPECIAL SKETCHBOOK.
Scratch
scribble
SLUMP
WHAT DOES IT SAY?

CHAPTER 11

Wednesday, June 23

   Today's playgroup ended hours ago and I'm still laughing about what went on. Now this is an example of something hilarious that probably could never have happened in New York City. . . . It started when David Michael brought Louie to the playgroup. Just to set things off on the wrong foot, it turns out that Jenny is afraid (and I mean terrified) of dogs. Remember that for the future, you guys.

Then Kristy decided we needed to give Louie a bath. That's when the trouble really began. When the morning was over, Louie was the only one who was both clean and dry. Thank goodness Jenny was wearing her smock.

   Claudia — we miss you!

                                    Stacey

CHAPTER 12

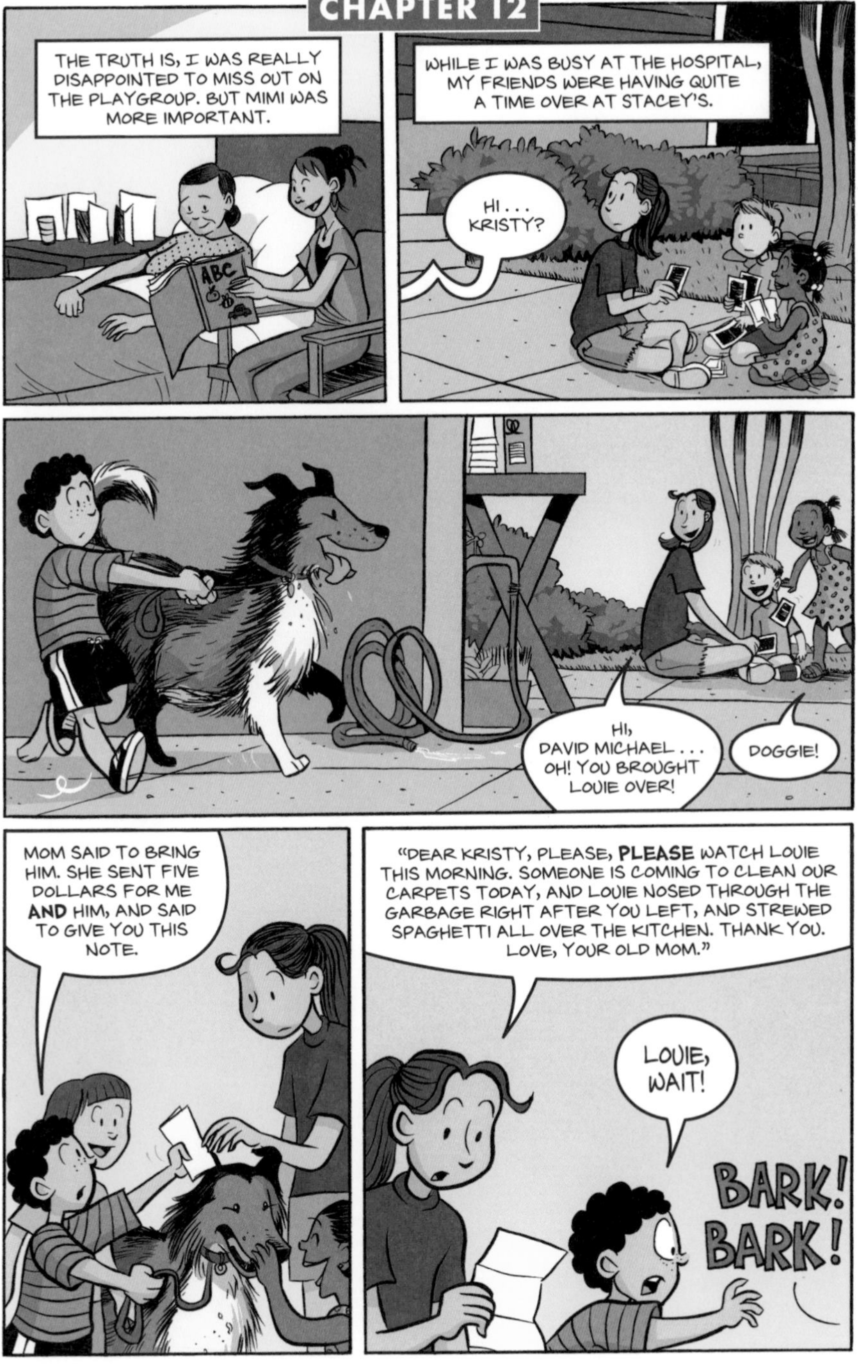

THE TRUTH IS, I WAS REALLY DISAPPOINTED TO MISS OUT ON THE PLAYGROUP. BUT MIMI WAS MORE IMPORTANT.
ABC
WHILE I WAS BUSY AT THE HOSPITAL, MY FRIENDS WERE HAVING QUITE A TIME OVER AT STACEY'S.
HI . . . KRISTY?
HI, DAVID MICHAEL . . . OH! YOU BROUGHT LOUIE OVER!
DOGGIE!
MOM SAID TO BRING HIM. SHE SENT FIVE DOLLARS FOR ME **AND** HIM, AND SAID TO GIVE YOU THIS NOTE.
"DEAR KRISTY, PLEASE, **PLEASE** WATCH LOUIE THIS MORNING. SOMEONE IS COMING TO CLEAN OUR CARPETS TODAY, AND LOUIE NOSED THROUGH THE GARBAGE RIGHT AFTER YOU LEFT, AND STREWED SPAGHETTI ALL OVER THE KITCHEN. THANK YOU. LOVE, YOUR OLD MOM."
LOUIE, WAIT!
BARK! BARK!

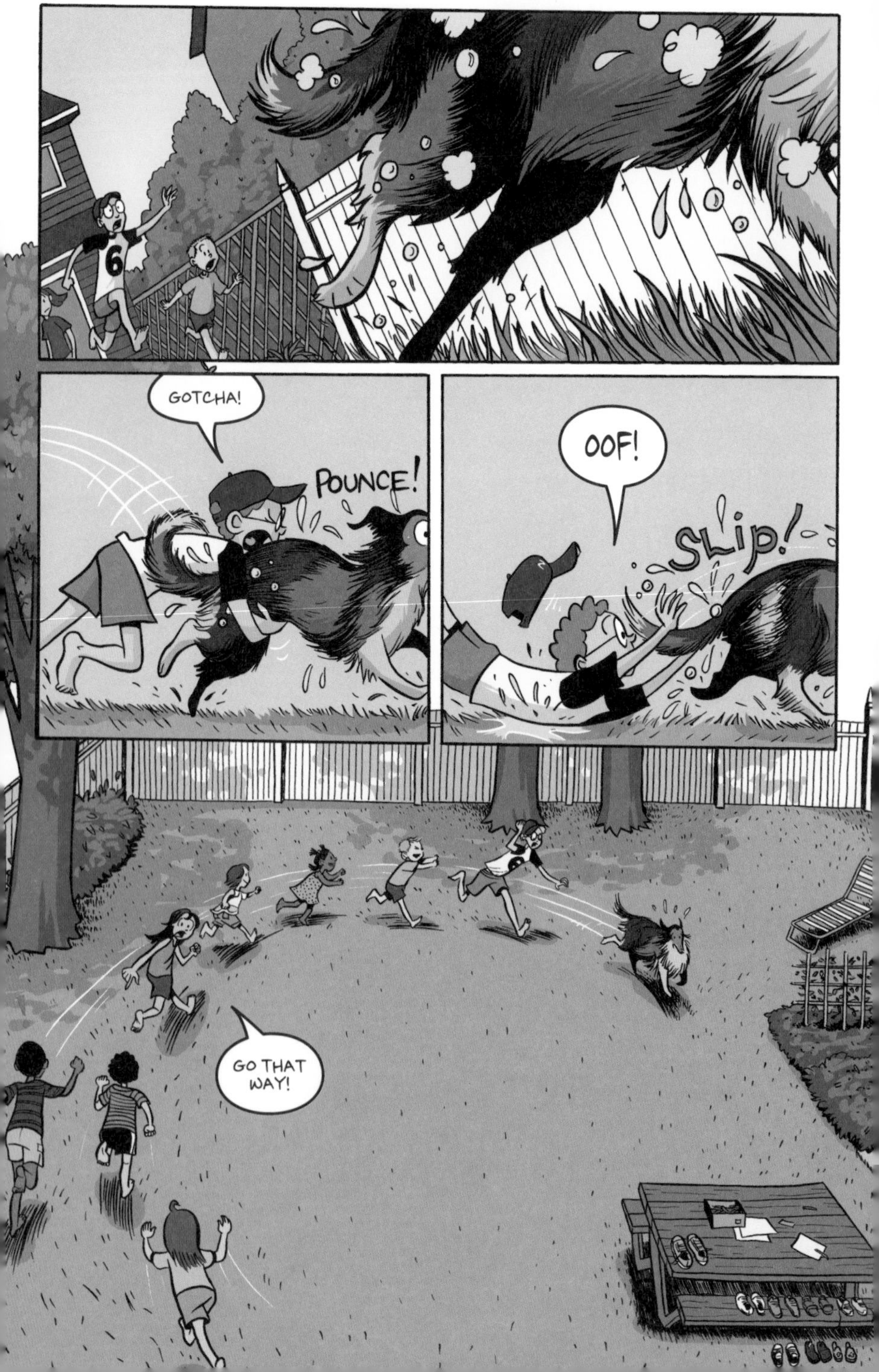
GOTCHA!
POUNCE!
OOF!
SLIP!
GO THAT WAY!

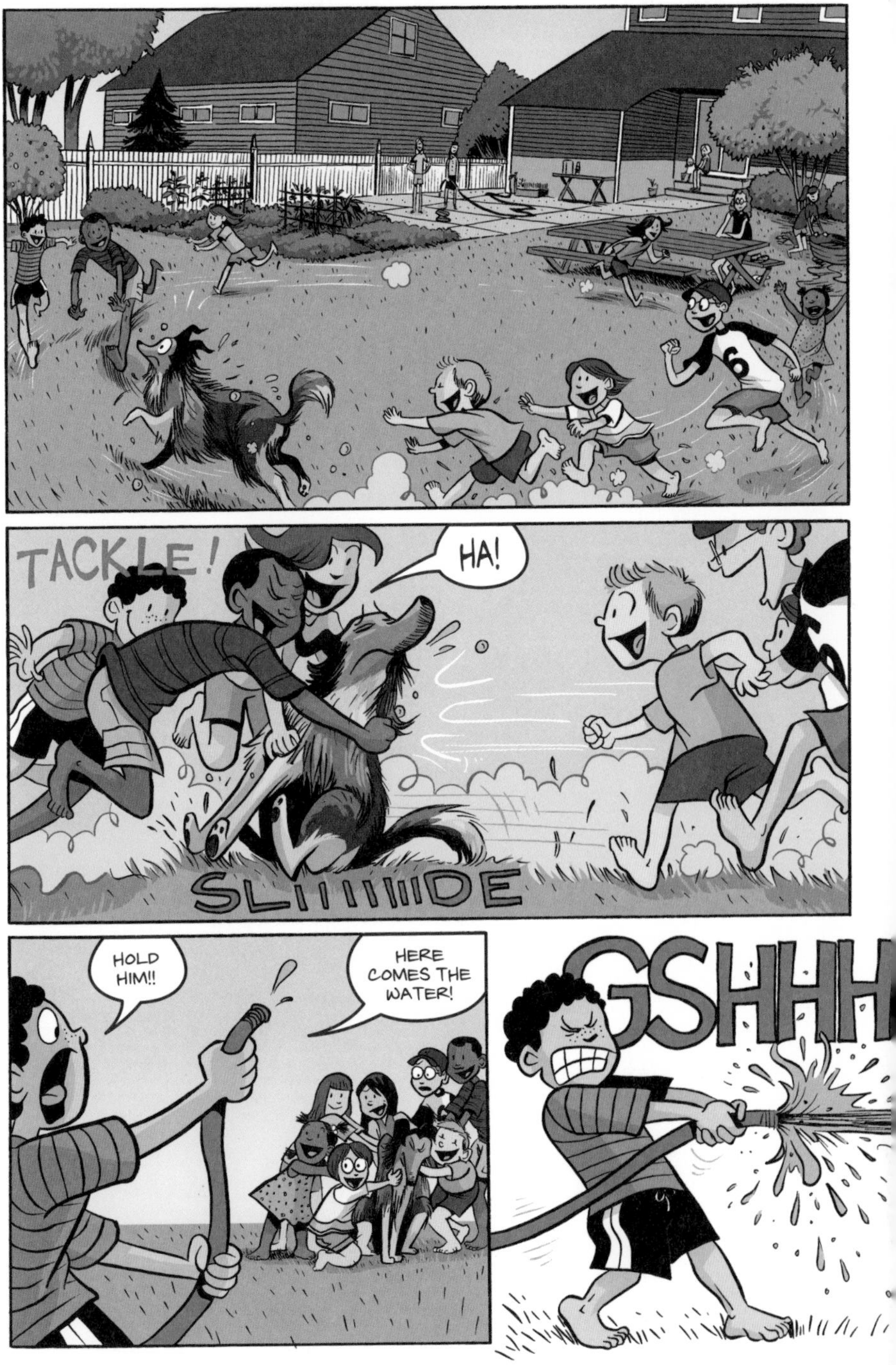
TACKLE!
HA!
SLIIIIIIDE
HOLD HIM!!
HERE COMES THE WATER!
GSHHH

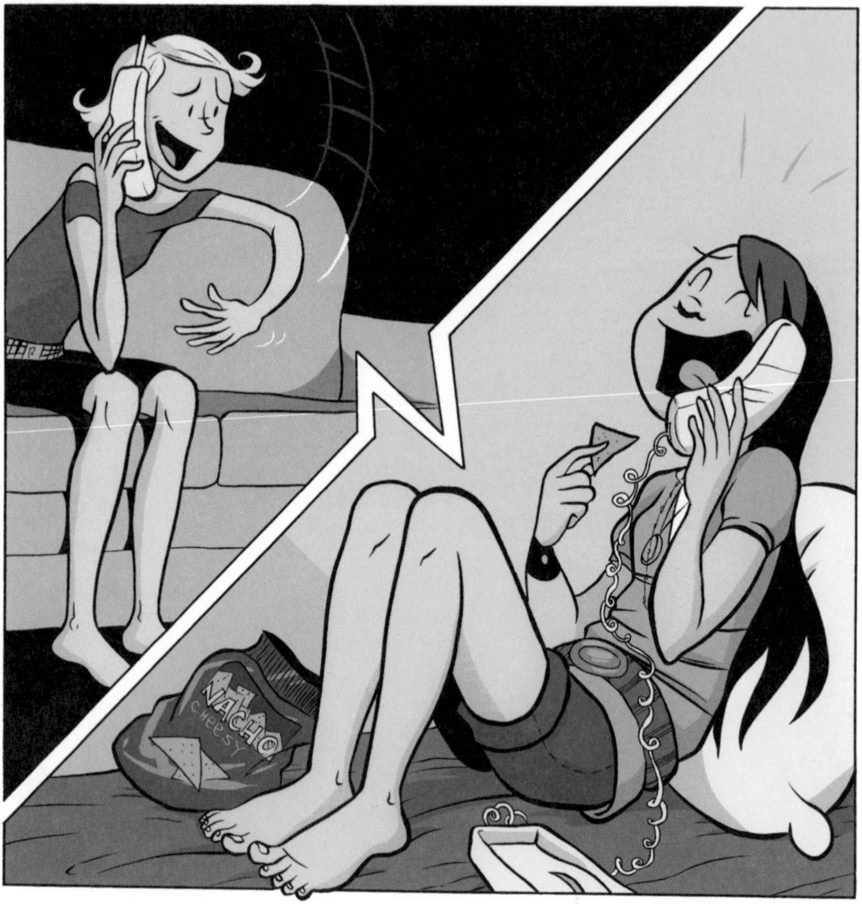
NACHO
CHEESY

CHAPTER 13

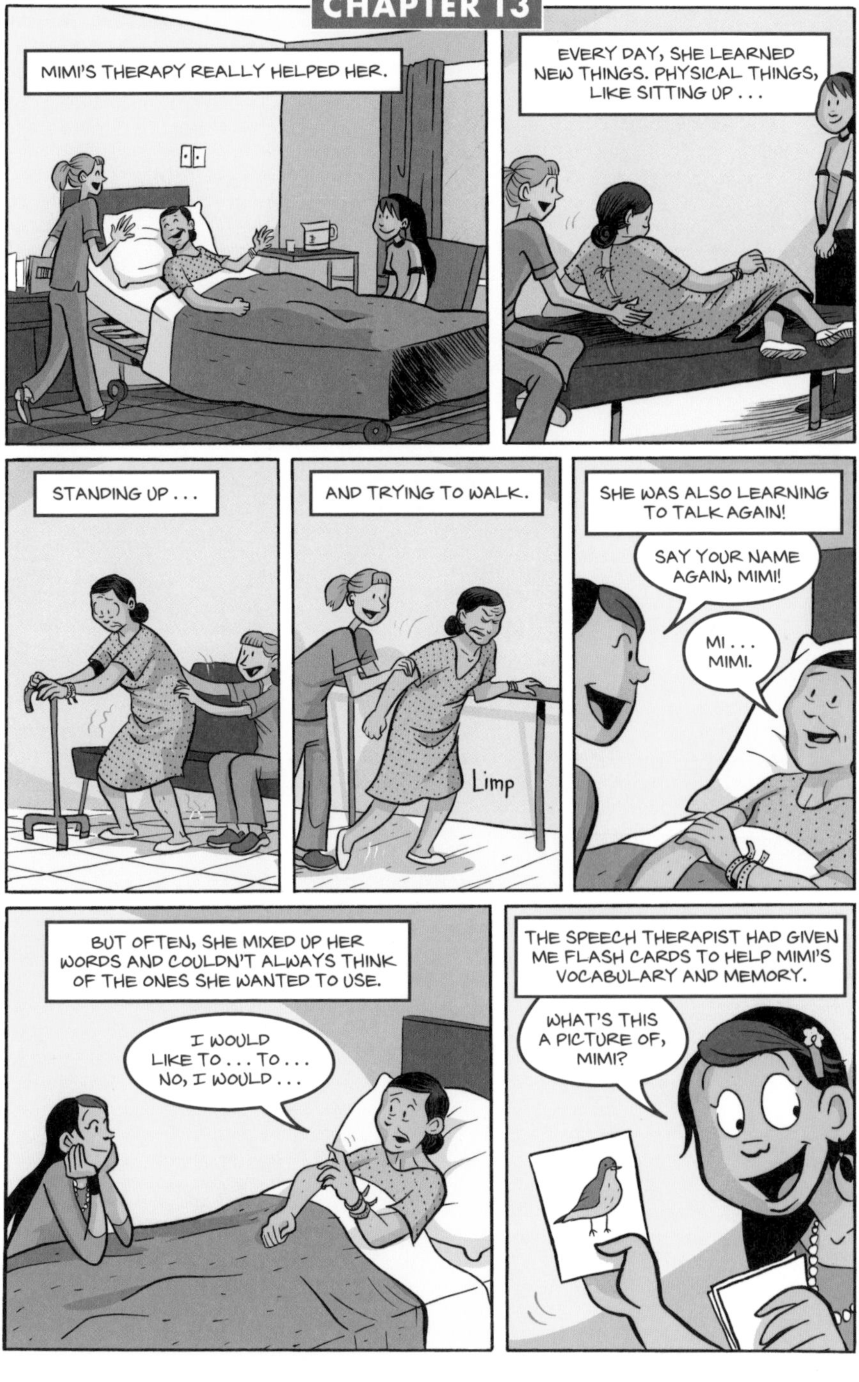
MIMI'S THERAPY REALLY HELPED HER.
EVERY DAY, SHE LEARNED NEW THINGS. PHYSICAL THINGS, LIKE SITTING UP . . .
STANDING UP . . .
AND TRYING TO WALK.
Limp
SHE WAS ALSO LEARNING TO TALK AGAIN!
SAY YOUR NAME AGAIN, MIMI!
MI . . . MIMI.
BUT OFTEN, SHE MIXED UP HER WORDS AND COULDN'T ALWAYS THINK OF THE ONES SHE WANTED TO USE.
I WOULD LIKE TO . . . TO . . . NO, I WOULD . . .
THE SPEECH THERAPIST HAD GIVEN ME FLASH CARDS TO HELP MIMI'S VOCABULARY AND MEMORY.
WHAT'S THIS A PICTURE OF, MIMI?

111

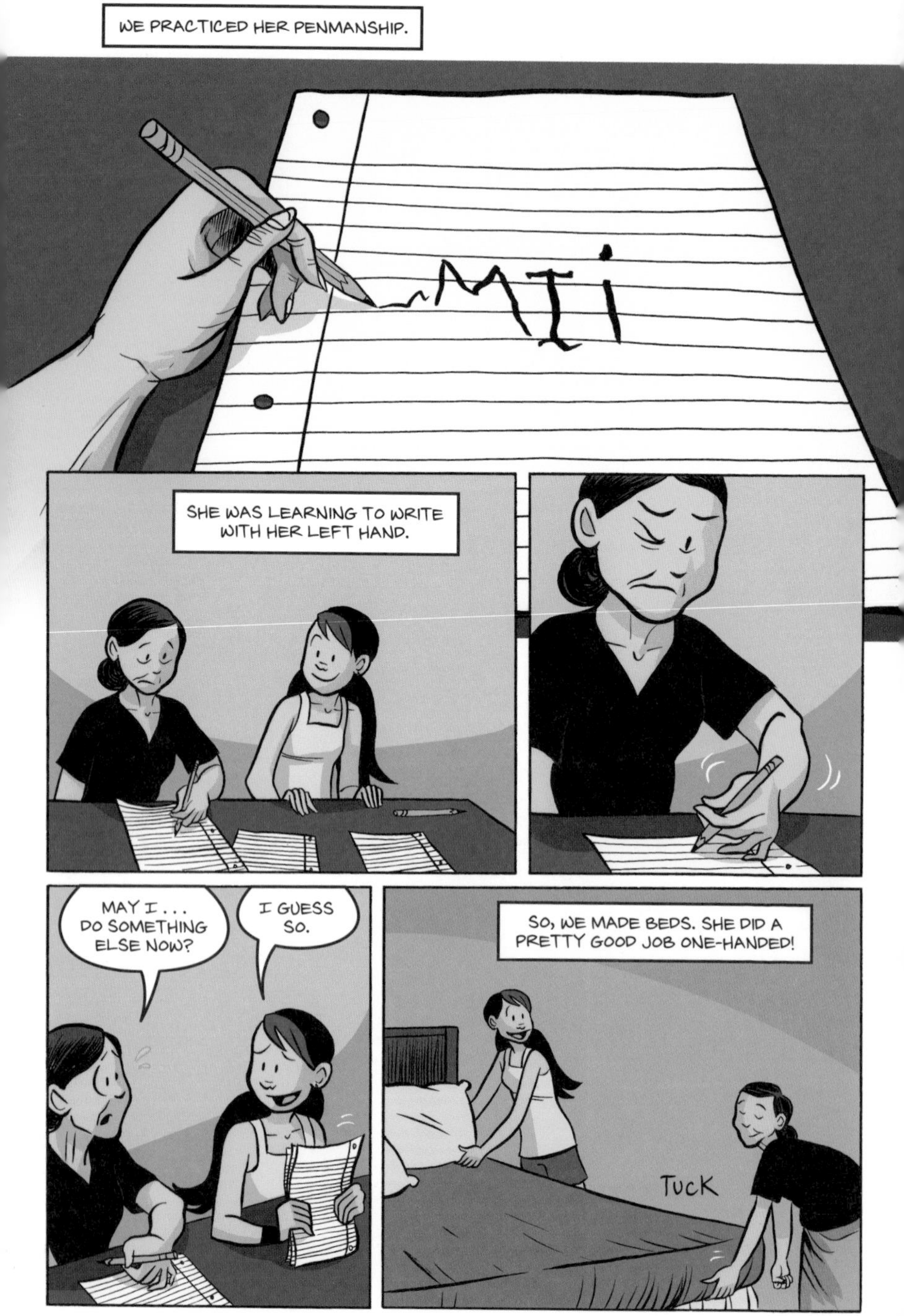
WE PRACTICED HER PENMANSHIP.
MII
SHE WAS LEARNING TO WRITE WITH HER LEFT HAND.
MAY I . . . DO SOMETHING ELSE NOW?
I GUESS SO.
SO, WE MADE BEDS. SHE DID A PRETTY GOOD JOB ONE-HANDED!
TUCK

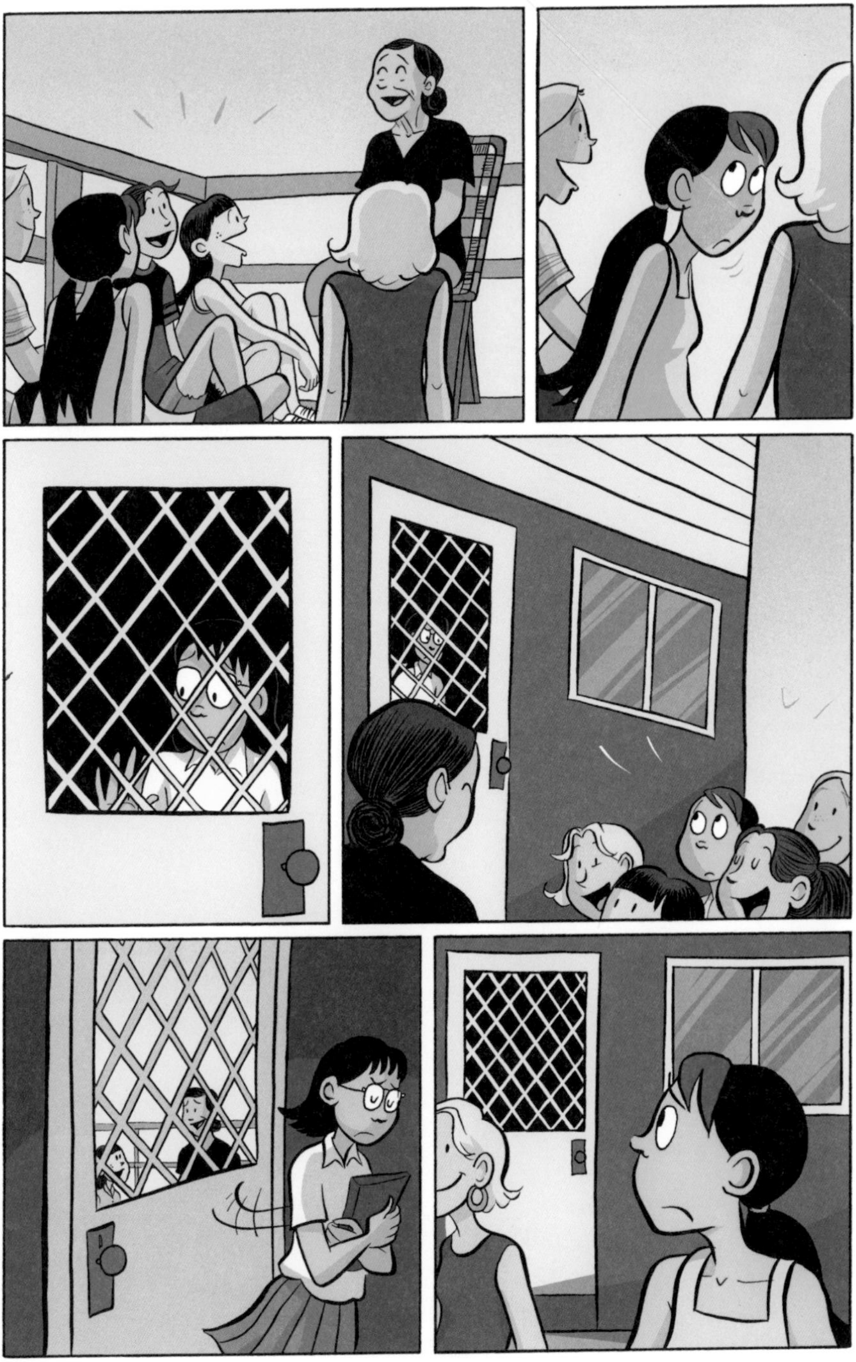

Friday, July 18

This morning I didn't baby-sit . . .

I _Mimi_-sat!

Claudia was helping out at the Newtons' all day, so Mrs. Kishi asked if I could stay with Mimi. I was happy to, of course, but I wasn't expecting Mimi to be so different. She can't even remember the simplest things sometimes.

In case any of you stays with Mimi while she's getting better, you should know that she gets upset easily. Frustrated, I guess. She yelled at me and Mimi has never, ever yelled at me. In fact, Claudia told me later that Mimi has never yelled at anyone in their family, so I assume Mimi was embarrassed about needing a sitter in the first place.

Mary Anne

CHAPTER 14

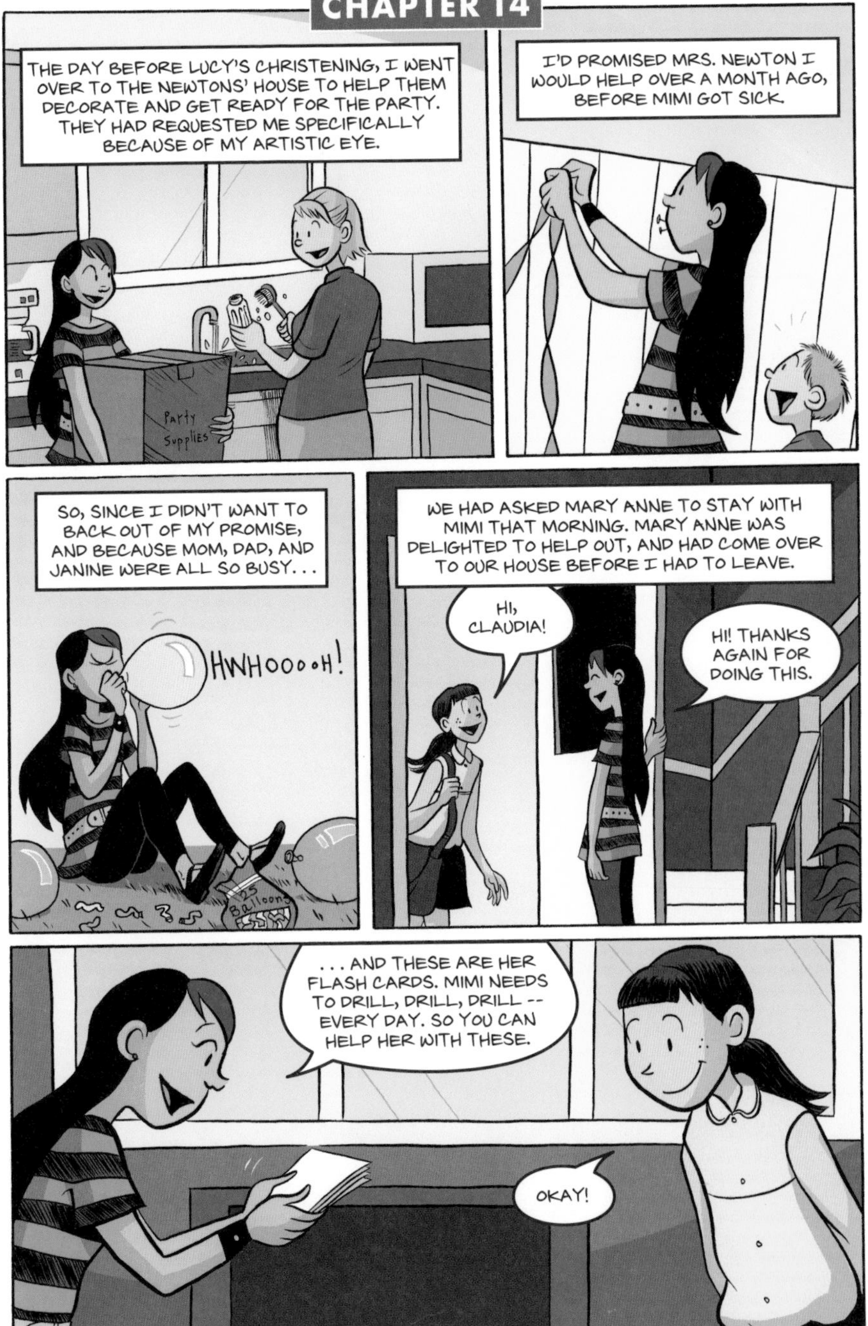
THE DAY BEFORE LUCY'S CHRISTENING, I WENT OVER TO THE NEWTONS' HOUSE TO HELP THEM DECORATE AND GET READY FOR THE PARTY. THEY HAD REQUESTED ME SPECIFICALLY BECAUSE OF MY ARTISTIC EYE.
Party Supplies
I'D PROMISED MRS. NEWTON I WOULD HELP OVER A MONTH AGO, BEFORE MIMI GOT SICK.
SO, SINCE I DIDN'T WANT TO BACK OUT OF MY PROMISE, AND BECAUSE MOM, DAD, AND JANINE WERE ALL SO BUSY. . .
HWHOOOoOH!
25 Balloons
WE HAD ASKED MARY ANNE TO STAY WITH MIMI THAT MORNING. MARY ANNE WAS DELIGHTED TO HELP OUT, AND HAD COME OVER TO OUR HOUSE BEFORE I HAD TO LEAVE.
HI, CLAUDIA!
HI! THANKS AGAIN FOR DOING THIS.
. . . AND THESE ARE HER FLASH CARDS. MIMI NEEDS TO DRILL, DRILL, DRILL -- EVERY DAY. SO YOU CAN HELP HER WITH THESE.
OKAY!

118

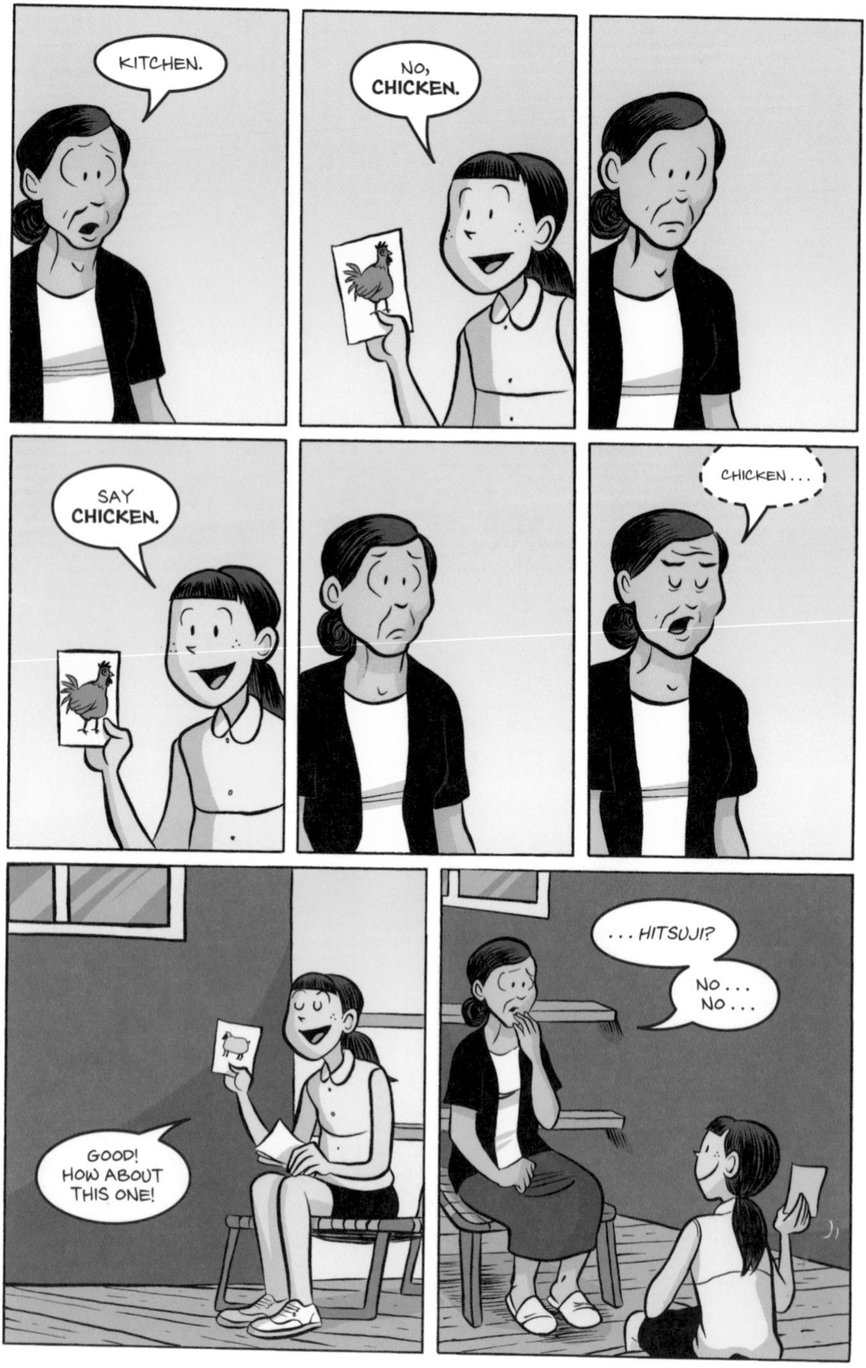
KITCHEN.
NO, **CHICKEN.**
SAY **CHICKEN.**
CHICKEN . . .
GOOD! HOW ABOUT THIS ONE!
. . . HITSUJI?
NO . . . NO . . .

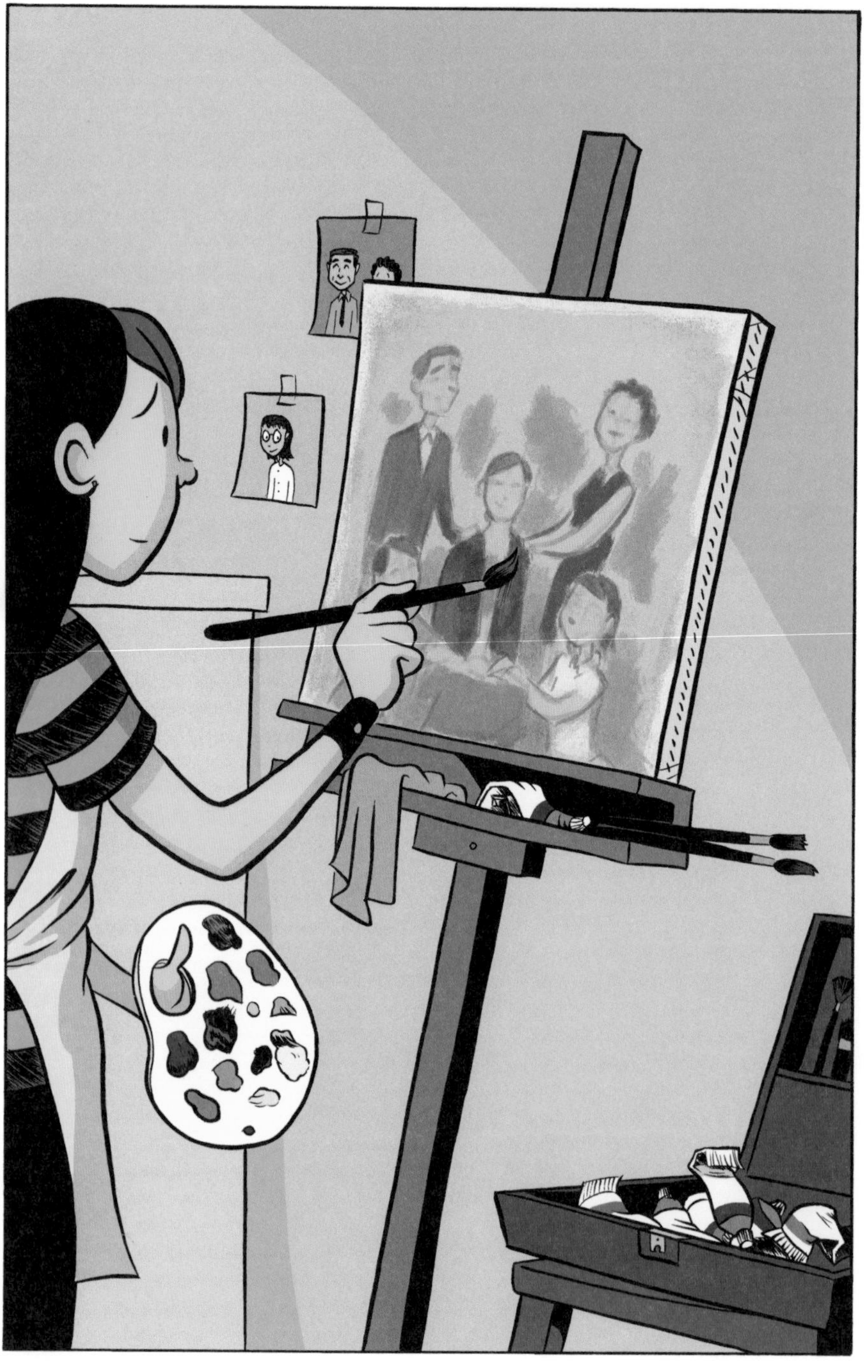

CHAPTER 15

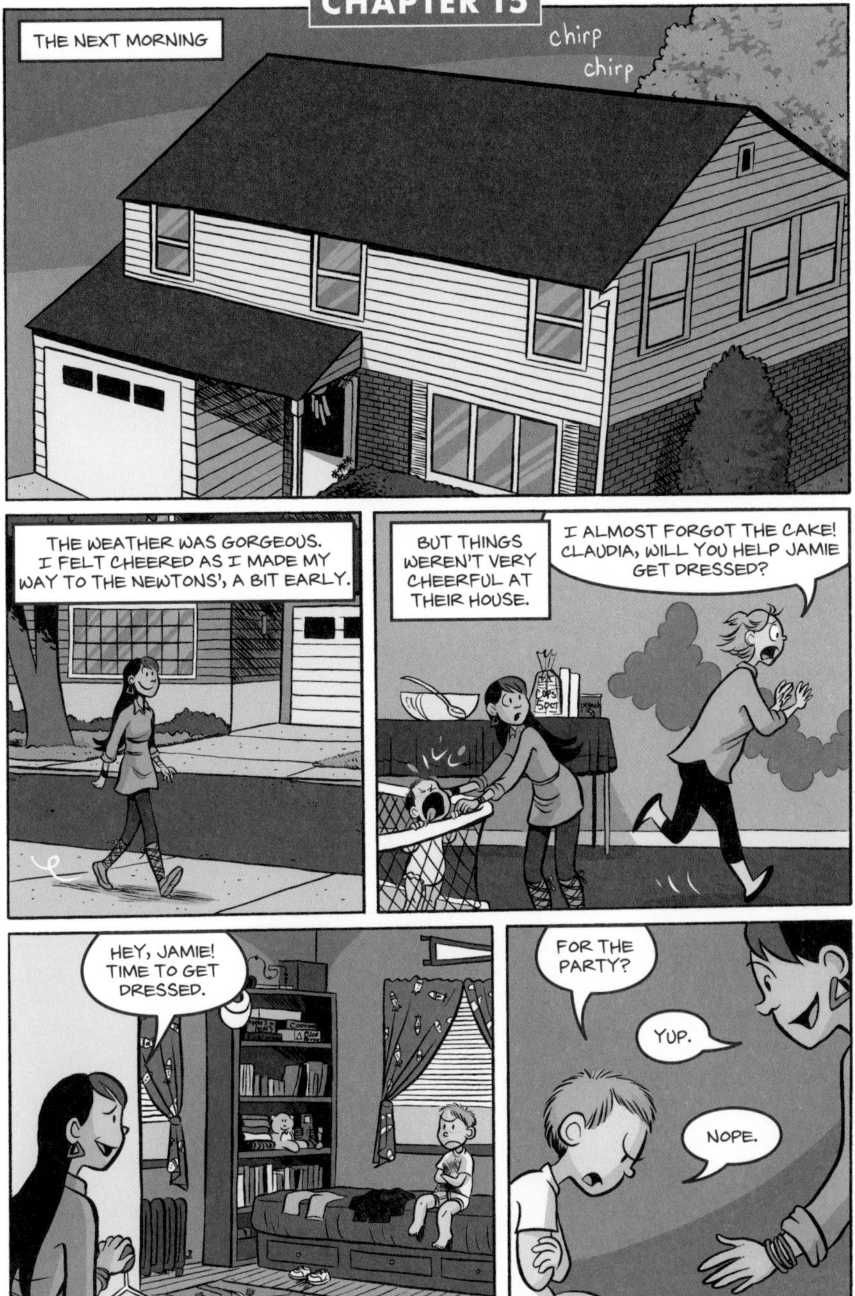

THE NEXT MORNING
chirp
chirp
THE WEATHER WAS GORGEOUS. I FELT CHEERED AS I MADE MY WAY TO THE NEWTONS', A BIT EARLY.
BUT THINGS WEREN'T VERY CHEERFUL AT THEIR HOUSE.
I ALMOST FORGOT THE CAKE! CLAUDIA, WILL YOU HELP JAMIE GET DRESSED?
HEY, JAMIE! TIME TO GET DRESSED.
FOR THE PARTY?
YUP.
NOPE.

128

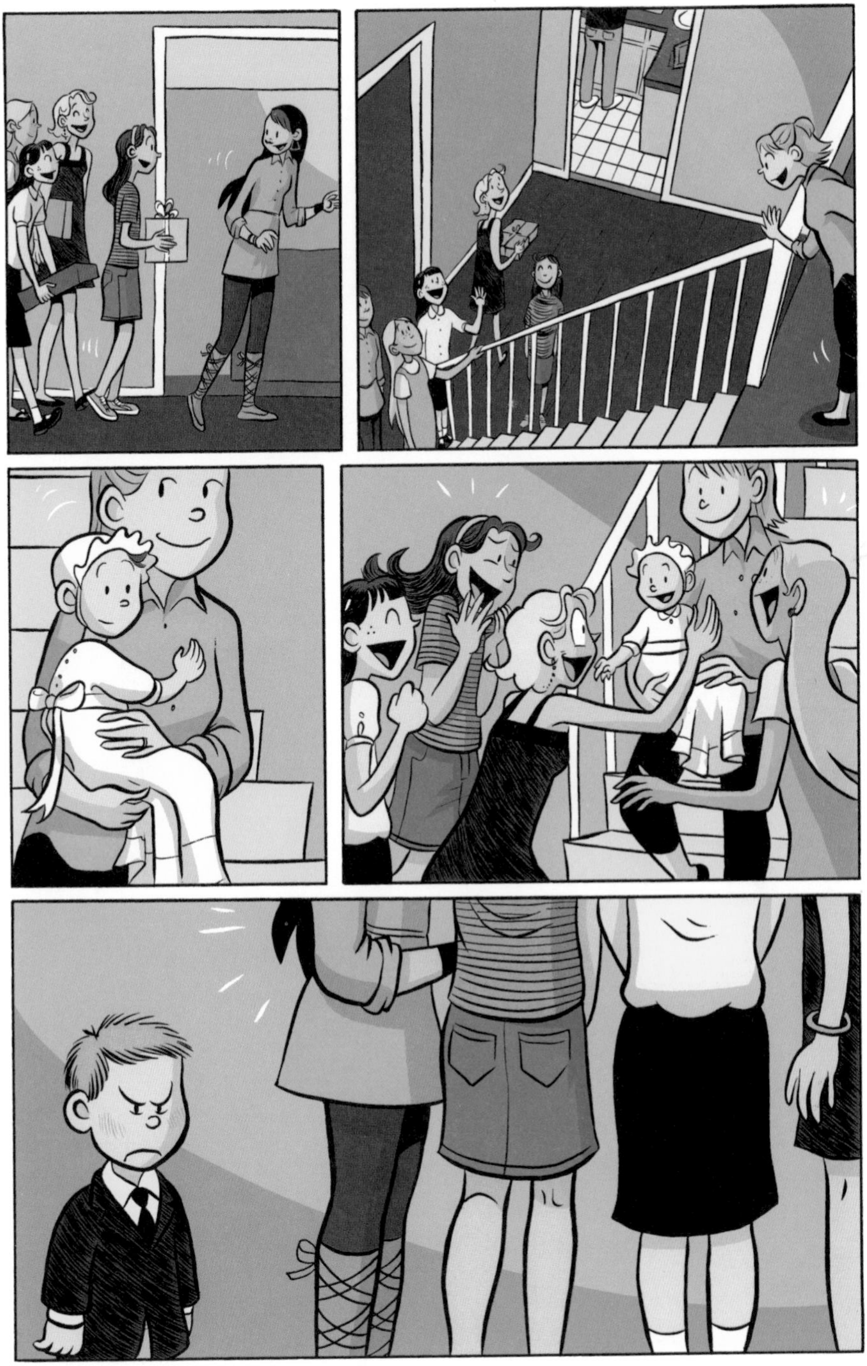

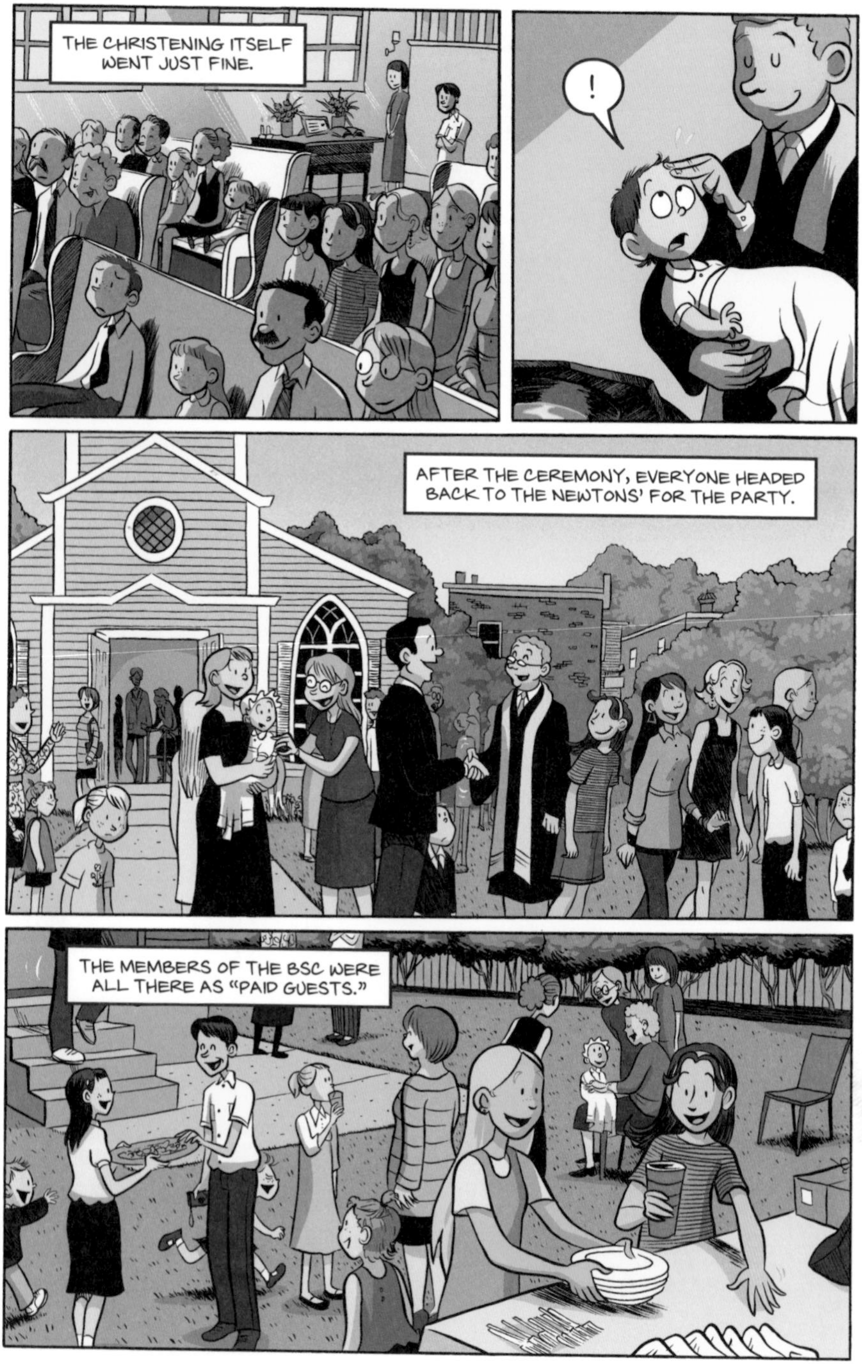
THE CHRISTENING ITSELF WENT JUST FINE.
!
AFTER THE CEREMONY, EVERYONE HEADED BACK TO THE NEWTONS' FOR THE PARTY.
THE MEMBERS OF THE BSC WERE ALL THERE AS "PAID GUESTS."

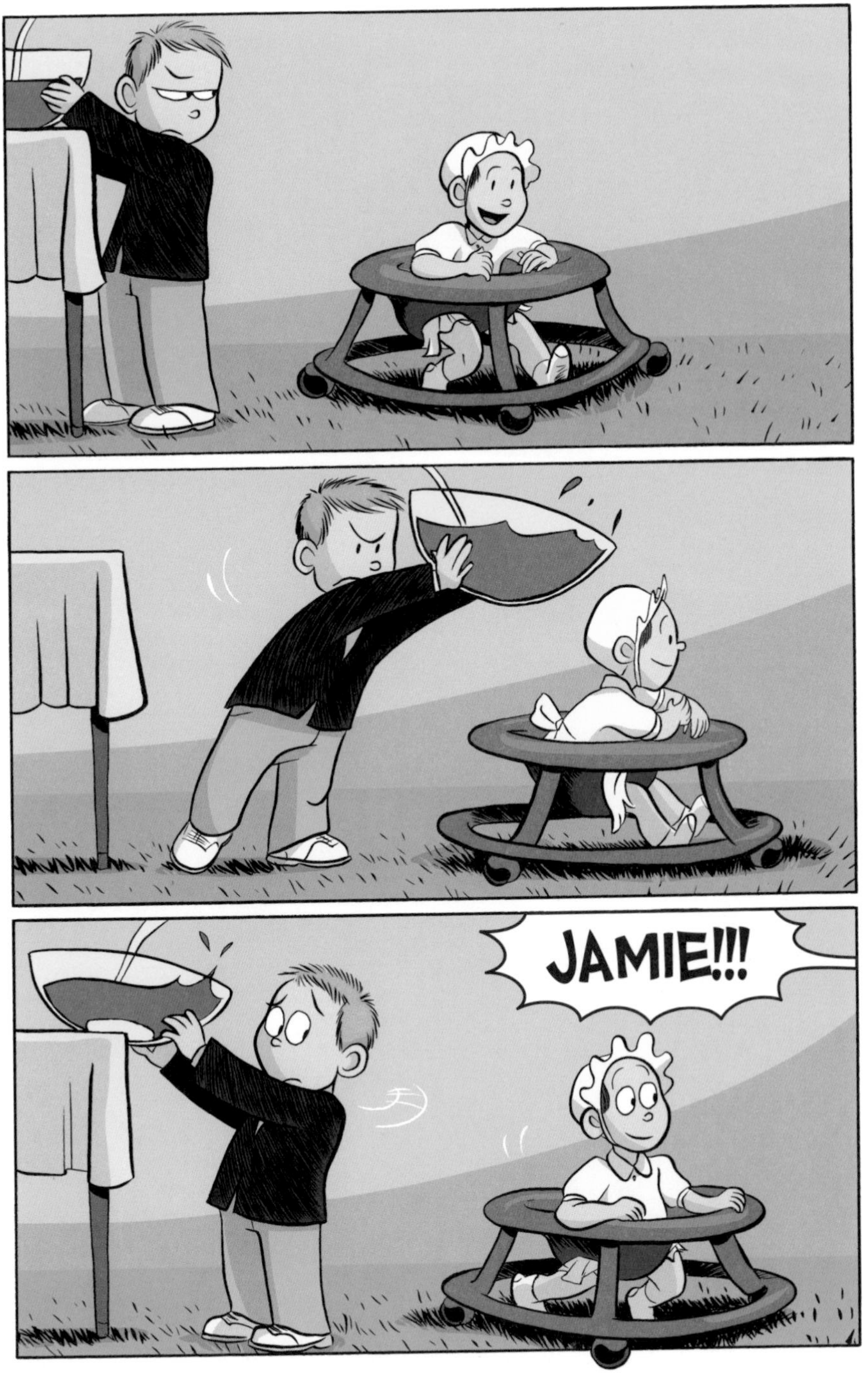
JAMIE!!!

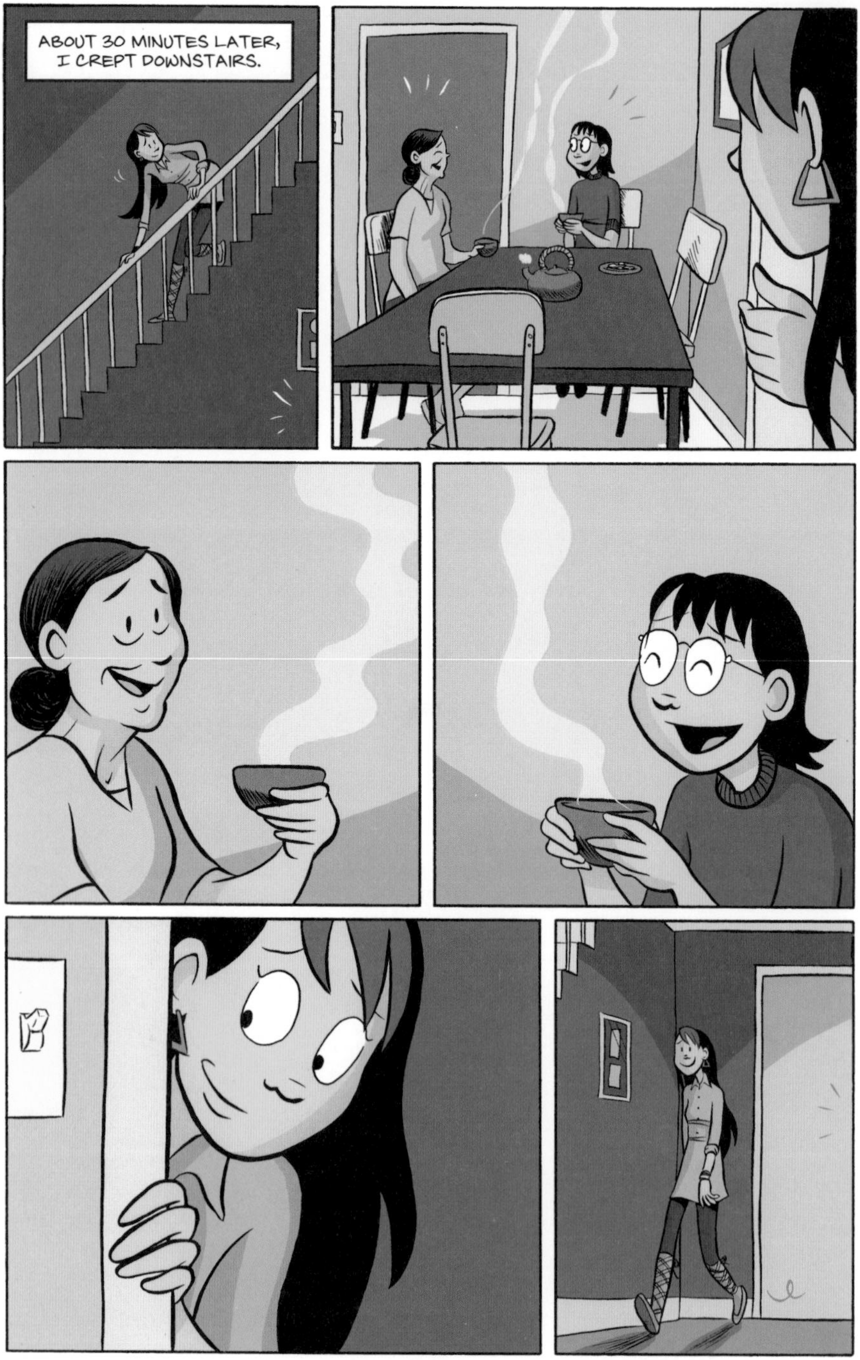
ABOUT 30 MINUTES LATER, I CREPT DOWNSTAIRS.

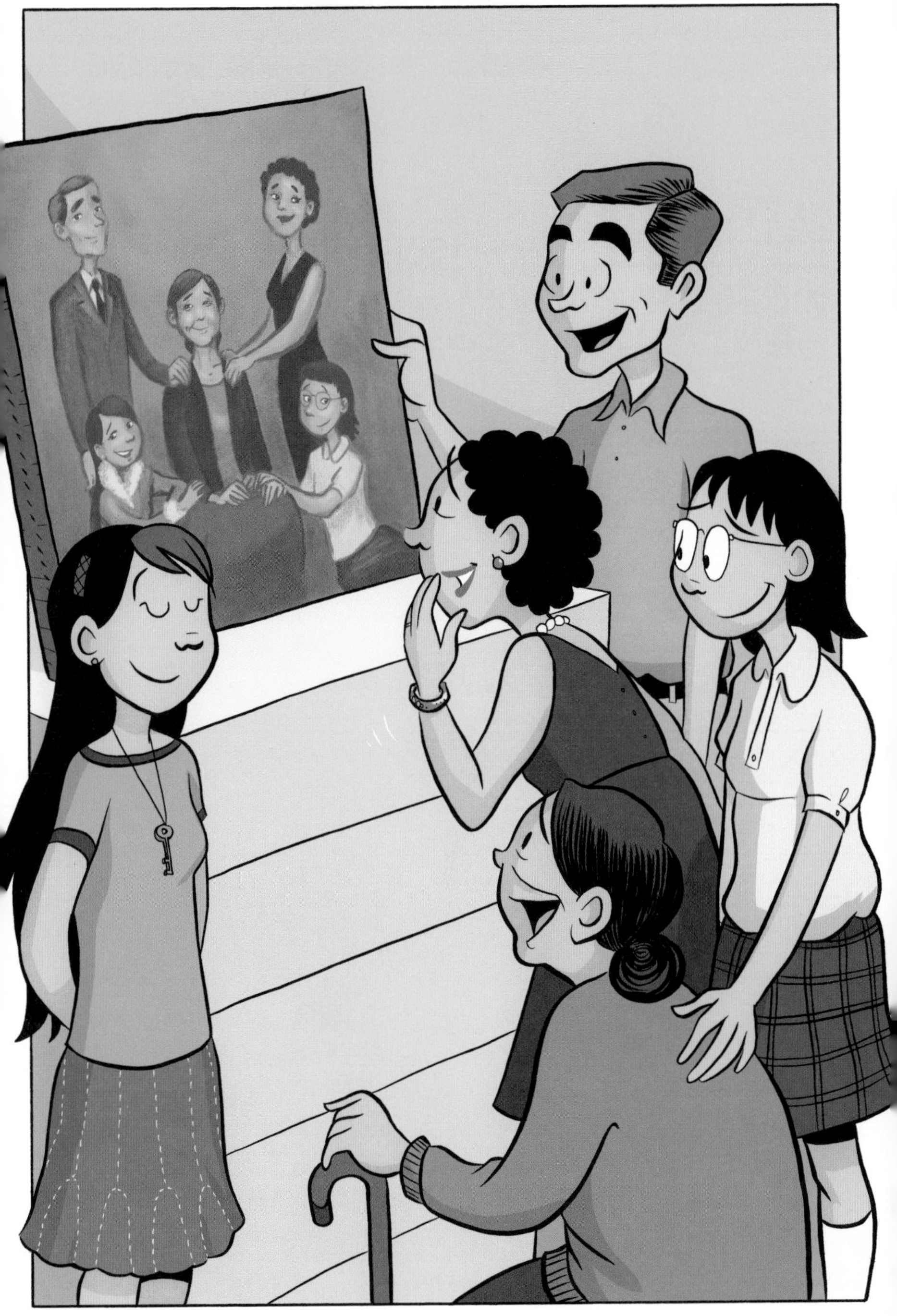

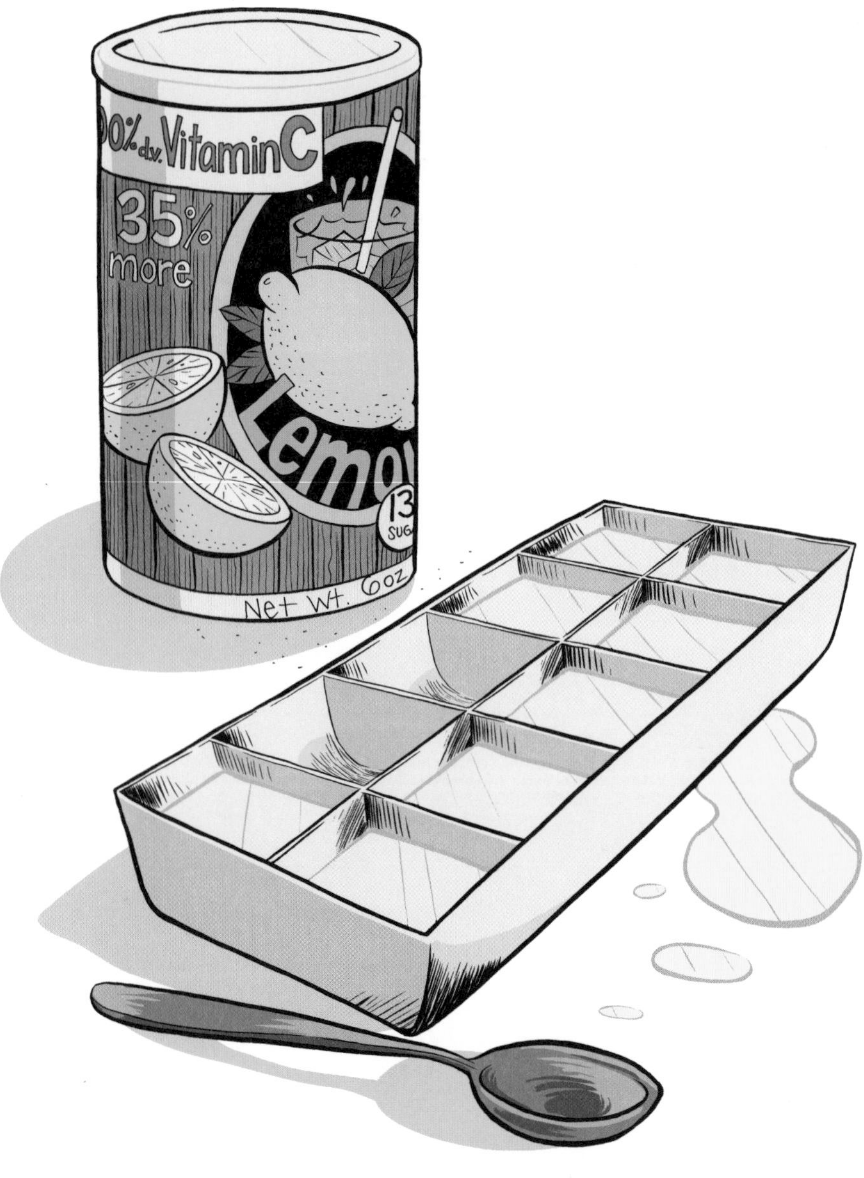

d.v. VitaminC
35% more
Net Wt. 6oz

CHAPTER 17

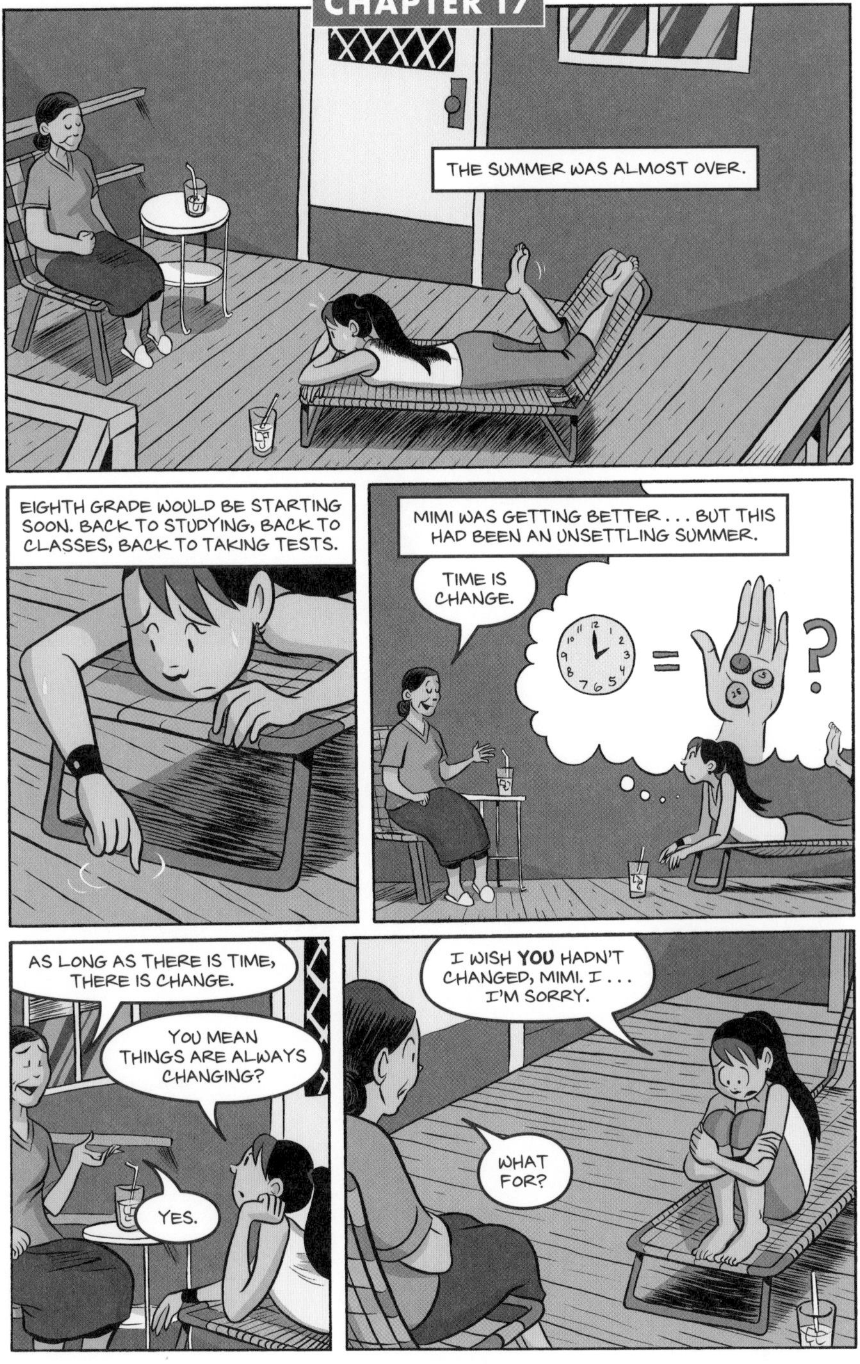

THE SUMMER WAS ALMOST OVER.
EIGHTH GRADE WOULD BE STARTING SOON. BACK TO STUDYING, BACK TO CLASSES, BACK TO TAKING TESTS.
MIMI WAS GETTING BETTER . . . BUT THIS HAD BEEN AN UNSETTLING SUMMER.
TIME IS CHANGE.
?
AS LONG AS THERE IS TIME, THERE IS CHANGE.
YOU MEAN THINGS ARE ALWAYS CHANGING?
YES.
I WISH YOU HADN'T CHANGED, MIMI. I . . . I'M SORRY.
WHAT FOR?

153

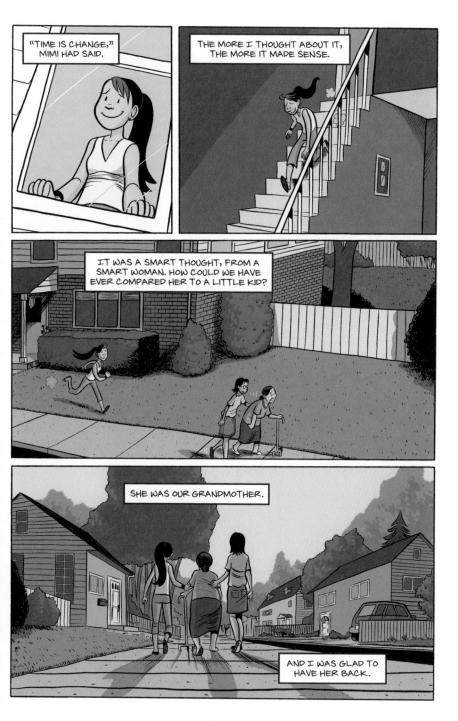

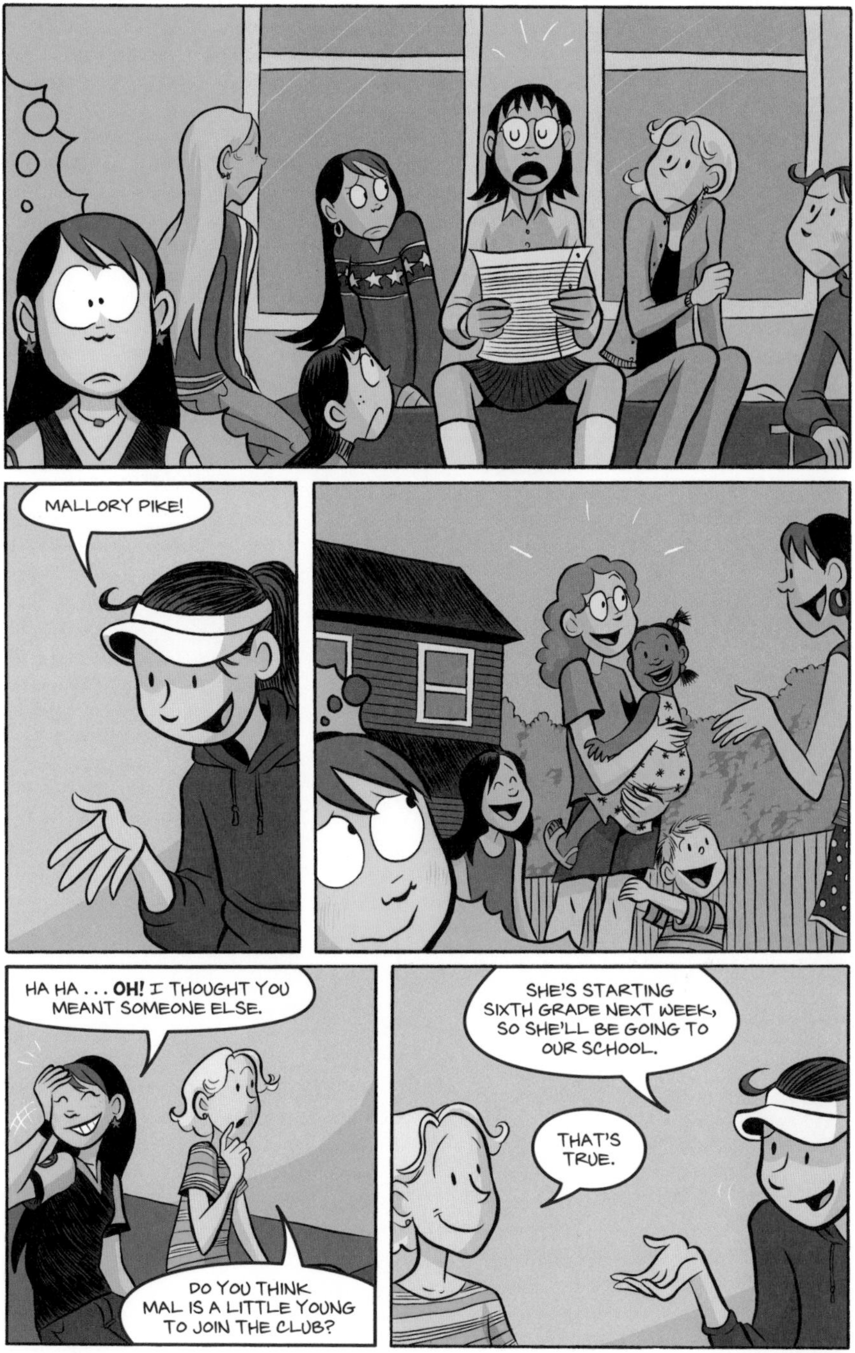
MALLORY PIKE!
HA HA . . . OH! I THOUGHT YOU MEANT SOMEONE ELSE.
DO YOU THINK MAL IS A LITTLE YOUNG TO JOIN THE CLUB?
SHE'S STARTING SIXTH GRADE NEXT WEEK, SO SHE'LL BE GOING TO OUR SCHOOL.
THAT'S TRUE.

THE MAKING OF

THE BABY-SITTERS CLUB

GRAPHIC NOVEL

STEP 1

Raina reads the original Baby-sitters Club book she is about to adapt several times before she starts working on the graphic novel. She underlines parts she especially likes, writes notes, and draws sketches of any new characters. Raina was a big fan of the BSC books when she was young, and often remembers things about the stories from the very first time she read them!

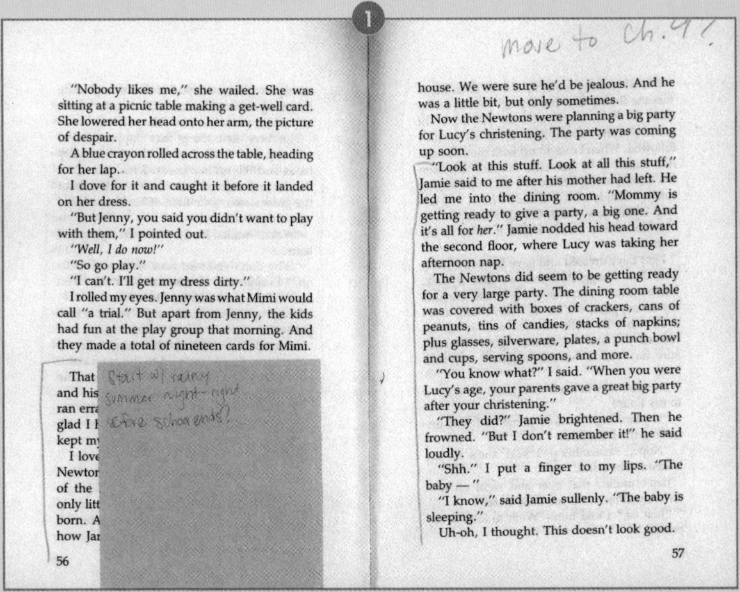

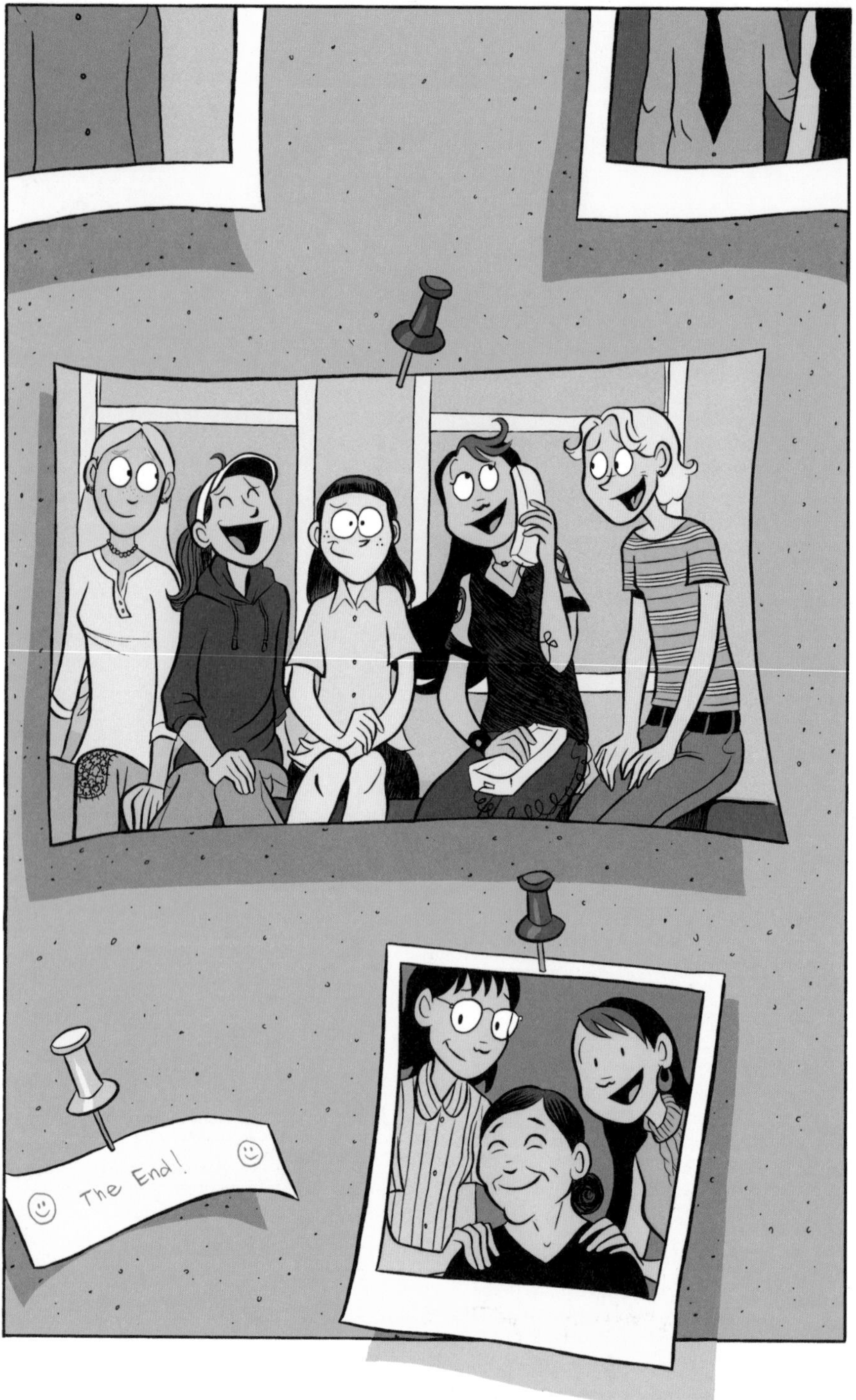
The End!

THE MAKING OF
THE
BABY-SITTERS
CLUB®
(GRAPHIC NOVEL)

STEP 1

Raina reads the original Baby-sitters Club book she is about to adapt several times before she starts working on the graphic novel. She underlines parts she especially likes, writes notes, and draws sketches of any new characters. Raina was a big fan of the BSC books when she was young, and often remembers things about the stories from the very first time she read them!

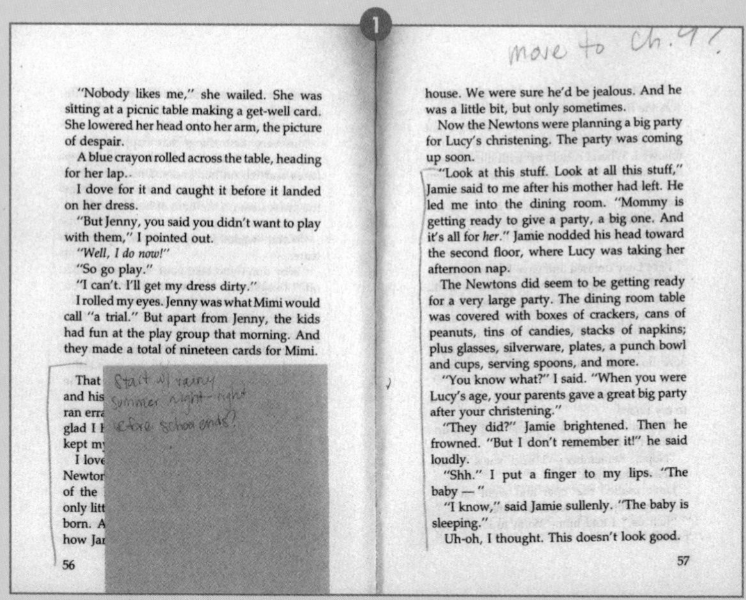

move to ch. 9!

"Nobody likes me," she wailed. She was sitting at a picnic table making a get-well card. She lowered her head onto her arm, the picture of despair.

A blue crayon rolled across the table, heading for her lap.

I dove for it and caught it before it landed on her dress.

"But Jenny, you said you didn't want to play with them," I pointed out.

"Well, I *do now!*"

"So go play."

"I can't. I'll get my dress dirty."

I rolled my eyes. Jenny was what Mimi would call "a trial." But apart from Jenny, the kids had fun at the play group that morning. And they made a total of nineteen cards for Mimi.

That [...] *Start all rainy*
and his [...] *summer night—right*
ran erra[...] *before school ends?*
glad I [...]
kept my [...]

I love[...]
Newton[...]
of the [...]
only litt[...]
born. A[...]
how Jar[...]

56

house. We were sure he'd be jealous. And he was a little bit, but only sometimes.

Now the Newtons were planning a big party for Lucy's christening. The party was coming up soon.

"Look at this stuff. Look at all this stuff," Jamie said to me after his mother had left. He led me into the dining room. "Mommy is getting ready to give a party, a big one. And it's all for *her*." Jamie nodded his head toward the second floor, where Lucy was taking her afternoon nap.

The Newtons did seem to be getting ready for a very large party. The dining room table was covered with boxes of crackers, cans of peanuts, tins of candies, stacks of napkins; plus glasses, silverware, plates, a punch bowl and cups, serving spoons, and more.

"You know what?" I said. "When you were Lucy's age, your parents gave a great big party after your christening."

"They did?" Jamie brightened. Then he frowned. "But I don't remember it!" he said loudly.

"Shh." I put a finger to my lips. "The baby —"

"I know," said Jamie sullenly. "The baby is sleeping."

Uh-oh, I thought. This doesn't look good.

57

Then, she begins to create thumbnails. These are small, simple, quick pages created on pieces of computer paper. Using a No. 2 pencil, Raina sketches out where the action and dialogue and drawings will appear on every page. She does this for the entire book, so she can see if the whole story works as well in comic form as it did in written form. It's easy to edit, shift things around, re-sketch, and rewrite at this stage. She also shows this to her editors and Ann M. Martin, the BSC's original author!

STEP 3

Once the thumbnails have been approved, Raina types up all the dialogue. This will be used when the book gets lettered (Step 8).

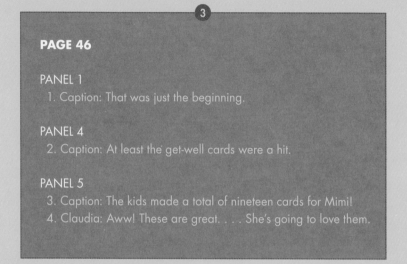

PAGE 46

PANEL 1
  1. Caption: That was just the beginning.

PANEL 4
  2. Caption: At least the get-well cards were a hit.

PANEL 5
  3. Caption: The kids made a total of nineteen cards for Mimi!
  4. Claudia: Aww! These are great. . . . She's going to love them.

STEP 4

Next, Raina uses a light blue pencil to do final layouts. She draws the panel borders and redraws her sketches onto large 11" x 14" Bristol board. It's a lot of work to redraw the sketches, even though they look very simple. This is where Raina works out perspective, composition, and general action in every panel. It also helps her see where the word balloons are going to go, so she can leave room for them. Being messy is no problem because blue pencil doesn't show up when the pages are scanned! See how this page changed between the thumbnail stage and the layout stage?

STEP 5

Now the real fun begins! Raina draws over her blue lines with a regular No. 2 pencil, this time going nice and slow and drawing in all the details. You can see how different the page is starting to look! The blue lines help guide the more finished art.

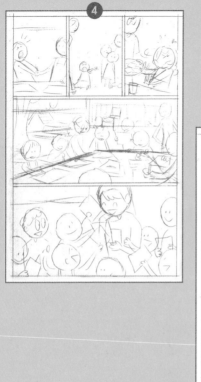

STEP 6

Raina's favorite stage is inking. She uses a Faber-Castell artist pen to draw the panel borders (using a ruler, of course!), and then a #2 Winsor & Newton watercolor brush and a bottle of waterproof India ink to ink the drawings. Little details like eyeballs and buttons are drawn with a tiny-tipped Micron pen, and are usually added last.

STEP 7

After the ink dries, Raina erases all the pencil lines. Each page is scanned into the computer at 64% its size, and then "cleaned up" in Photoshop. Instead of using Wite-Out, Raina just erases little mistakes digitally, which is faster. When each page file is clean, they are sent to the letterer!

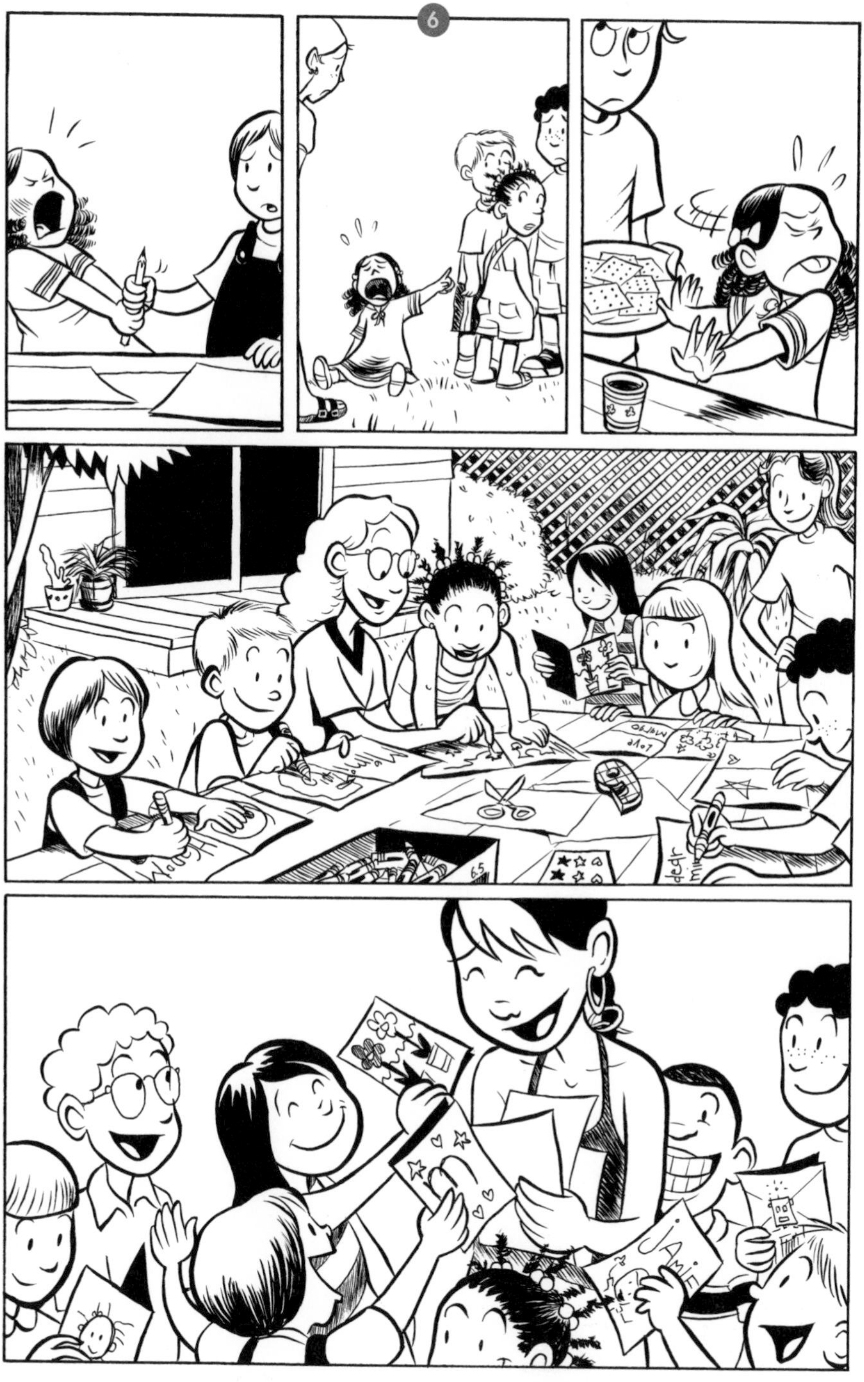
6
JAMIE

ANN M. MARTIN'S The Baby-sitters Club is one of the most popular series in the history of publishing — with more than 190 million books in print worldwide — and inspired a generation of young readers. Her novels include *Belle Teal, A Corner of the Universe* (a Newbery Honor book), *Here Today, A Dog's Life,* and *On Christmas Eve,* as well as the much-loved collaborations, *P.S. Longer Letter Later* and *Snail Mail No More,* with Paula Danziger, and *The Doll People* and *The Meanest Doll in the World,* written with Laura Godwin and illustrated by Brian Selznick. Ann lives in upstate New York.

RAINA TELGEMEIER is the #1 *New York Times* bestselling, multiple Eisner Award–winning creator of *Smile, Sisters,* and *Guts,* which are all graphic memoirs based on her childhood. She is also the creator of *Drama* and *Ghosts,* and is the adapter and illustrator of the first four Baby-sitters Club graphic novels. Raina lives in the San Francisco Bay Area. To learn more, visit her online at goraina.com.

STEP 9

In the final step, the colorist, Braden, uses Adobe Photoshop to add digital color to the black-and-white art. Now the finished pages are ready to go to the printer!

ANN M. MARTIN'S The Baby-sitters Club is one of the most popular series in the history of publishing — with more than 176 million books in print worldwide — and inspired a generation of young readers. Her novels include *Belle Teal*, *A Corner of the Universe* (a Newbery Honor book), *Here Today*, *A Dog's Life*, and *On Christmas Eve*, as well as the much-loved collaborations, *P.S. Longer Letter Later* and *Snail Mail No More*, with Paula Danziger, and *The Doll People* and *The Meanest Doll in the World*, written with Laura Godwin and illustrated by Brian Selznick. She lives in upstate New York.

RAINA TELGEMEIER is the #1 *New York Times* bestselling, multiple Eisner Award–winning creator of *Smile* and *Sisters*, which are both graphic memoirs based on her childhood. She is also the creator of *Drama*, which was named a Stonewall Honor Book and was selected for YALSA's Top Ten Great Graphic Novels for Teens. Raina lives in the San Francisco Bay Area. To learn more, visit her online at www.goRaina.com.